Baked with Love

OVER 100 ALLERGY-FRIENDLY VEGAN DESSERTS

BRITTANY BERLIN

VICTORY BELT PUBLISHING INC.

LAS VEGAS

Author photos by Brooke Berlin

Cover design by Justin-Aaron Velasco

Interior design and illustrations by Kat Lannom

Printed in Canada

TC 0121

Table of Contents

Introduction

Every morning, my alarm goes off at 4:30 a.m. While this is a fairly early start for most people, it's pretty normal for me. The earlier I rise, the sooner I get to start my day. I'm that in love with what I do: the recipes, the community, the writing, researching, testing, photo shoots—every single bit.

Even the challenges bring me joy and gratitude in the end. (Believe me, it's not always marshmallow clouds and rainbow sprinkles!) My long days spent working as a food blogger fly by compared to the twelve-hour days I spent working at other jobs. Don't get me wrong; it's hard work. A lot of sweat, love, passion, and, yes, a few tears go into building an online community that comes together around one very specific topic.

I wear multiple hats, sometimes hourly depending on the day, and I have built everything from scratch. Growing up as a more traditional artist (paints were my thing), I've always been inspired by those who really align with their work, and I aspired to do something creative that fulfilled my soul. This is my greatest masterpiece: the blog, every single recipe I share, the photos that capture each recipe's unique personality, connecting with hundreds of thousands of individuals out there experimenting with plant-based baking, and especially this book.

If you picked up this book and have no clue who the heck I am or why I'm talking about 4:30 a.m. wake-up calls and comparing painting to a food blog, hi! My name is Britt, and I'm the blogger behind *The Banana Diaries,* a wholesome vegan baking blog featuring plant-based recipes with Paleo and gluten-free twists.

That is a mouthful, but I often have a lot to say (which, if you read the blog, you'll quickly come to learn). Don't worry, though—all of those words are paired with drool-worthy photos of recipes made with a whole lot of love that you'd hardly believe are vegan. Oh, and I have the kindest and most loving readers ever—seriously, go read the comments section. I tear up every time!

I didn't always have this loving relationship with food or with life in general. I'll give you the abridged version.

I grew up loving to bake more traditionally—you know, with eggs, butter, sugar, the works. Like many, I relished the magic of baking—mixing together an array of ingredients and producing something completely distinct from its parts. It was a fun alchemical experiment and a welcome escape for an hour or two where I could play around and make something pretty and delicious.

But at twelve years old, after an accident during gymnastics that led to multiple intensive surgeries and being sidelined for a year, I developed anorexia, which soon became comorbid with depression, both of which I battled for nearly a decade. During that tumultuous time, my relationship with food mirrored all of my other relationships: everything felt hollow, empty, constricting, and painful. Truthfully, I feared every day.

I graduated college and started a corporate job, having mustered a half-hearted recovery from my eating disorder and still very much in the throes of depression. It felt a bit like the world was closing in on me (don't worry, there is a happy ending to this story): my partner, Jared, was struggling with chronic Lyme disease, I was trying to find my footing in a new city that never felt like home to me, and every day I felt like I needed an army and a half just to get me out of bed. Back in college, after losing a friend to depression, I had promised myself that I wouldn't waste my life. Yet here I was, feeling like there wasn't much to live for.

Me being me (if you follow me on Instagram, you'll see that I'm very much about finding light within the dark), I decided enough was enough. There had to be more to life. So I began diving into research about the mind, craving a better understanding of why I thought the way I did. Why had I failed to get better after years of traditional treatment, and why was it that others seemed to have avoided my current reality?

This led me to the research of Dr. Joe Dispenza, Dr. Kelly Brogan, Dr. Sue Morter, and others. I started to understand that the reality I was experiencing was directly caused by my thought patterns and subconscious beliefs. (I know you signed up for a cookbook here, not a quantum physics lesson, but trust me, we're getting there!) I began to work on reprogramming my thoughts and shifting my fear surrounding food, especially macronutrients, food types, and food groups.

I began embracing meditation to tap into my subconscious and change old beliefs that had been running the show since I was twelve (or younger). By rewiring these thoughts, I found freedom and safety in my own mind and body rather than feeling like I was trapped in a jail cell every day. With that inner freedom came outer freedom, and I no longer feared what was on my plate; rather, I enjoyed it—imagine that! And most importantly, I found the freedom to be the person I was originally put here to be. (I know, cheesy, but it's true.) I could be Britt, without the restrictions of an eating disorder, without the chains of depression, and without the worries of living by someone else's standards.

Okay, okay, this is great and all, but how is this related to *The Banana Diaries* and, more importantly, *Baked with Love*?

Well, my dear reader, let me explain.

You see, I felt food was the easiest place to start rewriting my beliefs. After all, I had struggled with an eating disorder before depression hit, and I felt it was the key to this buried lock I had been seeking for almost ten years. With this newfound freedom, I began to bake again—not traditionally, but with twists of vegan, dairy-free, gluten-free, and mainly Paleo. If you recall, Jared was struggling with chronic Lyme disease. While I felt free to eat whatever I pleased, I knew he couldn't. Oh, and to boot, Jared's sister had also been diagnosed with Lyme *and* has a nut allergy. I love a challenge, so I quickly took this one on.

I experimented. I started baking with "flours" other than all-purpose (though I still use traditional flour in a few recipes, as you'll see!), swapping real butter with a dairy-free plant-based version, and using coconut milk instead of heavy cream and ground flaxseed in lieu of eggs.

What started as a tiny "daily eats" Instagram in late spring of 2017 from the cramped confines of my tiny Brooklyn studio kitchen soon blossomed into publishing full recipes and eventually to a blog reaching and inspiring tens of thousands daily. And not just any recipes. What started as a healthy baking blog has evolved into a plant-based vegan healthy baking blog with twists of Paleo, gluten-free, and even keto options.

But you're probably wondering, am I actually recovered from an eating disorder if I'm still out here labeling everything?

Well, I've come to realize that most readers still choose to label themselves, and for good reasons—they're highly allergic to eggs, a drop of gluten will send their stomach into a maelstrom, or a whiff of nuts likely means life or death. So I've reached a point where I know that, even if I eat plant-based and choose not to label myself for my own sanity, others might not have that luxury. Thus all of my recipes on the blog and in this cookbook are labeled. They also include instructions for making swaps if the recipe doesn't quite fit your dietary needs as written.

You'll come to find that my recipes are more about inclusivity than exclusivity. We live our entire lives being closed into little boxes. We constantly create these "us versus them" scenarios of you're gluten-free or you're not, you're vegan or you're not, and many more non-food-related boxes that I don't have enough room to get into here. So I sought to create a space where all feel welcome, whether they're recovering from an eating disorder and rediscovering their freedom, they're struggling with a chronic illness or a life-threatening allergy, or they just want to enjoy delicious comfort food while honoring their values of a healthy lifestyle. What's more, I was determined to change the stigma that allergy-friendly foods had to be so dang tasteless!

I wholeheartedly believe that anything is possible in this life. I mean, I have no reason not to. I went from wishing the days would stop, too weak and hopeless to get out of bed much of the time, to being so eager to get started, I can't sleep past 4:30 a.m. (unless it's the weekend, and then it's more like 6:30—let's be real here).

So every single recipe in this book has been tested and retested and approved not only by eaters with allergies but also by more traditional eaters. I want each recipe on my blog to pass or even surpass its more traditional counterpart, and the same desire holds true for the recipes in this book.

You don't need to call yourself a vegan to enjoy gluten-free vegan Monster Cookies (page 116). Nor do you need to eat a Paleo diet to love my Paleo vegan Chocolate Hazelnut Cake. (If you're ready for chocolate overload, skip on over to that recipe on page 174.) But if you do adhere to a gluten-free or Paleo diet, this is the place to be. All are welcomed, and none are judged. You're free to live the life you want to live within and outside the pages of this cookbook.

Now, there's one last bit that I haven't talked about yet. You see, throughout this healing journey, I've found one core concept to be the foundation of everything: love. As cliché as it may sound, love is all there is. There can never be an absence of love, only an absence of the awareness of it. Do you remember a time when you baked something for someone you love? I can recall quite a few of those times from my childhood, and many more now that I've started my blog. There are countless ways to express love, but one of my favorite ways is through food.

Every single recipe in this cookbook has been created, baked, tested, retested, and shared with so much love. And that's what I intend for you to feel with every bite.

Hearing from readers like you through email, Facebook messages, and Instagram DMs or just seeing them share their creations on Pinterest is my biggest joy. The ones that really hit home for me are the ones that say, "I never thought I'd be able to eat this again," or, "I used to have so much fear surrounding this kind of food, but seeing you make it and making it myself, I feel so happy!"

That's my one goal. Whether you have no baking experience or you are a seasoned baker, and whether you know the ins and outs of a Paleo, vegan, dairy-free, gluten-free diet or you don't know what's what, I intend for you to have confidence and an insane amount of fun when making and devouring these recipes.

How to Bake with Success (and Love!)

Whether you're an avid baker or you're just buying a pair of oven mitts, you're in the right place. The recipes in this book are designed so that no matter your skill level, you can create something beautiful and delicious. If you haven't noticed, I have a big sweet tooth, so my favorite form of showing love is sharing something sweet with family and friends. However, baking is meant to be for yourself, too.

Even before I started my blog, while living in a cramped New York City apartment, it was not uncommon to find me making a batch of cupcakes for no other reason than the fact that baking brings me joy. And of course, anyone who happened to walk into my tiny kitchen could enjoy a cupcake as well! So, with that said, you can use these recipes in the ways that bring you the most joy. Whether that's bringing a dozen Chocolate Chip Banana Cupcakes (page 138) to a birthday party or making a batch of Caramel-Filled Brownies (page 58) on a Wednesday night because you had a long day at work, this cookbook is your handbook to baking with love.

Now, baking is also a bit of a science, so following directions and using precise measurements are very important. To ensure your success, I've included some nuts-and-bolts chapters that cover topics ranging from the ingredients and pans used to my prized baking tips (some learned the hard way). Before you dig into the recipes, I recommend that you give these early chapters a read to orient yourself to what you'll need to make the baked goods in this book and to avoid the mistakes I made when first learning to bake.

Of course, baking is not all about rules. I still want you to get creative and have fun, so feel free to decorate, garnish, and finish the recipes in your own creative way—especially the cakes and cupcakes. That's the best part in my opinion!

Above all, I hope that you will fall in love with every part of the process, not just the finished product. We often race through the journey just to get to the result, but the best part is truly in the time frame from where we start to where we end.

So, with that being said, go forth and bake (and enjoy!) with love.

Chapter 1
COMMON VEGAN & PALEO BAKING INGREDIENTS

Whether you're new to vegan or Paleo baking or you're a seasoned pro, it's important to go over ingredients and why they're used.

Vegan, or Paleo, baking is really not all that different from more traditional baking. Of course, there are some outliers in the mix—vegan cake recipes, for example, occasionally turn out gummy (but not the ones in this book!)—but I've figured out some one-to-one vegan and sometimes Paleo swaps that prove to be very useful (and delicious) for baking without the usual dairy and eggs. (Paleo baking recipes may, depending on the interpretation of Paleo, contain full-fat dairy products and eggs, but you will not find those ingredients in this book since it is 100 percent vegan.)

This chapter goes over the most common vegan and Paleo baking ingredients that are found in this cookbook. I mention which ingredients are Paleo specifically and which are both vegan and Paleo, but all of the ingredients mentioned here are plant-based. When an ingredient is noted as Paleo, this means it is also gluten-free and free of ingredients that are not Paleo-friendly, such as cane sugar, corn, and soy.

If you're new to this style of baking, I suggest you spend some time browsing the healthy baking aisle in your local grocery store to familiarize yourself with some of the ingredients you'll be using. There, you'll likely find almond flour, cassava flour, coconut flour, coconut sugar, maple syrup, and more. You might see a few ingredients that you're interested in experimenting with. The more you get to know what's available to vegan and Paleo bakers, the easier it will be to make a plant-based grain-free creation taste as good as (or even better than!) the traditional version.

Dry Ingredients

All-Purpose Flour and Cake Flour

Many recipes in this cookbook give the option of using either all-purpose flour/cake flour or gluten-free 1-to-1 baking flour. If you're not gluten-free, both all-purpose and cake flour are wonderful vegan options that are used in traditional baking. Some recipes, specifically the cake and cupcake recipes, call for cake flour. I recommend sticking with cake flour in those recipes if you're not gluten-free because it creates the desired tender crumb texture that you find in more traditional cakes.

However, you can use all-purpose flour if you don't have cake flour. Just note that you'll need to make an adjustment here. For every 1 cup of cake flour needed, take 1 cup of all-purpose flour, remove 2 tablespoons, and replace it with 2 tablespoons of arrowroot powder or cornstarch. Sift the flour and arrowroot powder or cornstarch together to ensure that they're evenly distributed.

Gluten-Free 1-to-1 Baking Flour

Much like the wet ingredients that I discuss later in this chapter, we're finally seeing gluten-free baking flours that are nearly identical to regular flour in terms of results. When a recipe lists gluten-free 1-to-1 baking flour as an alternative to all-purpose or cake flour, know that you will need to use a flour that contains some sort of gum or binder in the mix. For a gluten-free flour to work comparably to wheat flour in a recipe, it must contain one or more binding additives.

The brands that I recommend are Bob's Red Mill and King Arthur Flour. Both companies carry two different products: a gluten-free flour and a gluten-free 1-to-1 baking flour. Always use the baking flour for these recipes! If you don't, the results will be crumbly and cardboardlike— not the delicious vegan baked goods you're expecting.

Almond Flour

I try to make many of my recipes nut-free because I've found that people who have nut allergies are often unable to enjoy Paleo treats because so many of them are made with almond flour. As a result, only three recipes in this book use almond flour. Nonetheless, almond flour is a wonderful conventional flour substitute if you are Paleo and do not have a nut allergy. It's not quite like all-purpose flour (if you were to swap in almond flour in a recipe that calls for all-purpose flour, your baked good would be quite crumbly), but when crafted correctly, a Paleo vegan recipe can mimic the taste and texture of its more conventional counterpart.

When working with almond flour, keep in mind that there are a few different types. For the recipes in this book, I recommend using super-fine blanched almond flour (the skin is removed and the flour is ground almost to a powder). I do not recommend using unblanched almond flour, also called almond meal, or even regular blanched almond flour. Using the super-fine type ensures that there are no clumps of almonds in the flour, which yields less of a mealy texture. You can find various types of almond flour in the health food aisles at most grocery stores.

Keep in mind that nut flours tend to go rancid much quicker than all-purpose flour or even oat flour, so please store your almond flour in a cool, dry area and make sure the container is airtight.

Cassava Flour

Cassava flour is probably my favorite Paleo baking flour, the reason being that it can be used nearly 1-to-1 to conventional flour in almost all recipes. I've never seen anything like it. It binds and creates the traditional gumlike texture of regular flour without any added gums. If you're unfamiliar with cassava flour, it's actually ground-up cassava root, which is similar to a potato or sweet potato. The key differences between cassava flour and all-purpose flour are that cassava flour occasionally requires a little more liquid (hence it's not always 1-to-1), it's much finer than conventional flour (meaning it's a little dustier), and it is completely gluten- and grain-free. That means it won't rise in a yeasted bread recipe like all-purpose flour would, but it works very well in pie crust recipes and in many cookie and cake recipes (although you may need to use less cassava flour, depending on the recipe).

Cassava flour is becoming a lot more common in grocery stores. You can purchase it online or at Whole Foods and health food stores. I recommend the brands Anthony's Goods, Otto's Naturals, and Terrasoul Superfoods for the highest-quality cassava.

A final note: Cassava flour is not safe to eat raw (much like you shouldn't eat uncooked all-purpose flour).

Coconut Flour

When paired with cassava or oat flour, coconut flour helps create a more traditional, glutenlike texture. It's a fantastic flour for vegan and Paleo baking. However, you cannot use it as 1-to-1 gluten-free flour substitute. In most recipes, coconut flour is used in relatively small quantities—much less than you would normally assume for flour. This is because coconut flour absorbs a lot of liquid in the baking process, so if you don't want a very dry banana bread, for example, less really is more. Plus, using less means less of a coconut aftertaste, which can turn some people off. However, coconut flour can really add to the flavor of a dessert: think coconut cake. You can find coconut flour in almost every grocery store now as well as online.

Oats and Oat Flour

I use rolled oats a lot in this book. Sometimes I use them to give baked goods a chewy texture and a comforting oat-y flavor. Sometimes I grind rolled oats into a rustic flour to use as gluten-free flour substitute. Oat flour is a fantastic gluten-free flour that has a few similarities to all-purpose flour in that it can create a binding reaction when activated with wet ingredients. If you've ever had a bowl of hot oatmeal, you're familiar with that bit of sliminess that develops when you cook the oats. That's essentially what oat flour does, but to a much lesser degree, to create vegan breads and other baked goods with a texture that's close to the texture you get when using all-purpose flour.

More often than not, I make my own oat flour, which is an inexpensive and easy way to get a great-tasting and -acting gluten-free flour. That said, you can definitely purchase oat flour in stores; however, I don't feel the store-bought kind gives as good a result as homemade oat flour (although it's still decent).

Note that rolled oats and other oat products are sometimes subject to gluten contamination, depending on how they were processed. To be sure that the rolled oats (or oat flour) you are using are gluten-free, purchase only products that are certified gluten-free.

Arrowroot Powder

I love arrowroot powder because it's basically a Paleo-friendly substitute for cornstarch. Arrowroot powder acts much like cornstarch in that it helps thicken sauces, spreads, and jams. While both arrowroot powder and cornstarch are vegan, arrowroot powder is considered Paleo while cornstarch is not, since corn is not Paleo. However, when you come across a Paleo recipe in this book that calls for arrowroot powder, you can absolutely swap cornstarch for the arrowroot powder if you don't require it to be Paleo.

Leavening Agents

Baking soda and baking powder are the go-to leavening ingredients not only in traditional baking but in vegan baking as well. Baking soda is considered both vegan and Paleo; however, baking powder is considered only vegan because cornstarch is typically added to it. In Paleo recipes that call for baking powder, I give the option of using a homemade Paleo baking powder, which involves simply combining baking soda with apple cider vinegar to create a chemical reaction that causes baked goods to rise. For the leavener in my Chocolate Babka recipe (page 300), I use instant yeast to give it a great yeasty flavor and a classic breadlike texture. Otherwise, from muffins to quick breads, cookies, cakes, and more, I use baking soda and baking powder to add lift to baked goods.

Coconut Sugar

Coconut sugar, also known as coconut palm sugar, is a natural sugar made from coconut palm sap. It is my favorite alternative to cane sugar. Like cane sugar, it comes granulated but is more similar to brown sugar in taste and has a light tan color. It can be used interchangeably with cane sugar and can even be used to make powdered sugar (see page 36). You can find coconut sugar in most grocery stores as well as online. It is both vegan and Paleo.

Sugar, Granulated and Powdered

If you're a traditional baker, you're used to working with granulated sugar and powdered sugar (also known as confectioner's sugar). Though these sweeteners aren't Paleo, they are vegan, and most of my recipes are crafted to be lower in sugar than their more traditional counterparts.

Raw Cacao Powder

For all of my recipes, I recommend cacao powder over cocoa powder, the reason being that cacao powder is raw and less processed than cocoa powder; as a result, it has more nutritional benefits and a richer taste. This ingredient is both vegan and Paleo, meaning that you can have your chocolate and eat it, too!

Cashews

Truly my favorite "nut" that's not a nut! Technically, cashews are seeds, but however you classify them, they are a wonderful ingredient in many vegan recipes, especially vegan "cheesecakes." I love making homemade cashew butter and cashew milk, but I use cashews most often in my cheesecake recipes because blending cashews with a high-fat dairy-free substitute such as coconut cream creates a texture much like regular cheesecake.

Vegan Chocolate

Many people ask this question, and the answer is yes, chocolate can be vegan! In fact, cacao, the base of chocolate, is naturally vegan; it's the ingredients that are added to it, principally dairy products or perhaps a nonvegan sweetener such as honey, that render it not vegan. Likewise, chocolate can be Paleo if it does not contain soy or dairy and a Paleo-friendly sweetener is used. In my recipes, I most often use vegan dark chocolate chips, aka morsels, or chunks with a 55 to 70 percent cacao content, or chopped dark chocolate (about 80 percent cacao); occasionally, I even use 100 percent cacao chocolate baking chips. (Unsweetened chocolate seems very bitter at first, but you will learn what chocolate is supposed to taste like!)

Vegan chocolate occasionally has the certification of "Vegan" on it, but if it doesn't, you can check the ingredients to make sure it doesn't contain milk, milk solids, or milk fat and is not sweetened with honey. A couple of Paleo/vegan brands of chocolate that I like are Hu Kitchen and Pascha Chocolate. My go-to chocolate chips, though, are the dark chocolate chips from Lily's (55 percent cacao) and the dark morsels from Enjoy Life (69 percent cacao). There isn't much of a difference in taste between the two.

How to Melt Chocolate

Too many times I have started to melt chocolate, stepped away, and returned to a thick, burnt mess. It's awful! Let's melt chocolate the right way, shall we?

I use two methods for melting chocolate: using the microwave and using a double boiler setup on the stovetop. I use the former when I'm in a pinch and the latter when I have more time on my hands. You can use whichever method you prefer; most people find the microwave more convenient. If you're melting a chocolate bar rather than chips, be sure to chop it before attempting to melt it.

To melt chocolate in the microwave, place the chocolate in a microwave-safe bowl and heat it on high for 30 seconds. Remove the bowl and stir, then place the bowl back in the microwave for another increment of 30 seconds. At this point, the chocolate should be about halfway melted. Remove the bowl and continue to stir until it is entirely melted. Sometimes you'll need to stick the chocolate back in the microwave for a third interval. Depending on your microwave, the third interval could take 10 to 30 seconds, so watch the chocolate carefully (and start at the lower end of the time range). You never want to fully melt chocolate in the microwave; it should become fully melted during the final stir, relying on the heat of the bowl to finish melting it. After the chocolate is fully melted, use it as directed in the recipe.

To melt chocolate on the stovetop, pour a few inches of water into a small saucepan, then place a small heatproof glass mixing bowl on top. It should fit snugly on top of the saucepan to prevent steam from escaping around the edge of the bowl. The bottom of the bowl should not touch the water; if it does, pour out some of the water. Heat the water on high until it begins to boil, then immediately turn  off the heat and put the chocolate in the bowl. Gently stir as it begins to melt against the hot bowl, continuing to stir until it is entirely melted. Then use as directed.

Ground Flaxseeds

In this book, I use flaxseeds to make a vegan egg replacer (see page 34). When mixed with water, flaxseeds activate and become a bit gelatinous, allowing them to serve as an egg-free binder in recipes. Flaxseed eggs are a great option if you have issues with eggs and/or are working toward a more plant-based diet.

Finely Ground Sea Salt and Finishing Salt

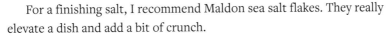

When I call for salt in my recipes, I always specify finely ground sea salt or, as a finishing salt, flaked sea salt. I prefer using sea salt over table salt in all instances. I like the taste better (and I promise it doesn't taste like seawater!), plus you may get some trace minerals in there due to the fact that sea salt is made by evaporating seawater. You can use whatever salt you have on hand, but keep in mind that when creating these recipes, I used sea salt.

For a finishing salt, I recommend Maldon sea salt flakes. They really elevate a dish and add a bit of crunch.

Wet Ingredients —————————————

Applesauce, Unsweetened

Applesauce is a wonderful substitute for both oil and eggs in traditional baking. I like to use some oil in my recipes to ensure that my baked treats are sufficiently moist, but applesauce is interesting because it not only adds moisture but also acts as a binder, much like an egg. Unsweetened applesauce, which is Paleo, adds a subtle natural sweetness to recipes. You can use your favorite store-bought applesauce or even make your own.

When baking cakes with applesauce, make sure that the applesauce is at room temperature; using cold applesauce may lead to a gummy cake.

Avocado Oil, Coconut Oil, and Olive Oil

Many traditional recipes call for canola or vegetable oil as a flavorless moisture additive, but a lot can be done with avocado oil, coconut oil, or olive oil. All three of these oils are Paleo and vegan, and they act just like canola or vegetable oil. Avocado oil is the most neutral tasting of the three, but sometimes olive oil adds a really nice flavor to baked treats. If you don't like the flavor of coconut, you can purchase triple-filtered coconut oil, which has almost no coconut flavor whatsoever. Unless a recipe directs you to melt coconut oil, it should be used at room temperature, where it is solid, like butter.

Dairy-Free Cream Cheese

While dairy-free cream cheese can be used as a substitute for real cream cheese in vegan cheesecake recipes, I prefer the texture of cashews and coconut yogurt in vegan cheesecakes. But in a vegan cream cheese frosting? That's another story! Dairy-free cream cheese is also wonderful smeared on a gluten-free bagel or a slice of toast. Some brands contain nuts (such as Miyoko's Creamery), but there are brands that are coconut oil–based and/or soy-based. Your best bet is to check out the dairy-free section at your market to see what's available locally.

Dairy-Free Milk and Cream

The dairy-free milk options that are available these days are incredible. Many of them are even Paleo! Of course, there are many different dairy-free milks, such as oat milk, soy milk, and even macadamia nut milk, but the three that I recommend for the recipes in this book are almond milk, cashew milk, and coconut milk. If you have a nut allergy, I highly recommend coconut milk, but oat milk is also a great option; it just won't be Paleo. (If you use oat milk and you require it to be gluten-free, be sure to buy a brand labeled as such to avoid milk made with oats that may have been contaminated with gluten.) For the recipes in this book, always choose an unsweetened dairy-free milk. Either plain or vanilla-flavored is fine.

Coconut cream is a dairy-free alternative to heavy cream. In some of my recipes, I ask you to use coconut cream from a can, but when not specified, you can use the nut and coconut milks found in the refrigerated section of the grocery store. Canned coconut cream comes in handy for making my Coconut Whipped Cream (page 49).

Dairy-Free Yogurt

Although dairy-free yogurt doesn't have quite the same protein count as regular yogurt, it does add a beautiful tanginess to recipes, along with moisture and a tender crumb that makes cakes, cupcakes, and baked goods irresistible. This is another ingredient that can be both Paleo and vegan, but it depends on the brand. When I call for dairy-free yogurt, I recommend that you use coconut yogurt, cashew yogurt, or almond yogurt. In a couple of recipes, I specify which type(s) of dairy-free yogurt should be used for the best results; otherwise, you can use whichever you like. These yogurts can be Paleo, too, but check the ingredients.

I recommend that you stick with plain unsweetened yogurt to keep the added sugars low in recipes.

Vegan Butter

We live in a day and age where vegan butter is nearly identical to regular butter. It's a wonderful substitute: wherever you would use regular butter, you can swap in vegan butter. If you're just beginning to switch out a few dairy-based ingredients for dairy-free options in baking, I'd start with vegan butter. My favorite brands include Daiya, Earth Balance, and Forager Project. The only brand I know of that is also considered Paleo is Miyoko's Creamery. I use Miyoko's for all of my Paleo vegan buttercream frostings. There are some great nut-free options as well, including Daiya, Earth Balance, and Tofutti. If using Earth Balance vegan butter, I recommend the buttery sticks rather than the tub of buttery spread—I find that the sticks work better for baking.

Apple Cider Vinegar

Apple cider vinegar is a fantastic ingredient for creating vegan buttermilk (see page 35) and Paleo baking powder (see page 37). Of course, you can use any neutral-flavored vinegar if you prefer, but apple cider vinegar is great because it is made from crushed apples and then fermented twice. You can find it in almost every grocery store. My preferred product is Bragg raw and unfiltered apple cider vinegar, but you can swap in your favorite if you have one.

Maple Syrup

I love maple syrup as an unrefined sweetener that's both vegan and Paleo. Of course, you definitely need to use the real deal. They call maple syrup liquid gold for a reason! It not only has a beautiful amber color, but the real good stuff is on the pricier end—mainly because the process of making maple syrup is pretty complicated and much different from just turning a sugar into a syrup. The good thing is that a little goes a long way!

There are various grades of maple syrup, but maple syrup purveyors are moving toward a system of classifying it by shade of color rather than grade. The lighter the color, the less the syrup tastes of maple, and the darker the color, the more robust the maple flavor. For most of my recipes, I typically go with an amber-colored maple syrup, but if you prefer a more detectable maple taste in your baked treats, you can definitely use the darker, more robust grades.

My all-time favorite brand of maple syrup is Crown Maple. The company offers a multitude of naturally infused flavors, including vanilla bean and cinnamon.

Medjool Dates

Though technically dates are a "dried" fruit, they retain some moisture, so they are used as a wet ingredient in many recipes. I specifically call for medjool dates (over Deglet and other varieties) because medjool dates not only have a very sweet almond-caramel flavor but also are the softest of the date varieties. As a result, they need only a relatively short soak in water to make them perfect for use as a binder in many recipes. For instance, for many of my vegan cheesecake crusts, I grind soaked dates into a sticky puree that helps bind together other dry ingredients.

Dates are also a wonderful natural sweetener; they taste almost like candy! For that reason, I like to have them around just for snacking.

Peanut Butter and Nut Butters

An ingredient that is always present in my kitchen is peanut butter (along with other nut butters, such as almond, pecan, and walnut). Peanut butter isn't considered Paleo, but other nut butters are if they contain no added sugar; just be sure to read the ingredients. If you avoid both nuts and peanuts, not a problem; feel free to swap in sunflower seed butter or coconut butter when peanut butter or nut butter is called for!

When purchasing peanut butter, nut butter, or sunflower seed butter for the recipes in this book, be sure to look for unsweetened and unsalted versions that have a creamy texture.

Vanilla Extract

Another ingredient you will always find in my cupboard is vanilla extract. If you omit the vanilla in any recipe that calls for it, the result will most definitely be subpar—that's how much of an effect just a teaspoon or two of vanilla can have! I use it not only for baked goods but also for general purposes: it's a wonderful addition to oatmeal and unsweetened dairy-free yogurt.

Choosing a high-quality vanilla extract is key. I know vanilla extract is expensive, but vanilla (along with maple syrup) is one of the select few ingredients that I tend to splurge on because the taste of the higher-quality stuff is so worth it to me. I really love Simply Organics' pure vanilla extract.

If you'd like to save money, there are some fun ways to make your own vanilla extract. Unfortunately, the process takes a few months, but the end result is well worth the wait.

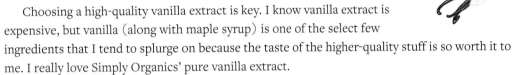

A Guide to the Recipe Icons

If you have to avoid certain ingredients because of food allergies or sensitivities or other dietary restrictions, not to worry! I've marked the recipes with icons to help you find the ones that suit you best. Here's a quick rundown:

 The recipe is gluten-free.

 The recipe is nut-free.

 The recipe is Paleo, which means that it is free of gluten, grains, legumes, and refined sugar.

 The recipe can be made peanut-free with the substitutions noted. (All other recipes are entirely peanut-free.)

If the word OPTION appears below an icon, look to the Notes section for modifications. As a reminder, all of the recipes in this book are free of dairy, eggs, and soy.

Chapter 2
ESSENTIAL
BAKEWARE & TOOLS

In this chapter, I go over the specific bakeware, tools, and other equipment you need to make perfect vegan cookies, cakes, and more. You'll find that the equipment listed here is pretty standard—vegan baking really isn't all that different from traditional baking, I promise! For all of you seasoned bakers who are just beginning to dabble in plant-based recipes, take comfort in knowing that you don't have to jettison your favorite baking pans. In fact, you probably already have almost everything you will need to get started on your vegan baking adventure.

Note that some pieces of bakeware as well as tools and equipment that I highlight in this chapter are truly essential: to make a layer cake, for example, you must have cake pans—they're not optional! Other items are strongly recommended, although you can generally find workarounds for these. You'll find many of the items listed here in the baking or paper goods aisle of your local grocery store; others can be found at specialty cooking stores or online.

Baking Pans and Tins

These will become your best friends when making vegan baked treats! There are all sorts and sizes of baking sheets, cake pans, and pie pans out there, so to make things less confusing, I've consolidated the following list to the types and sizes most useful for making the recipes in this book.

Typically, I use metal baking pans, but for some recipes, such as sheet cakes, brownies, bars, and breads, you can also use glass. It heats slightly differently in the oven, and treats take a bit longer to bake in glass, so keep that in mind if you're using glass baking dishes for these recipes.

For most brownies and bars, you'll need a 9 by 6-inch baking pan. If you want to make my Cookie Dough Fudge Bites (page 76), you'll need a 9-inch square baking pan, and for my Lemon Bars (page 82), you'll need an 8-inch square pan.

For cakes, I recommend having several nonstick cake pans; however, regular metal pans can be used if greased and floured. For the cake recipes in this book, you will need three 6-inch by 2-inch round cake pans, two 8-inch by 2-inch round cake pans, and one 9 by 12-inch rectangular pan for sheet cakes.

For Bundt cakes, I recommend using a 10-cup-capacity Bundt pan.

For cheesecakes, as well as the Blueberry Coffee Cake on page 218, you'll need an 8-inch springform pan.

For cookies, I recommend having at least one large baking sheet (aka cookie sheet) measuring at least 17 by 14 inches or two medium-sized baking sheets measuring at least 12 by 9 inches.

For cupcakes and muffins, you'll need a standard-size 12-cup muffin tin.

For pies and tarts, you'll need a 9-inch pie pan, a 9-inch tart pan with a removable bottom, and a 9-inch ceramic tart pan.

For quick breads, you'll need a loaf pan measuring 9 by 5 inches. (You'll need two of these pans for making my yeasted Chocolate Babka on page 300.)

Donut Pan

Though donuts traditionally are fried, I love to bake mine for a healthy treat. A donut pan is a useful piece of bakeware to have in case the craving strikes. (When it does, flip to my Baked Strawberry Donuts recipe on page 308!) I recommend getting two 6-cavity nonstick donut pans, but you can also purchase a 12-cavity nonstick donut pan. Silicone donut pans are also available, but I find them a hassle to use; given the soft, bendy nature of silicone, it's far too easy to squish a donut with oven mitts when removing the pan from the oven.

Cookie Scoop

I use cookie scoops to form and portion cookie dough as well as to divvy up cupcake and muffin batter evenly into muffin tins. My favorite cookie scoops are from OXO and KitchenAid. I believe KitchenAid has only one size, which holds about 1½ tablespoons of dough, but OXO offers several sizes ranging from 1 tablespoon to 3 tablespoons. For the most part, I use a 3-tablespoon and a 1½-tablespoon scoop.

If you don't have a cookie scoop, I also give you the option of using a measuring cup or measuring spoon, but I do recommend getting a cookie scoop!

Measuring Cups and Spoons

To get ultra-precise measurements, many bakers use a kitchen scale to weigh ingredients. For convenience, and because I realize that not everyone owns a kitchen scale, I prefer to use dry and liquid measuring cups. Dry measuring cups are made of metal or plastic and are designed so that you can easily level off a cup of flour, whereas liquid measuring cups are clear glass or plastic and are spouted. Having a full set of both is always helpful. Make sure you have a full set of measuring spoons, too, as you shouldn't eyeball even small quantities when baking.

Whisk

This tool might not seem essential, but trust me when I say that it is the key to getting your baked goods to come out right. Many bakers ignore the instruction to whisk and use a spoon instead when mixing dry ingredients, but the best way to ensure that dry ingredients are evenly distributed is to whisk rather than stir with a spoon. I use a 12-inch whisk and find it to be a good all-purpose size.

Electric Mixer

In all of the recipes in this book that require electric-powered mixing, save one, I use a hand mixer. These mixers are easy to find, are reasonably priced, and don't take up much storage or counter space. I use a hand mixer to beat together the wet ingredients for cookies and bars and to whip up frostings and creamy fillings for tarts. If you have a stand mixer, you can definitely use it if you prefer, but a hand mixer will take you far. The one recipe for which I suggest using a stand mixer for ease is the Eton Mess (page 206); that recipe involves making a meringue, which requires several minutes of mixing. But even there, with some patience, a hand mixer would work fine, too.

Food Processor

My food processors—yes, I have two!—are probably the most-used tools in my kitchen. Whether I'm making vegan ice cream, vegan cheesecake fillings, or homemade nut butter, I swear by this piece of equipment. My favorite food processors are made by Hamilton Beach and Oster Kitchen, and I use the two for different reasons. My Hamilton Beach food processor has lasted me nearly six years so far without issue; with a 12-cup capacity, it's large enough to process hefty amounts of cashews for cheesecake fillings or to coarsely grind oats into a rustic flour. My second food processor is made by Oster Kitchen, and its 4-cup capacity makes it ideal for finely processing small quantities of food, such as nuts, herbs, and sauces. A high-powered blender will work as well, but a small food processor is ideal for finely chopping ingredients.

Kitchen Thermometer

You need a kitchen thermometer for making yeasted breads like the Chocolate Babka on page 300. When I first started baking with yeast, I thought I could go by touch to judge how warm or cool the dairy-free milk was before adding the yeast to activate it, and I've since learned my lesson. A thermometer will help you accurately gauge when the heated liquid is at just the right temperature to add the yeast: too hot and you'll kill the yeast; too cold and it won't activate at all.

Parchment Paper

Parchment paper is essential for baking everything from cookies to bread loaves, and sometimes even cakes. It works much better than aluminum foil and saves you the effort of greasing baking sheets, which means that, without the added grease, your cookies won't spread as much as they bake. Aside from baking, I also use parchment paper to roll out pie dough and sometimes even to make DIY cupcake liners (see page 291). White and brown parchment paper work equally well, so there's no need to fret over the type or brand you buy.

Cupcake Liners

Many people don't realize this, but if a cupcake sticks to the paper liner too much, the problem could be the quality of the liner. Look for high-quality and/or nonstick cupcake liners for your baked goods. Some cupcake liners, such as silicone and certain parchment paper ones, are nonstick.

Piping Bag and Tips

For piping frosting, I prefer to use a piping bag and a Wilton #8B open star decorating tip or a plain Ateco decorating tube (size 808). I switch between the two depending on the design I feel like making. A tube is great if you want a clean look, whereas a star tip can be used to make fun ripples in your frosting swirl as well as intricate rosettes, shells, and stars. When piping meringue, a Wilton #32 open star tip is ideal.

Piping bags are easy to use, particularly the disposable type, but if you don't have a piping bag, you can snip off one corner of a large resealable plastic bag and insert the piping tip there. Even a piping tip isn't required—you can simply press the frosting through the small opening you created in the corner of the bag—but the frosting will not look as neat as it would if you had used a tip.

Cupcake Carrier

While a cupcake carrier isn't an essential item, it comes in handy if you're making dozens of cupcakes and need to transport them. When I worked at Georgetown Cupcakes in Washington, D.C., I ended up getting one to transport any leftover or "imperfect" cupcakes at the end of the day to friends and classmates rather than using a box (reducing the chance of the frosting being squashed!). You can find a cupcake carrier online.

Storage Containers

I highly recommend investing in a few good glass containers with tight-fitting lids for storing baked goods and treats. I love Pyrex and OXO Good Grips containers. You can use small, medium, and large containers to store anything from cupcakes to slices of coffee cake or cookies. Having proper containers also ensures that you're storing your creations in something that is airtight, which helps preserve their freshness. If you have only plastic containers, those will work, but glass is optimal.

Chapter 3
BAKING TIPS & TRICKS

In this chapter, I share my favorite baking tips and tricks that I've learned along the way to ensure that you get the best possible results when trying the recipes in this book!

Many of these pointers have been garnered either from advice passed on to me or through the best teacher of all: experience. Whether you're new to vegan or Paleo/gluten-free baking or you've been around the block a few times, it's always good to freshen up your knowledge and see if there are some new tips and tricks to be learned. After all, our baking skills grow the more we practice and learn from others.

I hope these tips and tricks are as useful to you as they have been for me!

Read through the steps before doing anything else.

When I first started baking, I was eager to jump right in. I quickly learned that for a recipe to come out as intended, it's important to read through the directions before beginning. This ensures that you have an understanding of what's to come in the process so that everything goes as the recipe writer intended, and it ensures fewer mistakes, if any. If you're already familiar with the steps, you'll be able to recognize if anything was skipped!

Measure out all of the ingredients in advance.

This simple organizational tip really does help. When you're constantly switching between the ingredient list and the directions, it's easy to mismeasure an ingredient—which could have drastic consequences for your baking creation. After you read the directions, measure out each ingredient before beginning. If you don't have enough measuring cups and/or spoons for all of the ingredients, you can place the premeasured ingredients in separate small bowls or cups so that you can continue to use the measuring cups and spoons until all of the ingredients are measured.

When a recipe says to bring ingredients to room temperature, doing so is necessary.

If an ingredient is listed as being at room temperature, it absolutely should be. That step is definitely not skippable! With vegan baking in particular, using ingredients at various temperatures—some chilled, some at room temperature—often leads to the dreaded gummy cake texture, which is probably why people think vegan baking is difficult. If all of the ingredients are at room temperature, you'll get the traditional cake texture that you know and love.

When baking cakes and cupcakes, use cake flour rather than all-purpose flour.

Cake flour isn't necessary for all baking (and this applies only if you eat gluten!), but I prefer cake flour to all-purpose flour for cakes and cupcakes. Cake flour yields a more tender crumb. I give a quick trick on how to make a DIY cake flour on page 10, so check that out if you don't have cake flour on hand.

If you're gluten-free, you can sift gluten-free 1-to-1 baking flour once or twice to ensure that there are no clumps and give the flour a lighter texture that more closely mimics cake flour.

Make Paleo baking powder by combining baking soda and vinegar.

This is a pretty cool trick that I learned when I first started my Paleo baking adventure, which actually came before my vegan baking adventure! Because corn is not considered Paleo and many store-bought baking powders contain cornstarch, I needed to find a way to get my baked goods to rise without using baking powder. I found it! You simply combine two parts baking soda with three parts apple cider vinegar to create a foamy mixture that acts like baking powder. It's a wonderful corn-free option for those who are following a strict Paleo diet. See page 37 for more detailed instructions for making and using this Paleo hack.

Ripen bananas in the oven.

This is one of my favorite tricks. I'm sure we've all been there: you want to make banana bread and your bananas aren't fully ripe (or worse, they're green!). An easy hack is to preheat the oven to 300°F and placing your unripened bananas on a baking sheet. Place the baking sheet in the oven for about 30 minutes, or until the banana peels turn black. When done, remove the bananas from the oven and allow them to cool for 10 minutes. Then use them as needed for baking.

Be sure to use unsweetened dairy-free milk and yogurt.

Not every carton of dairy-free milk or dairy-free yogurt is unsweetened. This trips up many first-time dairy-free product purchasers. You have to look for the "unsweetened" label. Using sweetened dairy-free products in a recipe that calls for unsweetened will alter the taste (and possibly your enjoyment) of the recipe. Thankfully, there are many unsweetened dairy-free products to be found in grocery stores.

Similarly, many unsweetened dairy-free milks and yogurts are flavored with vanilla; some are plain. You can use either vanilla-flavored or plain for the recipes in this book. I've used both, and I barely notice a difference in the final result.

Keep the oven door closed as much as possible.

I know you're eager to see how your baked creation is coming along, but try to keep the oven door closed. Each time you open the door, a draft of air at a drastically different temperature rushes into the oven, which lowers the oven temperature. This can result in increased baking times as well as foods just not baking properly. If you're nervous about burning something, use the oven light whenever possible. If your oven doesn't have a light, you can open the oven door near the very end of the baking time to gauge how much longer the food really needs.

Check baked goods for doneness near the end of the baking time.

This tip may seem contradictory to the preceding one, where I stress not opening the oven door during baking. But because all makes and models of ovens differ slightly, and because older ovens differ from newer ones, it's best to check the doneness of a baked good a few minutes before the end of the baking time stated in the recipe. It is preferable to use the oven light to do so, but if you must, you may open the oven door. Otherwise, even if you follow the recipe exactly, you could end up with overbaked cupcakes, cookies, and more.

The more recipes you make from a particular cookbook, the better you'll be able to judge if your oven bakes a little slower or faster than the cookbook author's oven. You can also use an oven thermometer to determine if your oven runs hot or cool and adjust the temperature as needed.

Allow baked goods to cool completely.

Way too many times, I've been so eager to finish a cake and get it decorated that I don't allow the cake layers to fully cool. This typically ends with the assembled cake going splat on the ground. And yes, I've shed a tear or two of frustration over it! Allowing cakes and cupcakes to fully cool before frosting them is crucial. Otherwise, the frosting will melt, and you'll have cake slipping and sliding all over the place.

Technically, cakes, cupcakes, and other baked goods continue to bake even after they come out of the oven, so it's best to let them cool at room temperature for as long as possible. If you're really in a hurry, once the cakes or cupcakes are nearly cool to the touch (with just a little warmth remaining in the center), you can pop them in the refrigerator to finish cooling. They should not be placed in the refrigerator right after they come out of the oven, however, as this will alter their texture and heat up your refrigerator.

I provide specific cooling instructions for all of the recipes in this book, but, as a general guideline, cookies or brownies might take 15 to 20 minutes to cool, whereas cakes will take 30 minutes or longer. As a reminder, nearly all baked goods require cooling, so make sure to allot time to cool your baked goods as directed when anticipating when you will be able to serve them.

Chapter 4
BASICS

Flaxseed Egg

YIELD: 1 flaxseed egg   **PREP TIME:** 1 minute, plus 9 minutes to activate

Flaxseed eggs come in handy when you need a binder and moisture but you don't want added sweetness from applesauce, my other go-to binder. If a recipe calls for multiple flaxseed eggs, simply double or triple this recipe as needed. For instance, if the recipe requires three flaxseed eggs, whisk together 3 tablespoons of ground flaxseeds with 9 tablespoons of water. Be sure to allow the flaxseeds to fully activate in the water; when activated, they become a bit gelatinous, which makes the mixture act like an egg in baking.

1 tablespoon ground flaxseeds
3 tablespoons water

1. In a small bowl, lightly whisk together the ground flaxseeds and water. Allow to sit for 5 to 9 minutes for the flaxseeds to fully activate; when activated, the mixture will appear gelatinized and thick, much like an egg white but thicker.

2. Use as you would a regular egg in baking.

Vegan Buttermilk

OPTION OPTION

YIELD: 1 cup   **PREP TIME:** 1 minute, plus 5 minutes to sit

If ever you're in need of vegan (or even regular) buttermilk, I hope you will try this simple recipe. It is one of my favorite off-the-beaten-path methods for making a baked treat vegan. This vegan buttermilk acts just like regular buttermilk and adds a wonderful flavor and texture to vegan cakes, cupcakes, and other treats. The recipe takes all of six minutes to make and is used quite a bit throughout the cake and cupcake chapters. Use whichever dairy-free milk you prefer: you have nut-free and/or Paleo options.

1 cup unsweetened dairy-free milk

1 tablespoon apple cider or white vinegar

1. In a small glass bowl or glass 1-cup liquid measuring cup, gently stir together the dairy-free milk and vinegar. Allow to sit for 5 minutes. The mixture will begin to thicken and curdle.

2. Use right away in any recipe that calls for buttermilk. This vegan buttermilk does not store well; make it fresh as needed.

Note

If you prefer a nut-free dairy-free milk, I recommend coconut or oat milk. (If using oat milk and you require it to be gluten-free, be sure to buy a brand labeled as such.) If you prefer Paleo, I recommend coconut, almond, or macadamia nut milk.

Paleo Powdered Sugar

YIELD: 1 cup   **PREP TIME:** 5 minutes

This has to be my favorite Paleo baking hack. Just by pulsing some coconut sugar in a food processor, you get a Paleo-friendly powdered sugar substitute. Give it a shot—it's mind-blowing when you put it in a recipe, and it comes together in about five minutes! Use this sugar in any frosting recipe in this book or even in your own recipe. Except for giving the frosting a slightly tan color and a bit of a sweet caramelized flavor, it acts just like regular powdered sugar.

1 cup coconut sugar

In a food processor, pulse the coconut sugar on high speed until it is pulverized into a fine powder, 2 to 3 minutes. Use as you would regular powdered sugar. If making a big batch to have on hand, store in a sealed glass container. If the powdered sugar begins to clump after a few days, simply pulse it in a food processor for 10 to 15 seconds or pass it through a sifter to remove any clumps before using.

Paleo Baking Powder

YIELD: equivalent to 2 teaspoons baking powder   **PREP TIME:** 2 minutes

This is the perfect substitute when you need a leavening agent in a Paleo recipe. Most baking powders contain corn, which is technically not Paleo.

2 teaspoons baking soda
1 tablespoon apple cider vinegar

1. Combine the baking soda and vinegar in a small bowl or ramekin. Stir and allow to sit for 1 minute.

2. Add to the wet ingredients in any recipe requiring baking powder for an easy Paleo baking powder swap.

Note

To increase or decrease this recipe, just remember these two rules: the ratio of the ingredients is two parts baking soda to three parts vinegar, and the quantity of baking soda used should match the amount of baking powder the recipe requires. So, if you need 1 tablespoon of baking powder, you simply combine 1 tablespoon of baking soda and 1½ tablespoons of vinegar.

Vegan Buttercream Frosting

OPTION   OPTION

YIELD: 4 cups (enough for one 3-layer, 6-inch cake; one 2-layer, 8-inch cake; or 16 cupcakes)   **PREP TIME:** 10 minutes, plus 2 hours to soften butter

Of all the frosting recipes on my blog, The Banana Diaries, *this easy vegan buttercream is by far my favorite. (I have few frostings there, but nothing beats a good buttercream.) This buttercream is an absolute dream; no one will know it's vegan! Truly! Whenever I use it, my taste testers (family and friends, of course) are shocked when I tell them it's dairy-free. It's a great time to be alive! The vegan products on the market these days make vegan baking that much easier and tastier. For this recipe, I use Miyoko's butter, which is vegan and Paleo, but I also recommend Forager Project's buttery spread and Earth Balance's vegan buttery sticks. I've included an option for a Paleo vegan buttercream frosting as well.*

1 cup vegan butter

4 cups powdered sugar, divided

1 teaspoon pure vanilla extract

1. Allow the vegan butter to soften and come nearly to room temperature; it should still be slightly cool to the touch. This will take about 2 hours.

2. In a large bowl, use a hand mixer to beat the vegan butter until creamy and whipped.

3. Sift in the powdered sugar 1 cup at a time and beat the sugar with the vegan butter, being sure to fully incorporate the sugar after each addition.

4. Continue to beat the frosting on high speed until it is fluffy and creamy, 2 to 3 minutes.

5. Add the vanilla extract and beat until fully incorporated.

6. Use immediately to frost a cake or pipe onto cupcakes.

7. To store, cover the frosting and keep in the refrigerator for up to 1 day, then allow it to sit at room temperature for 30 minutes before using. For the best results, rewhip the frosting with a hand mixer for 2 to 3 minutes.

Notes

To make this frosting nut-free, use Earth Balance's vegan buttery sticks.

To make it Paleo, use Miyoko's vegan butter and swap in 4 cups of Paleo powdered sugar (page 36).

Paleo Vegan Chocolate
BUTTERCREAM FROSTING

OPTION

YIELD: 4 cups (enough for one 3-layer, 6-inch cake; one 2-layer, 8-inch cake; or 16 cupcakes)   **PREP TIME:** 10 minutes, plus 2 hours to soften butter

Have I eaten this buttercream frosting by the spoonful? Yes, yes I have. It is that good. It comes together so easily, and the coconut sugar adds a delicious caramelized flavor—but don't worry, it doesn't taste like caramel, in case that's not your thing. This beautifully sweet frosting is a tasty addition to any baked treat. You can use it for any cake that calls for chocolate frosting, or whenever you feel that a cake or cupcake recipe could use some extra chocolate!

1 cup Miyoko's vegan butter

3 cups Paleo Powdered Sugar (page 36), divided

1 cup raw cacao powder

1. Allow the vegan butter to soften and come nearly to room temperature; it should still be slightly cool to the touch. This will take about 2 hours.

2. In a large bowl, use a hand mixer to beat the vegan butter until creamy and whipped.

3. Sift in the powdered sugar 1 cup at a time and beat the sugar with the vegan butter, being sure to fully incorporate the sugar after each addition.

4. Sift in the cacao powder and beat the frosting until the cacao powder is completely mixed in. Continue to beat on high speed until the frosting is fluffy and creamy, 2 to 3 minutes.

5. Add the vanilla extract and beat until the vanilla is fully incorporated.

6. Use immediately to frost a cake or pipe onto cupcakes.

7. To store, cover the frosting and keep in the refrigerator for up to 1 day, then allow it to sit at room temperature for 30 minutes before using. For the best results, rewhip the frosting with a hand mixer for 2 to 3 minutes.

Notes

Miyoko's is the only Paleo vegan butter that I know of on the market; however, if you find other options, feel free to use them here.

To make this frosting nut-free, use Earth Balance's vegan buttery sticks. However, this option is not Paleo.

If you do not require a Paleo frosting, you may replace the Paleo powdered sugar with regular powdered sugar and use any vegan butter you like.

Vegan Cream Cheese Frosting

OPTION OPTION

YIELD: 4 cups (enough for one 3-layer, 6-inch cake; one 2-layer, 8-inch cake; or 16 cupcakes)   **PREP TIME:** 10 minutes, plus 2 hours to soften butter and cream cheese

I don't know about you, but sometimes I want a frosting with a bit of a tang, in contrast to the über sweetness of buttercream. This frosting definitely fits that flavor preference! There are a few vegan cream cheeses on the market. Miyoko's and Kite Hill are my two favorite brands in terms of consistency and taste, but feel free to use your favorite instead.

1 cup vegan butter
½ cup vegan cream cheese
4 cups powdered sugar, divided
1 teaspoon pure vanilla extract

1. Allow the vegan butter and vegan cream cheese to soften and come nearly to room temperature; they should still be slightly cool to the touch. This will take about 2 hours.

2. In a large bowl, use a hand mixer to beat the vegan butter and vegan cream cheese until creamy and whipped.

3. Sift in the powdered sugar 1 cup at a time and beat the sugar with the vegan butter mixture, being sure to fully incorporate the sugar after each addition. Continue to beat on high speed until the frosting is fluffy and creamy, 2 to 3 minutes.

4. Add the vanilla extract and beat until the vanilla is fully incorporated.

5. Use immediately to frost a cake or pipe onto cupcakes.

6. To store, cover the frosting and keep in the refrigerator for up to 1 day, then allow it to sit at room temperature for 30 minutes before using. For the best results, rewhip the frosting with a hand mixer for 2 to 3 minutes.

Notes

To make this frosting nut-free, use Earth Balance's vegan buttery sticks and a nut-free vegan cream cheese. The two nut-free brands that I know of are Daiya and Tofutti.

To make it Paleo, use Miyoko's vegan butter and vegan cream cheese and swap in 4 cups of Paleo powdered sugar (page 36).

Chocolate Hazelnut Spread

YIELD: 1 cup   **PREP TIME:** 7 minutes   **COOK TIME:** 10 minutes

Once you try this spread, you'll never go back to store-bought. This homemade Paleo and vegan take on Nutella is made with the purest and simplest ingredients around, yet it still yields that flavor combination we all know and love. Chocolate hazelnut lovers, be warned—one spoonful and you won't be able to stop!

16 ounces raw hazelnuts

5 ounces unsweetened baking chocolate (100% cacao), chopped (about ½ cup)

2 tablespoons maple syrup

1 tablespoon coconut oil, melted

1 tablespoon raw cacao powder

¼ teaspoon finely ground sea salt (optional)

1. Preheat the oven to 350°F. Line a rimmed baking sheet with aluminum foil.

2. Spread the hazelnuts on the prepared baking sheet and toast in the oven for 10 minutes. This brings out their aroma and oils and makes it easier to remove the skins and blend the nuts.

3. Wrap the toasted hazelnuts while still warm in a clean kitchen towel and begin rubbing the towel over the nuts to remove the skins. This step helps to make a really smooth hazelnut butter. Don't worry if not all of the skins come off, though. Removing most of the skins will yield a deliciously creamy spread.

4. Place the hazelnuts in a food processor and blend until semi-smooth but rather clumpy.

5. Melt the chocolate in the microwave or on the stovetop, following the instructions on pages 14 and 15.

6. Pour the melted chocolate into the food processor and add the maple syrup, coconut oil, cacao powder, and salt, if using. Puree until the spread is completely smooth and creamy. This step will take about 5 minutes, depending on the power of your food processor.

7. Pour the spread into an airtight jar and store on the countertop for up to 5 days or in the refrigerator for up to a month.

Coconut Caramel Sauce

OPTION OPTION

YIELD: 2½ cups   **PREP TIME:** 5 minutes, plus 2 hours to chill
COOK TIME: 20 minutes

When I first started eating a plant-based diet, I figured I'd never taste a good caramel sauce again. Yes, I adore date caramel, but let's be real: it does taste a bit date-y. Not that there's anything wrong with that, but when you're craving true caramel, you want something that's as close to the real deal as possible. (Spoiler alert: I believe all things are possible.) So I created this delicious sauce that you can use just as you would a traditional caramel. It has that deliciously rich sweetness and beautiful light brown color you'd expect. What's even better, this recipe is pretty straightforward—no fancy techniques required! You just need a bit of patience while the caramel is chilling in the refrigerator.

1 (13.5-ounce) can unsweetened coconut cream

2 cups coconut sugar

2 tablespoons vegan butter (optional)

1 teaspoon pure vanilla extract

1. In a large soup pot over high heat, bring the coconut cream to a boil.

2. Reduce the heat to medium and add the coconut sugar, vegan butter (if using), and vanilla extract. Stir until the coconut sugar has dissolved. Then reduce the heat to low and continue to stir the sauce for 10 minutes. It will begin to thicken.

3. Remove the pot from the heat and allow the sauce to cool for 5 minutes before pouring into an airtight container. Let it cool completely before placing it in the refrigerator to chill for 2 hours. It will thicken to the consistency of traditional caramel sauce.

4. Use in any recipe calling for caramel, or use as a topping for ice cream or your favorite desserts.

5. Pour the sauce into an airtight jar and store in the refrigerator for up to 5 days. The longer it is stored, the thicker it will become. To reheat to a regular caramel consistency, scoop the desired amount of sauce into a microwave-safe bowl and reheat for 30 seconds.

Note

The vegan butter is optional, but it gives the sauce a richer flavor. Note that some vegan butters are made with nuts; be sure to use a nut-free vegan butter if you need a nut-free caramel. Additionally, not all vegan butters are considered Paleo. The only brand I know of that is both vegan and Paleo is Miyoko's.

Berry Jam

YIELD: 1 cup   **PREP TIME:** 3 minutes, plus 1 hour to chill
COOK TIME: 10 minutes

What I love about this recipe is that it's easily customizable. I use this jam in a few of the recipes in the book, where I call for specific versions, like raspberry or blueberry. However, feel free to use your preferred berry! It's such an easy jam recipe and is 100 percent preservative-free. Plus, you can spread this jam on toast, add it to your morning oatmeal, or smear some on top of a shortcake for the easiest sweet treat.

1½ cups fresh raspberries, blueberries, or sliced strawberries

½ cup water

2 tablespoons arrowroot powder

1. Rinse the berries thoroughly.

2. In a medium soup pot, heat the berries and water on high until the water begins to boil. Once boiling, reduce the heat to low and cook the berries for 5 minutes. While the berries are cooking, use a fork to mash them into a pulp.

3. Add the arrowroot powder and stir until there are no clumps of powder left.

4. Remove the pot from the heat and let cool for 5 minutes before pouring the jam into an airtight container. Place the container in the refrigerator for 1 hour to allow the jam to gel. Store in the refrigerator for up to a week.

Coconut Whipped Cream

YIELD: 2½ cups   **PREP TIME:** 5 minutes, plus 1 hour to chill coconut cream

If you don't have store-bought dairy-free whipped cream on hand, not to worry! This easy whipped cream comes together in five minutes and is a perfect topping for pies, ice cream sundaes, and just about any dessert in this book. What's great about this recipe is that it uses just two ingredients—just as simple as, if not simpler than, a traditional whipped cream.

1 (13.5-ounce) can unsweetened coconut cream, chilled for 1 hour

2 tablespoons maple syrup

1. Remove the can of coconut cream from the refrigerator and open the can. The cream should be solid on top, and the water will have settled on the bottom.

2. Scoop the coconut cream from the can into a large bowl. Reserve 2 tablespoons of the coconut water in the can; discard the rest or save it for a smoothie.

3. Add the maple syrup and use a hand mixer to whip at high speed for 5 minutes. The coconut cream will begin to thicken. Add the reserved coconut water and continue whipping until the coconut whipped cream becomes fluffy and voluminous.

4. Use the coconut whipped cream as stated in recipes or on ice cream, pie, etc. To store, spoon it into an airtight container and store in the refrigerator for up to 2 days. Alternatively, you can freeze it for up to 3 months. When ready to use, allow the whipped cream to thaw at room temperature for 2 to 2½ hours. If needed, you can rewhip it once thawed for 5 minutes to fluff it up again. Then use as desired.

Vegan Oat Crust

YIELD: One single 9-inch crust   **PREP TIME:** 10 minutes

If you love oats, you're going to love this crust. It is one of my favorite tart and pie crusts of all time. It's not like a traditional crust in that it has a bit of a rustic flavor and a chewiness to it. I think using oats makes anything taste a little more homey. Plus, this recipe calls for simple ingredients without the need for a rolling pin. This crust is perfect for cheesecakes, tarts, and pies alike, so it is used in abundance in the Pies, Tarts & Cheesecakes chapter. You can even add a pinch of cinnamon to the dough if the flavors of the pie filling you're using would go well with that!

2 cups gluten-free rolled oats

1 teaspoon baking soda

½ cup coconut oil, softened

¼ cup maple syrup

1 teaspoon pure vanilla extract

4 to 6 tablespoons chilled water

1. In a large food processor, pulse the oats until they become almost a fine powder. Add the baking soda and pulse once or twice to combine.

2. Add the coconut oil, maple syrup, and vanilla extract and blend until the dough becomes thick and sticky.

3. Add 4 tablespoons of chilled water to the dough and blend again. The dough should be soft and spoonable and slightly sticky to the touch. If needed, add the remaining 2 tablespoons of chilled water, 1 tablespoon at a time, and blend again until the dough has the right consistency. Use as directed in the recipe you are making.

Paleo Vegan Pie Crust

YIELD: One single 9-inch crust **PREP TIME:** 20 minutes, plus 1 hour to chill
COOK TIME: 12 minutes if par-baked or 20 minutes if prebaked

Who says you can't have pie while following a Paleo vegan diet? This crust is similar to a traditional pie crust, making it the perfect switch-up if you or someone you love needs a gluten-free, grain-free, dairy-free, and/or egg-free crust. The cool part is that even traditional eaters will love this crust! My mom is one of them; when she first tried it, she couldn't believe it was vegan, let alone not made with all-purpose flour. This crust is also nut-free, so those with nut allergies finally have a solution when they want an allergy-friendly pie that's also Paleo. This crust is perfect for everything from pumpkin pie to berry pies, so swap it for the traditional crust in your favorite pie recipe!

1¼ cups cassava flour

2 tablespoons arrowroot powder

1 teaspoon baking soda

¼ cup coconut sugar

½ cup coconut oil, softened

5 to 7 tablespoons chilled water

1. In a large bowl, whisk together the flour, arrowroot powder, baking soda, and coconut sugar.

2. Cut the coconut oil into the dry ingredients until it resembles clumpy sand. Add 5 tablespoons of chilled water and mix until the dough is thick. If needed, add the remaining 2 tablespoons of water, 1 tablespoon at a time, to help with the mixing process. You should be able to form the dough into a sticky ball.

3. Form the dough ball into a disc. Wrap it in plastic wrap and chill the dough for 1 hour. Take the dough out of the refrigerator and allow it to soften at room temperature for 15 to 20 minutes before rolling it out.

4. Place the dough between 2 pieces of parchment paper and roll it out to a circle about 12 inches in diameter and ½ inch thick. Smooth out any cracks with your fingers and continue rolling until smooth. Carefully place the dough in a 9-inch pie or tart pan by removing the top sheet of parchment and gently flipping the dough over into the pan using the bottom sheet. Remove the bottom sheet, now on top, trim off any crust overhanging the edge of the pan, and then crimp the edge of the crust with your fingers or a fork. Use the crust as directed in the recipe you are making; if the recipe requires the crust to be blind baked before being filled, complete Steps 5 through 7.

5. To blind bake the crust, preheat the oven to 350°F and use a fork to prick the bottom of the crust in several places. Chill the crust in the refrigerator for 15 minutes while the oven preheats.

6. When the oven is ready, lay a piece of parchment paper over the crust and place a handful of pie weights on top of the paper. For a prebaked crust, bake for 20 minutes, until it is fully baked and slightly golden; for a partially baked, or par-baked, crust, bake for 10 to 12 minutes, until it no longer looks raw and is slightly golden.

7. Remove from the oven and let cool for 15 minutes before filling.

Note

When blind baking a crust, most recipes call for either docking the crust or using pie weights to keep it flat. However, with this recipe, I've found that when docking alone is used, the crust sometimes still blisters or buckles a bit. I like to use both methods for extra insurance!

Chapter 5

BROWNIES & BARS

Peanut Butter Swirl Brownies

YIELD: 12 brownies   **PREP TIME:** 10 minutes   **COOK TIME:** 30 minutes

Think it's impossible to have a Paleo vegan brownie that tastes identical to the classic Ghirardelli? Think again! I've actually had several self-proclaimed Ghirardelli connoisseurs taste-test this brownie base (with and without the peanut butter swirl), and they were all speechless. It's truly the most über-rich brownie you will ever taste, and you won't be able to detect an ounce of grain-free flour in here. Plus, as you know, my love for chocolate and peanut butter runs deep, so why not get extra "fancy" and throw a swirl in there? These brownies are the definition of easy yet elegant—a combo I really love. You get the beautiful swirl of peanut butter without having to spend all day in the kitchen (it's literally just peanut butter; no mixing required), which leaves you plenty of time to enjoy these beauts (although I don't think that'll take you too long, either).

4 Flaxseed Eggs (page 34)

1 cup coconut sugar

½ cup coconut oil, melted

1 teaspoon pure vanilla extract

1 cup cassava flour

1 cup raw cacao powder

2 teaspoons baking powder

¼ teaspoon finely ground sea salt

⅓ cup maple syrup

1 cup unsweetened baking chips (100% cacao)

⅓ cup creamy unsalted peanut butter

1. Preheat the oven to 350°F. Line a 9 by 6-inch baking pan with parchment paper.

2. In a large bowl, vigorously whisk the flaxseed eggs with the coconut sugar, coconut oil, and vanilla extract.

3. Sift the flour, cacao powder, baking powder, and salt into a medium bowl.

4. Fold the dry ingredients into the wet until the mixtures are combined. Gently stir in the maple syrup. The batter will be thick but spoonable.

5. Fold in the chocolate chips.

6. Spoon the batter into the prepared baking pan. Spread the batter to the edges and smooth out the top.

7. Place 4 or 5 dollops of peanut butter on top of the brownie batter and use a butter knife to gently create swirls of peanut butter in the brownie batter. Be careful not to overswirl.

8. Bake for 25 to 30 minutes, until a toothpick inserted in the middle comes out clean.

9. Allow the brownies to cool for 15 minutes before slicing and serving. Store in an airtight container at room temperature for up to 5 days or in the refrigerator for up to a week.

Note ————————————————————

To make these brownies Paleo and peanut-free, swap sunflower seed
butter for the peanut butter. For Paleo, also use the Paleo baking
powder on page 37, but add it to the wet ingredients in Step 2.

Caramel-Filled Brownies

OPTION

YIELD: 12 brownies   **PREP TIME:** 10 minutes   **COOK TIME:** 30 minutes

There's nothing quite like the combination of a rich and bold caramel sauce and ultra-fudgy brownies. These chocolate squares of decadence are the ultimate indulgence, yet they are completely grain-free and vegan. How? Honestly, this recipe took so much work, but it paid off. The brownies are so decadent that you'd think this was a regular ol' recipe filled with milk, butter, eggs, and flour. What I love most about these brownies is that are they allergy-friendly, not only for those who can't consume gluten, dairy, or eggs but also for those who are allergic to nuts. You can make these brownies without swaps and rest assured that you have a delicious and safe dessert.

4 Flaxseed Eggs (page 34)

1 cup coconut sugar

½ cup coconut oil, melted

2 teaspoons Paleo Baking Powder (page 37) (see Notes)

1 teaspoon pure vanilla extract

1 cup cassava flour

1 cup raw cacao powder

¼ teaspoon finely ground sea salt

⅓ cup maple syrup

1 cup unsweetened baking chips (100% cacao)

½ cup Coconut Caramel Sauce (page 46)

1 teaspoon flaked sea salt, for garnish (optional)

1. Preheat the oven to 350°F. Line a 9 by 6-inch baking pan with parchment paper.

2. In a large bowl, vigorously whisk the flaxseed eggs with the coconut sugar, coconut oil, baking powder, and vanilla extract.

3. Sift the flour, cacao powder, and salt into a medium bowl.

4. Fold the dry ingredients into the wet until the mixtures are combined. Gently stir in the maple syrup. The batter will be thick but spoonable.

5. Fold in the chocolate chips.

6. Spoon half of the batter into the prepared baking pan and spread it to the edges.

7. Pour ⅓ cup of caramel on top of the brownie batter and use a butter knife to gently spread the caramel over the brownie, until it's evenly coated.

8. Spoon the second half of the batter on top of the caramel sauce and spread the batter to the edges of the pan.

9. Drizzle the remaining caramel sauce on top of the brownie batter.

10. Bake for 25 to 30 minutes, until a toothpick inserted in the middle comes out clean.

11. Allow the brownies to cool for 15 minutes before slicing and serving. Garnish with the flaked sea salt, if desired. Store in an airtight container at room temperature for up to 5 days or in the refrigerator for up to a week.

Notes

To make these brownies nut-free, follow the nut-free option for the Coconut Caramel Sauce.

If you do not need the brownies to be 100 percent Paleo, you can use any store-bought baking powder in place of the homemade version. Add it to the dry ingredients in Step 3.

Birthday Cake Bars

OPTION

YIELD: 12 bars **PREP TIME:** 10 minutes **COOK TIME:** 30 minutes

If you're not a fan of cake but you still want something fun to celebrate a birthday, these birthday cake bars are right up your alley! Incredibly easy to make and dotted with vegan sprinkles, these bars taste just like cake in square form. If you really want to go all-out, you can smear some Vegan Buttercream Frosting (page 38) on top, but these bars are absolutely delicious on their own.

¾ cup coconut sugar

½ cup coconut oil, softened

⅓ cup unsweetened applesauce

1 tablespoon pure vanilla extract

2 teaspoons Paleo Baking Powder (page 37)

2 cups gluten-free 1-to-1 baking flour or all-purpose flour

1 teaspoon baking soda

¼ teaspoon finely ground sea salt

3 to 6 tablespoons unsweetened dairy-free milk, room temperature

½ cup vegan sprinkles

1. Preheat the oven to 350°F. Line a 9 by 6-inch baking pan with parchment paper.

2. In a large bowl, use a hand mixer to beat the coconut sugar, coconut oil, applesauce, vanilla extract, and Paleo baking powder until creamy.

3. Sift the flour, baking soda, and salt into a medium bowl.

4. Fold the dry ingredients into the wet until the mixtures are combined. The batter will be thick but spoonable. If the batter seems too dry and is not coming together easily, gently stir in the dairy-free milk, starting with 3 tablespoons and adding up to 3 tablespoons more, 1 tablespoon at a time, as needed.

5. Fold in the sprinkles.

6. Spoon the batter into the prepared baking pan and smooth it out to the edges.

7. Bake for 25 to 30 minutes, until a toothpick inserted in the middle comes out clean.

8. Allow to cool for 15 minutes before slicing and serving. Store in an airtight container at room temperature for up to 5 days or in the refrigerator for up to a week.

Note

To make these bars nut-free, use either coconut milk or oat milk. (If using oat milk and you require it to be gluten-free, be sure to buy a brand labeled as such.)

Oatmeal Chocolate Chunk Bars

OPTION

YIELD: 8 bars   **PREP TIME:** 10 minutes   **COOK TIME:** 30 minutes

Full of sweet chocolate chunks with a texture that will make you drool, this is not your average oatmeal recipe. Many people associate oats with being healthy (and thus not so exciting on the flavor front), but I can assure you that these bars are anything but boring. Even non-oatmeal lovers will love them! They're reminiscent of chocolate chip blondies, but even chewier and gooier.

3 cups gluten-free rolled oats, divided

2 teaspoons baking powder

1 teaspoon baking soda

¼ teaspoon finely ground sea salt

½ cup coconut sugar

½ cup coconut oil, melted

½ cup unsweetened dairy-free milk

⅓ cup maple syrup

3 Flaxseed Eggs (page 34)

1 teaspoon pure vanilla extract

⅔ cup vegan dark chocolate chunks or chips or coarsely chopped vegan dark chocolate (55% to 70% cacao)

½ cup vegan dark chocolate chips (55% to 70% cacao), melted (see pages 14 and 15), for drizzling (optional)

1. Preheat the oven to 350°F. Line a 9 by 6-inch baking pan with parchment paper.

2. To make a rustic oat flour, place 2 cups of the rolled oats in a food processor or high-powered blender and pulse until most of the oats have been pulverized into a fine flour but with some larger pieces remaining, about 5 seconds. There should not be any whole oats remaining. You should have 1½ cups of rustic oat flour.

3. In a medium bowl, whisk together the oat flour, the remaining 1 cup of rolled oats, the baking powder, baking soda, and salt.

4. In a large bowl, vigorously whisk together the coconut sugar, coconut oil, dairy-free milk, maple syrup, flaxseed eggs, and vanilla extract.

5. Fold the dry ingredients into the wet until the mixtures are combined. The batter will be thick but spoonable.

6. Fold in the chocolate chunks.

7. Spoon the batter into the prepared baking pan and spread it to the edges. Bake for 25 to 30 minutes, until a toothpick inserted in the middle comes out clean.

8. Allow to cool for 15 minutes before slicing and serving. Drizzle the bars with melted chocolate, if desired. Store in an airtight container at room temperature for up to 5 days or in the refrigerator for up to a week.

Notes

To make these bars nut-free, use coconut milk or oat milk. (If using oat milk and you require it to be gluten-free, be sure to buy a brand labeled as such.)

For this recipe, I used Enjoy Life's semi-sweet mega chunks. Feel free to use chopped dark chocolate or chocolate chips if you don't have chunks.

Kitchen Sink Blondies

OPTION OPTION

YIELD: 12 blondies   **PREP TIME:** 10 minutes   **COOK TIME:** 30 minutes

One thing I know for sure: the salty pretzel and sweet chocolate combination will never get old. These blondies taste like a chocolate chip cookie in bar form, with a sweet and salty twist. Pretzels are basically a snack, so the fact that these blondies contain pretzels makes it acceptable to have them anytime, right?

1 cup coconut sugar

½ cup coconut oil, softened

⅓ cup unsweetened applesauce

1 teaspoon pure vanilla extract

2 cups all-purpose flour

2 teaspoons baking powder

1 teaspoon baking soda

¼ teaspoon finely ground sea salt

3 to 6 tablespoons unsweetened dairy-free milk (if needed)

¾ cup vegan dark chocolate chips (55% to 70% cacao)

1 cup pretzels, broken into small pieces

1. Preheat the oven to 350°F. Line a 9 by 6-inch baking pan with parchment paper.

2. In a large bowl, use a hand mixer to beat the coconut sugar, coconut oil, applesauce, and vanilla extract until combined.

3. In a medium bowl, whisk together the flour, baking powder, baking soda, and salt.

4. Add the dry ingredients to the wet and use a rubber spatula to fold the mixtures together into a thick but spoonable batter. If the batter seems too dry and is not coming together easily, gently stir in the dairy-free milk, starting with 3 tablespoons and adding up to 3 tablespoons more, 1 tablespoon at a time, as needed.

5. Fold in the chocolate chips and pretzel pieces.

6. Spoon the batter into the prepared baking pan and spread it to the edges. Bake for 25 to 30 minutes, until a toothpick inserted in the middle comes out clean.

7. Allow the blondies to cool for 15 minutes before slicing and serving. Store in an airtight container at room temperature for up to 5 days or in the refrigerator for up to a week.

Notes

To make these blondies gluten-free, swap the all-purpose flour with gluten-free 1-to-1 baking flour and use gluten-free pretzels.

For a nut-free dairy-free milk, I recommend coconut or oat milk. (If using oat milk and you require it to be gluten-free, be sure to buy a brand labeled as such.)

S'mores Brownies

YIELD: 16 brownies   **PREP TIME:** 10 minutes   **COOK TIME:** 30 minutes

Who says you need a roaring campfire to enjoy the classic combo of marshmallows and chocolate? These gooey and fudgy brownies topped with melted vegan marshmallows make the perfect indoor treat whether it's a rainy day or you just want to pretend you're camping without changing out of your PJs. Either way, these brownies certainly bring back memories! I like to smear the melted marshmallows just after they come out of the oven in case there are any spots of brownie popping out, but you can let the marshmallows set as is. They'll still have that beautiful pull-apart stretch when you slice the brownies.

4 Flaxseed Eggs (page 34)

1 cup coconut sugar

½ cup coconut oil, melted

1 teaspoon pure vanilla extract

1 cup cassava flour

1 cup raw cacao powder

2 teaspoons baking powder

¼ teaspoon finely ground sea salt

⅓ cup maple syrup

1 cup unsweetened baking chips or coarsely chopped unsweetened baking chocolate (100% cacao)

1 cup vegan marshmallows

1. Preheat the oven to 350°F. Line an 8-inch square baking pan with parchment paper.

2. In a large bowl, vigorously whisk the flaxseed eggs with the coconut sugar, coconut oil, and vanilla extract.

3. Sift the flour, cacao powder, baking powder, and salt into a medium bowl.

4. Fold the dry ingredients into the wet until the mixtures are combined. Gently stir in the maple syrup. The batter will be thick but spoonable.

5. Fold in the chocolate chips.

6. Spoon the batter into the prepared baking pan and spread it to the edges. Bake for 25 to 30 minutes, until a toothpick inserted in the middle comes out clean.

7. Set the oven to high-broil. While the oven is heating, place the vegan marshmallows on top of the baked brownies.

8. Place the brownies back in the oven for 30 to 45 seconds, until the marshmallows start to brown.

9. Remove the brownies from the oven. If desired, use a butter knife to smear the marshmallows to cover any spots of brownie showing. Allow the brownies to cool for 15 minutes before slicing and serving. Store in an airtight container at room temperature for up to 5 days or in the refrigerator for up to a week.

Red Velvet Brownies

OPTION

YIELD: 12 brownies   **PREP TIME:** 10 minutes   **COOK TIME:** 30 minutes

What I love most about these brownies is that their reddish hue comes entirely from beets. They taste just like red velvet cake without the cream cheese frosting—but don't worry! Because of the fudginess of these brownies, you won't even miss it! I used Forager Project's sour cream for this recipe, which at the time of this writing is the only vegan sour cream that I know of on the market. However, your favorite dairy-free yogurt (keep it nut-free if needed) will yield equally delicious results.

2 Flaxseed Eggs (page 34)

¾ cup coconut oil, melted

⅔ cup coconut sugar

½ cup vegan sour cream

1½ cups gluten-free 1-to-1 baking flour or all-purpose flour

3 tablespoons beet powder

2 tablespoons raw cacao powder

1 tablespoon baking powder

1 teaspoon baking soda

1 tablespoon maple syrup

1. Preheat the oven to 350°F. Line a 9 by 6-inch baking pan with parchment paper.

2. In a large bowl, vigorously whisk the flaxseed eggs with the coconut oil, coconut sugar, and vegan sour cream.

3. Sift the flour, beet powder, cacao powder, baking powder, and baking soda into a medium bowl.

4. Fold the dry ingredients into the wet until the mixtures are combined. Gently stir in the maple syrup.

5. Spoon the batter into the prepared baking pan and spread it to the edges. Bake for 25 to 30 minutes, until a toothpick inserted in the middle comes out clean.

6. Allow the brownies to cool for 15 minutes before slicing and serving. Store in an airtight container at room temperature for up to 5 days or in the refrigerator for up to a week.

Almond Butter Blondies

OPTION

YIELD: 12 blondies   **PREP TIME:** 10 minutes   **COOK TIME:** 30 minutes

These blondies are incredibly gooey and delicious and basically taste like a chocolate chip cookie disguised as a brownie. Swap in sunflower seed butter for the almond butter and you have a Paleo nut-free blondie. Before you get too freaked out, sunflower seed butter occasionally turns green when combined with coconut flour. Do not panic! Your blondies will still be edible; they'll just have a bit of a ghoulish glow.

⅔ cup coconut sugar

½ cup creamy unsalted almond butter or sunflower seed butter

½ cup unsweetened dairy-free milk

2 Flaxseed Eggs (page 34)

2 tablespoons maple syrup

2 teaspoons Paleo Baking Powder (page 37) (see Notes)

1 tablespoon pure vanilla extract

1½ cups cassava flour

½ cup coconut flour

1 teaspoon baking soda

¼ teaspoon finely ground sea salt

1 cup vegan dark chocolate chips (55% to 70% cacao)

1 teaspoon flaked sea salt, for garnish (optional)

1. Preheat the oven to 350°F. Line a 9 by 6-inch baking pan with parchment paper.

2. In a large bowl, vigorously whisk together the coconut sugar, almond butter, dairy-free milk, flaxseed eggs, maple syrup, baking powder, and vanilla extract.

3. Sift the flours, baking soda, and salt into a medium bowl.

4. Fold the dry ingredients into the wet until the mixtures are combined. The batter will be thick but spoonable.

5. Fold in the chocolate chips.

6. Spoon the batter into the prepared baking pan and spread it to the edges. Bake for 25 to 30 minutes, until a toothpick inserted in the middle comes out clean.

7. Allow the blondies to cool for 15 minutes before slicing and serving. Garnish with the flaked sea salt, if desired. Store in an airtight container at room temperature for up to 5 days or in the refrigerator for up to a week.

Notes

To make these blondies nut-free, use sunflower seed butter and either coconut milk or oat milk. (If using oat milk and you require it to be gluten-free, be sure to buy a brand labeled as such.)

If you do not need the blondies to be 100 percent Paleo, you can use any store-bought baking powder in place of the homemade version. Add it to the dry ingredients in Step 3, along with the baking soda.

Chocolate Cheesecake Bars

YIELD: 12 bars   **PREP TIME:** 15 minutes, plus 2 to 3 hours to soak cashews and 1 hour to chill   **COOK TIME:** 35 minutes

My motto is always "save room for dessert." But if having a whole slice of cheesecake sounds like too much, you might enjoy these cheesecake bars instead! They deliver just the right amount of cheesecake, perfect for an after-dinner treat or a snack. I love how you can get the taste and texture of cheesecake from vegan ingredients. The trick is using dairy-free yogurt. Many cheesecake recipes call for lemon, but I get the best results with a bit of yogurt. That way, you get a real tang rather than the acidic punch of lemon, making these bars way more decadent and indulgent! The chocolatey date-sweetened oat crust is a perfect substitute for the usual plain graham cracker base.

OAT CRUST:

1 cup gluten-free rolled oats

1 cup raw cacao powder

½ cup pitted medjool dates

⅓ cup water

CHEESECAKE FILLING:

1 cup raw cashews, soaked in water for 2 to 3 hours and drained

½ cup plain unsweetened dairy-free yogurt

⅓ cup maple syrup

¼ cup arrowroot powder

1 cup vegan dark chocolate chips (55% to 70% cacao)

To make the crust:

1. Preheat the oven to 350°F. Line a 9 by 6-inch baking pan with parchment paper.

2. In a large food processor, pulse the oats and cacao powder until the oats turn into a rustic flour.

3. Add the dates and water and pulse again until a sticky dough has formed.

4. Press the dough into the baking pan, pushing it to the edges. Place the pan in the freezer to firm up the crust as you prepare the filling.

To make the filling:

5. In a large food processor, puree the cashews until smooth, 2 to 3 minutes.

6. Add the dairy-free yogurt, maple syrup, and arrowroot powder and pulse again until completely mixed.

7. Melt the chocolate chips in the microwave or on the stovetop, following the instructions on pages 14 and 15.

8. Pour the melted chocolate into the food processor and puree the filling until the chocolate is evenly distributed.

9. Remove the crust from the freezer and pour the filling over the crust. Spread it to the edges of the pan.

10. Bake for 30 to 35 minutes, until the edges and almost all of the filling have set. The center will be slightly jiggly.

11. Remove from the oven and let cool for 15 minutes, then place the pan in the refrigerator to chill and set, at least 1 hour. Once set, slice and serve. Store in an airtight container in the refrigerator for up to a week.

Pecan Pie Bars

YIELD: 8 to 16 bars   **PREP TIME:** 15 minutes, plus 2 hours to chill
COOK TIME: 30 minutes

If you're a fan of pecan pie, then you will love this Paleo vegan version of the holiday classic in bar form. Made with a simple grain-free crust and topped with the easiest pecan pie filling you could ever imagine, this is an elegant dessert to grace a dessert table, and truly anyone can make it. I will warn you, though: it is hard to stop at one bar!

CASSAVA FLOUR CRUST:

¾ cup coconut oil, softened

1½ cups cassava flour

¼ cup maple syrup

4 to 6 tablespoons water, chilled

PECAN PIE FILLING:

¾ cup unsweetened coconut cream

½ cup maple syrup

¼ cup coconut sugar

¼ cup arrowroot powder

1 teaspoon pure vanilla extract

2 cups raw pecan halves

To make the crust:

1. Line an 8 by 6-inch baking pan with parchment paper.

2. In a large bowl, use a fork to cut the coconut oil into the flour until it's crumbly.

3. Add the maple syrup and water, starting with 4 tablespoons of water and adding more if needed, and continue to mix until you have thick dough.

4. Evenly press the dough into the prepared baking pan and place the pan in the refrigerator to chill for 20 minutes.

5. While the crust is chilling, preheat the oven to 350°F.

6. When the oven is ready, place the crust in the oven to blind bake for 10 minutes. It will be slightly soft but not gooey and should be just lightly golden in color.

7. Remove the crust from the oven and set it aside while you prepare the filling. Keep the oven at 350°F.

To make the filling:

8. In a large bowl, whisk together the coconut cream, maple syrup, coconut sugar, arrowroot powder, and vanilla extract. Add the pecans and lightly toss to evenly coat the pecans.

9. Pour the filling over the par-baked crust, place the pan back in the oven, and bake for 20 minutes, or until the middle is entirely set.

10. Remove the pan from the oven and let cool for 20 to 30 minutes, then place the pan in the refrigerator until the bars are fully chilled, 1 to 2 hours.

11. Once chilled, slice into 8, 9, or 16 bars. Store in an airtight container in the refrigerator for up to a week.

Cookie Dough Fudge Bites

OPTION

YIELD: 24 or 36 squares   **PREP TIME:** 8 minutes, plus 35 minutes to freeze

This is the only recipe in the book (aside from some of the basics) that doesn't require an oven! These bites of cookie dough fudge are incredibly easy and absolutely heavenly; it truly does taste like you're eating a square of frozen cookie dough. Minus the eggs. And the butter. And the flour. Basically, this is cookie dough you actually want to eat. Even better, you can store these bites in the freezer for a while and take one out whenever you need a little pick-me-up!

1 cup raw unsalted creamy cashew butter or sunflower seed butter

½ cup coconut oil, melted

⅓ cup maple syrup

1 tablespoon pure vanilla extract

¾ cup coconut flour

¼ teaspoon finely ground sea salt

½ cup vegan dark chocolate chips (55% to 70% cacao)

1. Line the bottom and sides of a 9-inch square baking pan with parchment paper, allowing some paper to overhang the sides of the pan. (This will help you easily remove the fudge from the pan after it's set.)

2. In a large bowl, mix together the cashew butter, coconut oil, maple syrup, and vanilla extract.

3. Add the flour and salt and mix until well combined.

4. Fold in the chocolate chips.

5. Pour the mixture into the prepared baking pan and place in the freezer to chill for 35 minutes.

6. Remove the fudge from the freezer and allow it to come to room temperature for 5 to 7 minutes.

7. Using the edges of the parchment paper, lift up and remove the fudge from the pan. Slice into 24 or 36 squares. Store in an airtight container in the freezer for up to a month.

Chocolate Granola Bars

OPTION

YIELD: 8 bars   **PREP TIME:** 10 minutes, plus 2 hours to soak dates
COOK TIME: 30 minutes

Growing up, I was a big fan of granola bars. I would request one in my lunch and as an after-school snack whenever my mom purchased them (which was pretty much weekly). These bars are every bit as chewy and delicious as the ones I grew up with, but with minimal and natural ingredients (and quite possibly an even better taste than I remember). They make the perfect sweet treat for a work or school snack, and they can even serve as a healthier dessert!

1 cup pitted medjool dates, soaked in water for 2 hours and drained

⅓ cup unsweetened dairy-free milk

⅓ cup raw unsalted cashew butter or coconut butter

1½ cups gluten-free rolled oats

½ cup raw cacao powder

½ teaspoon finely ground sea salt

½ cup vegan dark chocolate chips (55% to 70% cacao)

1 teaspoon flaked sea salt, for garnish (optional)

1. Preheat the oven to 350°F. Line a 9 by 6-inch baking pan with parchment paper.

2. In a food processor, pulse the dates with dairy-free milk and cashew butter until smooth.

3. In a medium bowl, whisk together the oats, cacao powder, and salt.

4. Scrape the date mixture from the food processor into the bowl with the dry ingredients. Fold the dry ingredients into the wet until the mixtures are combined. The mixture will be thick but spoonable.

5. Fold in the chocolate chips.

6. Spoon the mixture into the prepared baking pan, then use your fingers to evenly press it to the edges. Bake for 25 to 30 minutes, until the granola mixture looks dry.

7. Allow to cool for 15 minutes before slicing and serving. Garnish with the flaked sea salt, if desired. Store in an airtight container at room temperature for up to 5 days, in the refrigerator for up to a week, or in the freezer for up to a month.

Note

For a nut-free dairy-free milk, I recommend coconut or oat milk. (If using oat milk and you require it to be gluten-free, be sure to buy a brand labeled as such.)

Chocolate Peppermint Bars

YIELD: 12 bars   **PREP TIME:** 15 minutes   **COOK TIME:** 35 minutes

I wanted to push the envelope and make something that is undeniably fudgy and rich but doesn't contain nuts. Despite my partner, Jared, being an avocado addict, I had never come up with an avocado dessert! These bars were the first of their kind, and they've been the gateway to turning me into another millennial who loves avocados. But only for sweet recipes, rest assured. (I cannot get on the avocado toast train!) These bars are packed with a refreshing hit of peppermint that makes them perfect for the wintertime. But don't worry, you don't have to wait for the colder months to come around before making them! If you don't want a peppermint flavor, simply omit the extract, and you'll have ultra-rich fudge bars with a delicious oat-y crust.

OAT CRUST:

1 cup gluten-free rolled oats

1 cup raw cacao powder

½ cup coconut oil, softened

⅓ cup maple syrup

Raw cacao powder, for garnish (optional)

CHOCOLATE PEPPERMINT FILLING:

2 large ripe avocados, pitted

1 cup raw cacao powder

½ cup maple syrup

½ cup coconut oil, melted

¼ cup cassava flour

1 tablespoon peppermint extract

To make the crust:

1. Preheat the oven to 350°F. Line a 9 by 6-inch baking pan with parchment paper.

2. In a food processor, pulse the oats and cacao powder until the oats are ground into a rustic flour.

3. Add the coconut oil and maple syrup and pulse until a sticky dough has formed.

4. Press the dough evenly into the baking pan, pushing it to the edges. Place the pan in the freezer to firm up the crust while you prepare the filling.

To make the filling:

5. In a food processor, pulse the avocados until smooth.

6. Add the cacao powder, maple syrup, coconut oil, flour, and peppermint extract and blend until smooth.

7. Remove the crust from the freezer and spoon the filling over the crust. Spread it to the edges of the pan.

8. Bake for 30 to 35 minutes, until almost all of the filling has set. The center will be slightly jiggly.

9. Remove from the oven and let cool for 15 minutes before slicing. If desired, dust the tops of the bars with cacao powder before serving. Store in an airtight container in the refrigerator for up to a week.

OPTION

YIELD: 8 to 16 bars   **PREP TIME:** 15 minutes, plus 2 hours to chill
COOK TIME: 40 minutes

If you've ever had a traditional lemon bar, then you will go crazy for this Paleo vegan version. I've never met a lemon-flavored treat that I didn't like, but I have to say, there is something about these bars that makes them incredibly light and has me going back for seconds and thirds. Even better, these bars are tinted yellow with nothing other than turmeric. But don't worry, if you're not a fan of turmeric, you won't taste a bit of it in here. It adds a nice yellow hue, and the combination of lemon and sweetness takes care of the rest.

CASSAVA FLOUR CRUST:

¾ cup coconut oil, softened

1½ cups cassava flour

¼ cup maple syrup

4 to 6 tablespoons water, chilled

TOPPINGS (OPTIONAL):

½ cup Berry Jam (page 48), made with blueberries

½ cup fresh blueberries

½ cup powdered sugar (see Note)

LEMON FILLING:

2 cups unsweetened coconut cream

¾ cup freshly squeezed lemon juice (about 4 lemons)

½ cup maple syrup

1 teaspoon pure vanilla extract

½ cup arrowroot powder

2 teaspoons turmeric powder

To make the crust:

1. Line an 8-inch square baking pan with parchment paper.

2. In a large bowl, use a fork to cut the coconut oil into the flour until it's crumbly.

3. Add the maple syrup and water, starting with 4 tablespoons of water and adding more if needed, and continue to mix until you have thick dough.

4. Press the dough evenly into the pan and place the pan in the refrigerator to chill for 20 minutes.

5. While the crust is chilling, preheat the oven to 350°F.

6. When the oven is ready, place the crust in the oven to blind bake for 10 minutes. It will be slightly soft but not gooey and should be just lightly golden in color.

7. Remove the crust from the oven and set it aside while you prepare the filling. Keep the oven at 350°F.

To make the filling:

8. In a large bowl, whisk together the coconut cream, lemon juice, maple syrup, and vanilla extract. Sift in the arrowroot powder and turmeric and whisk again until there are no clumps.

9. Pour the filling over the par-baked crust and bake for 20 minutes, or until the edges have started to set and the middle is still slightly jiggly.

10. Remove the pan from the oven and let cool for 20 to 30 minutes, then place the pan in the refrigerator until the bars are fully chilled, 2 to 3 hours.

11. Once chilled, slice into 8, 9, or 16 bars. Top with the jam, blueberries, and/or powdered sugar, if desired. Store in an airtight container in the refrigerator for up to a week.

Note ───────────────────────────
The optional powdered sugar is not considered Paleo.

Flourless Chickpea Brownies

YIELD: 12 brownies   **PREP TIME:** 5 minutes   **COOK TIME:** 35 minutes

This is the ultimate easy brownie recipe. Not only are these brownies entirely flourless, but you don't even have to do any of the hard mixing work. Yep, these brownies are basically blender brownies, except you use a food processor to get the batter ultra-creamy and smooth. Plus, there's a little bit of added nutritional benefit thanks to the protein that comes from the chickpeas. All you need to do: purée, blend, and bake! I love to make these brownies as my healthy meal prep dessert at the beginning of each week. It's the perfect recipe that requires minimal effort yet still provides the taste and nutritional satisfaction.

1 (15-ounce) can unsalted chickpeas, rinsed and drained

¼ cup coconut oil, softened

¾ cup coconut sugar

½ cup raw cacao powder

½ cup unsweetened applesauce, room temperature

1 tablespoon baking powder

1 teaspoon baking soda

1 teaspoon pure vanilla extract

½ teaspoon finely ground sea salt

1. Preheat the oven to 350°F. Line a 9 by 6-inch baking pan with parchment paper.

2. In a food processor, blend the chickpeas and coconut oil until smooth and creamy, almost like hummus. Add the remaining ingredients and blend until smooth.

3. Spoon the batter into the prepared pan and spread it to the edges. Bake for 30 to 35 minutes, until a toothpick inserted in the middle comes out clean.

4. Allow the brownies to cool for 15 minutes before slicing and serving. Store in an airtight container at room temperature for up to 5 days or in the refrigerator for up to a week.

Vegan Shortbread Millionaire Bars

OPTION

YIELD: 8 to 16 bars   **PREP TIME:** 15 minutes, plus 2 hours to chill
COOK TIME: 15 minutes

The combination of crisp and sweet shortbread, gooey caramel sauce, and rich chocolate fudge makes these bars absolutely irresistible. While eating one might not make you a millionaire, they're so rich that they deserve the title! Sprinkling them with a little flaked sea salt cuts the sweetness and adds an elegant finish, making these a wonderful treat for parties.

CASSAVA FLOUR CRUST:

¾ cup coconut oil, softened

1½ cups cassava flour

¼ cup maple syrup

4 to 6 tablespoons water, chilled

1 cup vegan dark chocolate chips (55% to 70% cacao)

⅓ cup coconut oil, melted

1 batch Coconut Caramel Sauce (page 46)

½ teaspoon flaked sea salt, for garnish (optional)

To make the crust:

1. Line an 8-inch square baking pan with parchment paper.

2. In a large bowl, use a fork to cut the coconut oil into the flour until it's crumbly.

3. Add the maple syrup and water, starting with 4 tablespoons of water and adding more if needed, and continue to mix until you have a thick dough.

4. Evenly press the dough into the prepared baking pan and place the pan in the refrigerator to chill for 20 minutes.

5. While the crust is chilling, preheat the oven to 350°F.

6. When the oven is ready, place the crust in the oven to blind bake for 15 minutes. It will be slightly soft but not gooey and should be lightly golden in color.

7. Remove the crust from the oven and set it aside while you prepare the filling.

To make the bars:

8. Melt the chocolate in the microwave or on the stovetop, following the instructions on pages 14 and 15. Add the coconut oil to the melted chocolate and mix together. Set aside.

9. Pour the caramel sauce over the prebaked crust, smoothing it out to the edges. Top with the melted chocolate mixture and spread the chocolate to completely cover the caramel.

10. Place the bars in the freezer to set for 2 hours. When ready to serve, remove from the freezer and allow the chocolate to thaw for 15 minutes before slicing. Slice into 8, 9, or 16 bars. Sprinkle the bars with the flaked sea salt, if desired, and serve. Store in an airtight container in the refrigerator for up to a week.

Note ————————————————————————————————————

To make these bars nut-free, follow the nut-free option for the
Coconut Caramel Sauce.

Candy Bar Blondies

OPTION OPTION OPTION

YIELD: 12 blondies   **PREP TIME:** 10 minutes   **COOK TIME:** 30 minutes

This is the type of recipe you need for the day after Halloween, when you don't know what to do with all that leftover candy. These deliciously chewy and decadent blondies packed with all sorts of vegan candies are incredibly easy and an all-around crowd-pleaser, from kids to adults. Plus, they're so customizable: I give recommendations for the candy to use, but feel free to swap in whichever candy you like! Make these your favorite candy bar blondies.

1 cup coconut sugar

½ cup coconut oil, softened

⅓ cup unsweetened applesauce

1 teaspoon pure vanilla extract

2 cups all-purpose flour or gluten-free 1-to-1 baking flour

2 teaspoons baking powder

1 teaspoon baking soda

¼ teaspoon finely ground sea salt

3 to 6 tablespoons unsweetened dairy-free milk (if needed)

¾ cup vegan dark chocolate chips (55% to 70% cacao)

½ cup UnReal Dark Chocolate Crispy Gems (see Notes)

½ cup crushed vegan peanut butter cups or coconut butter cups

1. Preheat the oven to 350°F. Line a 9 by 6-inch baking pan with parchment paper.

2. In a large bowl, use a hand mixer to beat the coconut sugar, coconut oil, applesauce, and vanilla extract until combined.

3. In a medium bowl, whisk together the flour, baking powder, baking soda, and salt.

4. Add the dry ingredients to the wet and use a rubber spatula to fold the mixtures together into a thick but spoonable batter. If the batter seems dry and isn't coming together easily, gently stir in the dairy-free milk, starting with 3 tablespoons and adding more as needed, 1 tablespoon at a time.

5. Fold in the chocolate chips, candy gems, and crushed peanut butter cups.

6. Spoon the batter into the prepared baking pan and spread it to the edges. Bake for 25 to 30 minutes, until a toothpick inserted in the middle comes out clean.

7. Allow the blondies to cool for 15 minutes before slicing and serving. Store in an airtight container at room temperature for up to 5 days or in the refrigerator for up to a week.

Notes

UnReal is the only brand I know of that makes vegan candy-coated chocolate gems. They are available in supermarkets and online. However, you can absolutely make your own; there is a plethora of recipes online!

To make these blondies nut-free, use coconut milk or oat milk. (If using oat milk and you require it to be gluten-free, be sure to buy a brand labeled as such.)

Snickerdoodle Blondies

OPTION

YIELD: 16 blondies   **PREP TIME:** 10 minutes   **COOK TIME:** 30 minutes

As soon as September 1 rolls around, I crave all things cinnamon. (Okay, so the craving actually starts in August, but I try to hold out for September…"try" being the operative word.) These snickerdoodle blondies are just as deliciously chewy and warm as a traditional snickerdoodle, and they're at the top of my list to make and enjoy alongside a homemade dairy-free chai latte—because the more spice, the better, right?

¾ cup plus 1 tablespoon coconut sugar, divided

½ cup coconut oil, softened

⅓ cup unsweetened applesauce

1 tablespoon pure vanilla extract

2 cups gluten-free 1-to-1 baking flour or all-purpose flour

3 tablespoons ground cinnamon, divided

2 teaspoons baking powder

1 teaspoon baking soda

1 teaspoon cream of tartar

¼ teaspoon finely ground sea salt

3 to 6 tablespoons unsweetened dairy-free milk, room temperature, as needed

1. Preheat the oven to 350°F. Line an 8-inch square baking pan with parchment paper.

2. In a large bowl, use a hand mixer to beat ¾ cup of the coconut sugar, the coconut oil, applesauce, and vanilla extract until combined.

3. Sift the flour, 2 tablespoons of the cinnamon, the baking powder, baking soda, cream of tartar, and salt into a medium bowl.

4. Fold the dry ingredients into the wet until the mixtures are combined. The batter will be thick but spoonable. If it seems dry and isn't coming together easily, gently stir in the dairy-free milk, starting with 3 tablespoons and adding more as needed, 1 tablespoon at a time.

5. Spoon the batter into the prepared baking pan and spread it to the edges.

6. In a separate small bowl, whisk together the remaining 1 tablespoon of cinnamon and the remaining 1 tablespoon of coconut sugar. Sprinkle the cinnamon sugar evenly on top of the batter.

7. Bake for 25 to 30 minutes, until a toothpick inserted in the middle comes out clean.

8. Allow the blondies to cool for 15 minutes before slicing and serving. Store in an airtight container at room temperature for up to 5 days or in the refrigerator for up to a week.

Note ————————————————————————

To make these blondies nut-free, use coconut milk or oat milk. (If using oat milk and you require it to be gluten-free, be sure to buy a brand labeled as such.)

Chapter 6

COOKIES

Chai-Spiced Snickerdoodles

OPTION OPTION

YIELD: 20 cookies   PREP TIME: 10 minutes   COOK TIME: 15 minutes

I love anything chai flavored, so I thought it would be fun to spice up the traditional snickerdoodle. Of course, these cookies are vegan and have a gluten-free option, so maybe there was nothing traditional about them to begin with. Regardless, these chewy and spicy cookies are the perfect fall treat!

1¾ cups all-purpose flour or gluten-free 1-to-1 baking flour

1 tablespoon chai spice blend, store-bought or homemade (see Notes)

1 teaspoon baking soda

1 teaspoon cream of tartar

¼ teaspoon finely ground sea salt

1 cup coconut sugar

½ cup coconut oil, softened

⅓ cup unsweetened applesauce, room temperature

1 teaspoon pure vanilla extract

2 tablespoons unsweetened dairy-free milk, room temperature (if needed)

CHAI SUGAR COATING:

¼ cup chai spice blend

¼ cup granulated sugar

1. Place an oven rack in the middle position and preheat the oven to 350°F. Line a large baking sheet (at least 17 by 14 inches) with parchment paper. Alternatively, you can bake the cookies in batches using 2 medium baking sheets.

2. In a medium bowl, whisk together the flour, chai spice, baking soda, cream of tartar, and salt.

3. In a large bowl, use a hand mixer to beat the coconut sugar, coconut oil, applesauce, and vanilla extract until creamy.

4. Gradually add the dry mixture to the wet mixture while stirring; continue stirring until the mixtures are well combined. You should have a sticky and thick dough. Add 2 tablespoons of dairy-free milk if needed to help the dough form. Set aside.

5. Make the chai sugar coating: Whisk together the chai spice and sugar in a small bowl.

6. Use a 1½-tablespoon cookie scoop to form a dough ball and roll it between your hands. Lightly roll the ball in the spiced sugar mixture. Repeat with the remaining dough to create 20 cookies, placing them on the prepared baking sheet, about 1½ inches apart. (If you don't have a medium cookie scoop, scoop up heaping tablespoons of the dough and form them into balls between your hands.)

7. Bake for 12 to 15 minutes, until the tops are lightly golden and the cookies have spread slightly.

8. Remove from the oven and let the cookies cool for 15 minutes before removing from the pan. Store in an airtight container at room temperature for up to 5 days or in the refrigerator for up to a week.

Notes

To make your own chai spice blend for this recipe, combine 1 teaspoon ground cinnamon, 1 teaspoon ginger powder, ½ teaspoon allspice, ½ teaspoon ground cardamom, ½ teaspoon ground cloves, and ½ teaspoon ground nutmeg.

For a nut-free dairy-free milk, I recommend coconut or oat milk. (If using oat milk and you require it to be gluten-free, be sure to buy a brand labeled as such.)

Macadamia Nut Cookies

OPTION

YIELD: 24 cookies   **PREP TIME:** 10 minutes   **COOK TIME:** 12 minutes

What I love most about these cookies is that they're no-chill—you simply make the dough and then bake it! Which means you get to enjoy these deliciously decadent and tropically nutty cookies (macadamia nuts always make me think of Hawaii) even sooner than more traditional recipes. I've made these cookies with both all-purpose flour and gluten-free 1-to-1 baking flour, and both options work fabulously.

1 cup coconut sugar

¾ cup coconut oil, softened

½ cup unsweetened applesauce

2 teaspoons pure vanilla extract

1¾ cups gluten-free 1-to-1 baking flour or all-purpose flour

2 tablespoons unsweetened dairy-free milk (if needed)

½ cup raw macadamia nut halves and/or pieces

1. Place an oven rack in the middle position and preheat the oven to 350°F. Line a large baking sheet (at least 17 by 14 inches) with parchment paper. Alternatively, you can bake the cookies in batches using 2 medium baking sheets.

2. In a large bowl, use a hand mixer to beat the coconut sugar, coconut oil, applesauce, and vanilla extract until creamy.

3. Add the flour gradually, stirring it into the coconut sugar mixture until well combined and you have a thick and sticky dough. If needed, add the dairy-free milk to help the dough form. Then fold in the chopped nuts.

4. Using a tablespoon, scoop up the dough and roll into 24 balls using your hands. Place on the prepared baking sheet(s), about 2 inches apart. Using the back of a spoon, lightly flatten the cookies to help them spread.

5. Bake on the middle rack for 10 to 12 minutes, until the cookies are lightly golden and have spread slightly.

6. Remove from the oven and let cool completely before removing the cookies from the pan. Store in an airtight container at room temperature for up to 5 days or in the refrigerator for up to a week.

Peanut Butter Cup Cookies

OPTION OPTION OPTION

YIELD: 12 cookies   **PREP TIME:** 10 minutes   **COOK TIME:** 15 minutes

These cookies are reminiscent of delicious peanut butter blossoms, but with an extra dash of fun. I mean, who wouldn't want to have a little candy with their cookie? You start with a vegan and gluten-free peanut butter cookie dough, and then you top each warm cookie with a mini peanut butter cup. If you'd like to enjoy these with a molten filling, as shown, break into the cookies while they are still warm, and the peanut butter will ooze right out of them. If you don't eat peanut butter, see the recipe for homemade Paleo vegan almond butter cups on my blog; I've tested it here, and it works wonderfully! However, you should feel free to use your favorite brand or recipe.

1 cup coconut sugar

½ cup unsweetened applesauce

⅓ cup coconut oil, softened

⅓ cup creamy unsalted peanut butter

2 teaspoons pure vanilla extract

2 cups gluten-free 1-to-1 baking flour or all-purpose flour

2 tablespoons unsweetened dairy-free milk (if needed)

12 mini vegan peanut butter cups

1. Preheat the oven to 350°F. Line a baking sheet with parchment paper.

2. In a large bowl, use a hand mixer to beat the coconut sugar, applesauce, coconut oil, peanut butter, and vanilla extract until creamy.

3. Add the flour gradually, stirring it into the coconut sugar mixture until well combined and you have a thick and sticky dough. If needed, add the dairy-free milk to help the dough form.

4. Scoop up 2 tablespoons of the dough and roll it between your hands into a ball. Repeat with the rest of the dough to make 12 balls, placing them on the prepared baking sheet about 1 inch apart. Lightly press your thumb into the middle of each dough ball to create a space for the peanut butter cups.

5. Bake for 12 to 15 minutes, until the cookies are lightly golden and have spread slightly.

6. Remove from the oven and let cool on the pan for 10 minutes before removing the cookies. When still slightly warm, lightly press a peanut butter cup into the center of each cookie. Store in an airtight container at room temperature for up to 5 days or in the refrigerator for up to a week.

To make these cookies nut-free, use a nut-free dairy-free milk (coconut and oat milk are good options). (If using oat milk and you require it to be gluten-free, be sure to buy a brand labeled as such.)

To make them peanut-free, swap in sunflower seed butter for the peanut butter and replace the peanut butter cups with almond butter cups. The recipe for Paleo vegan almond butter cups on my blog works wonderfully here, as do any number of the good-quality almond butter cup brands found in grocery stores.

Brownie Chocolate Chip Cookies

OPTION   OPTION

YIELD: 8 to 10 large cookies   **PREP TIME:** 10 minutes   **COOK TIME:** 15 minutes

What's better than a double chocolate chip cookie and a regular chocolate chip cookie? The two combined into one! These look more complicated than they are: you simply divide the dough in half, flavor one half with cacao powder, form into balls, and then press the two doughs together and bake. The double chocolate chip portion of these cookies reminds me an awful lot of brownie dough, giving these mash-ups a whole 'nother delicious dimension. Both kids and adults love these—my taste-testers confirmed.

1¾ cups all-purpose flour or gluten-free 1-to-1 baking flour

1 teaspoon baking soda

¼ teaspoon finely ground sea salt

1 cup coconut sugar

½ cup coconut oil, softened

⅓ cup unsweetened applesauce, room temperature

1 teaspoon pure vanilla extract

3 tablespoons unsweetened dairy-free milk, room temperature, divided

¼ cup raw cacao powder

⅔ cup vegan dark chocolate chips (55% to 70% cacao)

1. Place an oven rack in the middle position and preheat the oven to 350°F. Line a large baking sheet (at least 17 by 14 inches) with parchment paper. If you don't have a large baking sheet, you can bake the cookies in batches using 2 medium baking sheets.

2. In a medium bowl, whisk together the flour, baking soda, and salt.

3. In a large bowl, use a hand mixer to beat the coconut sugar, coconut oil, applesauce, and vanilla extract until creamy.

4. Gradually add the dry mixture to the wet mixture while stirring; continue stirring until the mixtures are well combined. You should have a sticky and thick dough. Add 2 tablespoons of dairy-free milk if needed to help the dough form. Then fold in the chocolate chips.

5. Divide the dough in half, placing one half in a separate medium bowl. To one bowl, add the cacao powder and 1 tablespoon of dairy-free milk and gently mix the cacao powder into the dough with your hands.

6. Use a 1½-tablespoon cookie scoop to scoop one dough ball from the regular chocolate chip dough and another dough ball from the chocolate dough. Using your hands, gently press the 2 balls together and roll to create one giant dough ball. Repeat with the remaining dough to create 8 to 10 cookies, placing them on the prepared baking sheet, about 1½ inches apart. (If you don't have a medium cookie scoop, scoop up heaping tablespoons of the dough and form the portions of dough into balls between your hands.)

7. Bake for 12 to 15 minutes, until the regular chocolate chip portion of the cookie is lightly golden and the cookies have spread slightly.

8. Remove from the oven and let the cookies cool for 15 minutes before removing from the pan. Store in an airtight container at room temperature for up to 5 days or in the refrigerator for up to a week.

Note —————————————————————————————

For a nut-free dairy-free milk, I recommend coconut or oat milk. (If using oat milk and you require it to be gluten-free, be sure to buy a brand labeled as such.)

Oatmeal Raisin Cookies

OPTION

YIELD: 20 cookies   **PREP TIME:** 10 minutes   **COOK TIME:** 12 minutes

This might sound crazy, but oatmeal raisin cookies were my all-time favorite growing up. My mom used to buy the ones with the vanilla icing that came in the red sealed package, and I'd secretly try to sneak one before dinner every night. I know, I know. Naturally, I'm the rare one who goes for the oatmeal raisin over the chocolate chip. What can I say, I like to march to the beat of my own drum! This vegan version tastes just like that favorite cookie of my childhood. And it's gluten-free as well, which means that even more people can enjoy these deliciously cinnamon-y and chewy delights!

2 cups gluten-free rolled oats, divided

2 teaspoons ground cinnamon

1 teaspoon baking soda

⅓ cup vegan butter, softened

½ cup coconut sugar

1 teaspoon pure vanilla extract

3 Flaxseed Eggs (page 34)

⅔ cup raisins

1. Place an oven rack in the middle position and preheat the oven to 350°F. Line a large baking sheet (at least 17 by 14 inches) with parchment paper. Alternatively, you can bake the cookies in batches using 2 medium baking sheets.

2. To make a rustic oat flour, place 1 cup of the rolled oats in a food processor or high-powered blender and pulse until most of the oats have been pulverized into a fine flour but with some larger pieces remaining, about 5 seconds. There should not be any whole pieces of oats remaining. You should have ¾ cup of rustic oat flour.

3. In a medium bowl, whisk together the remaining 1 cup of rolled oats, the rustic oat flour, cinnamon, and baking soda.

4. In a large bowl, use a hand mixer to beat the vegan butter, coconut sugar, vanilla extract, and flaxseed eggs until creamy.

5. Gradually add the dry mixture to the wet mixture while stirring; continue stirring until the mixtures are well combined. Then fold in the raisins.

6. Use a 1-tablespoon cookie scoop to form the dough into 20 balls and place 1½ inches apart on the prepared baking sheet. If you don't have a small cookie scoop, use a tablespoon to scoop up the dough and form it into balls between your hands.

7. Bake for 10 to 12 minutes, until the cookies are golden brown.

8. Remove from the oven and let cool on the pan for 15 minutes before removing the cookies. Store in an airtight container at room temperature for up to 5 days or in the refrigerator for up to a week.

Notes

If you prefer, you can swap the rustic oat flour with gluten-free 1-to-1 baking flour. If you're not gluten intolerant, you can substitute all-purpose flour.

To make these cookies nut-free, use a nut-free vegan butter, such as Earth Balance.

Peanut Butter–Filled

CHOCOLATE COOKIES

OPTION OPTION OPTION

YIELD: 10 cookies   **PREP TIME:** 12 minutes   **COOK TIME:** 15 minutes

If there ever was a way to make the blissful marriage of peanut butter and chocolate even better, it's these cookies. They're easily my most devoured treat in the whole book. My wonderful taste-testers went crazy for them. (I mean, they love all of the recipes, but I think I got a crew of the peanut butter obsessed!) A rich and decadent chocolate cookie filled with oozing peanut butter makes for a truly indulgent vegan treat.

1 cup all-purpose flour or gluten-free 1-to-1 baking flour

¾ cup raw cacao powder

½ cup coconut oil, softened

½ cup coconut sugar

1 teaspoon pure vanilla extract

3 Flaxseed Eggs (page 34)

2 tablespoons unsweetened dairy-free milk (if needed)

10 tablespoons creamy unsalted peanut butter, divided

1. Preheat the oven to 350°F. Line a baking sheet with parchment paper.

2. Sift the flour and cacao powder into a medium bowl.

3. In a large bowl, use a hand mixer to beat the coconut oil, coconut sugar, vanilla extract, and flaxseed eggs until creamy.

4. Gradually add the dry mixture to the wet mixture while stirring; continue stirring until the mixtures are well combined and you have a thick and sticky dough. Add the dairy-free milk if needed to help the dough form.

5. Use a 1½-tablespoon cookie scoop to form 2 balls. (If you don't have a medium cookie scoop, scoop up 2 heaping tablespoons of the dough and form them into 2 balls between your hands.)

6. Use your thumb to press into the middle of both dough balls to create a pocket for the peanut butter. Spoon 1 tablespoon of peanut butter into the middle of one of the dough balls and use the other to seal the peanut butter into a large cookie dough ball. Place on the prepared baking sheet and repeat with the remaining dough and peanut butter to make a total of 10 cookies.

7. Bake for 12 to 15 minutes, until the cookies have spread slightly.

8. Remove from the oven and let cool for 15 minutes before removing the cookies from the pan. Store in an airtight container at room temperature for up to 5 days or in the refrigerator for up to a week.

Notes

For a nut-free dairy-free milk, I recommend coconut or oat milk. (If using oat milk and you require it to be gluten-free, be sure to buy a brand labeled as such.)

To make these cookies peanut-free, swap in a nut butter or sunflower seed butter for the peanut butter.

Everything but the Kitchen Sink

COOKIES

OPTION   OPTION

YIELD: 20 cookies   **PREP TIME:** 10 minutes   **COOK TIME:** 15 minutes

One of my all-time favorite cookies. I absolutely love the chunks of slightly salty pretzel combined with the sweet punch of chocolate. Now, typically, Everything but the Kitchen Sink Cookies contain toffee bits. However, those are hard to find vegan, so I decided to omit them altogether. Of course, I could have you make your own toffee bits, but that's a lot of extra effort for one recipe! These cookies taste so good that you won't miss that toffee flavor. I like to garnish them with a bit of flaked sea salt—yes, it definitely adds to the aesthetic, but I also like a bit of extra saltiness. If you are a fan of the "kitchen sink" theme, also check out my recipe for Kitchen Sink Blondies on page 64.

1¾ cups all-purpose flour or gluten-free 1-to-1 baking flour

1 teaspoon baking soda

¼ teaspoon finely ground sea salt

1 cup coconut sugar

½ cup coconut oil, softened

⅓ cup unsweetened applesauce

1 teaspoon pure vanilla extract

2 tablespoons unsweetened dairy-free milk (if needed)

1½ cups pretzels, broken into small pieces

⅔ cup vegan dark chocolate chips (55% to 70% cacao)

1. Place an oven rack in the middle position and preheat the oven to 350°F. Line a large baking sheet (at least 17 by 14 inches) with parchment paper. Alternatively, you can bake the cookies in batches using 2 medium baking sheets.

2. In a medium bowl, whisk together the flour, baking soda, and salt.

3. In a large bowl, use a hand mixer to beat the coconut sugar, coconut oil, applesauce, and vanilla extract until creamy.

4. Gradually add the dry mixture to the wet mixture while stirring; continue stirring until the mixtures are well combined and you have a sticky and thick dough. Add the dairy-free milk if needed to help the dough form. Then fold in the pretzels and chocolate chips.

5. Use a 1½-tablespoon cookie scoop to form the dough into 20 balls and place on the prepared baking sheet, about 1½ inches apart. (If you don't have a medium cookie scoop, scoop up heaping tablespoons of the dough and form the portions of dough into balls between your hands.)

6. Bake for 12 to 15 minutes, until lightly golden and the cookies have spread slightly.

7. Remove from the oven and let cool for 15 minutes before removing the cookies from the pan. Store in an airtight container at room temperature for up to 5 days or in the refrigerator for up to a week.

Notes ————————————

To make these cookies gluten-free, swap the all-purpose flour with gluten-free 1-to-1 baking flour and use gluten-free pretzels.

For a nut-free dairy-free milk, I recommend coconut or oat milk. (If using oat milk and you require it to be gluten-free, be sure to buy a brand labeled as such.)

Chocolate Chip Biscotti

OPTION

YIELD: 20 cookies   **PREP TIME:** 15 minutes   **COOK TIME:** 47 minutes

Every time I see the word biscotti, *I vividly remember my grade school Italian teacher (lovingly) correcting us for calling a single cookie a "biscotti" rather than a "biscotto." Non dire "biscotti," ma "biscott-o" per uno biscotto! she would say. Either way, I suspect she would greatly approve of these vegan chocolate chip biscotti. In fact, I know she would, because my Sicilian grandmother loves them, and she's had her fair share of biscotti. They're a little more work, but well worth it. They pair perfectly with a cappuccino, I might add!*

2 cups gluten-free 1-to-1 baking flour or all-purpose flour

½ cup super-fine blanched almond flour

2 teaspoons baking soda

½ cup coconut oil, melted

⅓ cup maple syrup

⅓ cup coconut sugar

1 tablespoon pure vanilla extract

3 Flaxseed Eggs (page 34)

½ cup coarsely chopped vegan dark chocolate (80% cacao) (about 3 ounces)

1. Preheat the oven to 350°F. Line a baking sheet with parchment paper.

2. Sift the flours and baking soda into a medium bowl.

3. In a large bowl, whisk together the melted coconut oil, maple syrup, coconut sugar, vanilla extract, and flaxseed eggs until well combined.

4. Sift the dry mixture into the wet mixture and stir until just combined, being careful not to overmix the dough. Then fold in the chopped chocolate.

5. Divide the dough in half and form each portion into a 12-inch-long loaf, measuring about 2½ inches wide. Make the loaves as even as possible to ensure that all of the cookies turn out the same. Place the loaves on the prepared baking sheet.

6. Bake for 25 to 27 minutes, until slightly firm to the touch and lightly golden brown.

7. Remove from the oven and let the loaves cool slightly, about 5 minutes. Use a serrated knife to cut each loaf crosswise into ¾-inch-wide slices, about 10 biscotti per loaf.

8. Carefully place the biscotti slices back on the baking sheet, cut side down, and bake for another 20 minutes, flipping the biscotti after 10 minutes.

9. Remove from the oven and let cool for another 15 minutes before removing the biscotti from the pan. Store in an airtight container at room temperature for up to 5 days or in the refrigerator for up to a week.

Double Chocolate Chip Cookies

OPTION OPTION

YIELD: 20 cookies   **PREP TIME:** 10 minutes   **COOK TIME:** 15 minutes

In my opinion, the only thing better than chocolate is double chocolate, and these cookies are a testament to that. They are the perfect balance of gooey and chewy with melted chocolate in every bite. I can feel my stomach rumbling! The espresso powder is optional, but I highly recommend using it. It amplifies the chocolate flavor and makes the cookies more robust. However, these cookies are still decadent sans espresso powder. Every chocolate lover in your life will go crazy for these vegan masterpieces, even those who don't eat gluten-free.

1½ cups gluten-free 1-to-1 baking flour or all-purpose flour

½ cup raw cacao powder

¼ teaspoon finely ground sea salt

¾ cup coconut sugar

½ cup coconut oil, softened

⅓ cup unsweetened applesauce

1 teaspoon pure vanilla extract

1 teaspoon espresso powder (optional)

2 tablespoons unsweetened dairy-free milk (if needed)

⅔ cup vegan dark chocolate chips (55% to 70% cacao)

1. Place an oven rack in the middle position and preheat the oven to 350°F. Line a large baking sheet (at least 17 by 14 inches) with parchment paper. Alternatively, you can bake the cookies in batches using 2 medium baking sheets.

2. In a medium bowl, whisk together the flour, cacao powder, and salt.

3. In a large bowl, use a hand mixer to beat the coconut sugar, coconut oil, applesauce, vanilla extract, and espresso powder, if using, until creamy.

4. Gradually stir the dry mixture into the wet mixture; continue stirring until the mixtures are well combined and you should have a thick and sticky dough. Add the dairy-free milk if needed to help the dough form. Then fold in the chocolate chips.

5. Use a 1½-tablespoon cookie scoop to form the dough into 20 balls and place on the prepared baking sheet, about 1 inch apart. (If you don't have a medium cookie scoop, scoop up heaping tablespoons of the dough and form the portions of dough into balls between your hands.)

6. Bake for 12 to 15 minutes, until the edges appear set and the cookies have spread slightly.

7. Remove from the oven and let the cookies cool for 15 minutes before removing from the pan. Store in an airtight container at room temperature for up to 5 days or in the refrigerator for up to a week.

Note

For a nut-free dairy-free milk, I recommend coconut or oat milk. (If using oat milk and you require it to be gluten-free, be sure to buy a brand labeled as such.)

Frosted Soft Sugar Cookies

OPTION

YIELD: 20 cookies   **PREP TIME:** 10 minutes   **COOK TIME:** 15 minutes

I have so many memories of the famous Lofthouse cookies. My mom would buy them for family celebrations, whether it was the Fourth of July, a birthday, or even Thanksgiving! These frosted sugar cookies are an ode to the ones of my childhood. Many of my recipes are, really. I make these treats so that those who can't have the traditional version of a favorite food can still enjoy it in some form. With a pinch of cream of tartar, which adds a subtle tang and a bit of lift, these cakelike cookies are downright addicting! (For those who have never used cream of tartar, don't worry; it's completely vegan! It's derived from fermenting grapes.) Plus, you can frost them however you like. Go with pink, blue, green, yellow—the choice is yours! I give a few suggestions in the Notes.

1½ cups gluten-free 1-to-1 baking flour or all-purpose flour

1 teaspoon cream of tartar

¾ cup coconut sugar

½ cup vegan butter, softened

¼ cup unsweetened applesauce

2 teaspoons pure vanilla extract

2 Flaxseed Eggs (page 34)

½ batch Vegan Buttercream Frosting (page 38)

1 teaspoon all-natural food coloring (see Notes)

½ cup vegan sprinkles

1. Place an oven rack in the middle position and preheat the oven to 350°F. Line a large baking sheet (at least 17 by 14 inches) with parchment paper. Alternatively, you can bake the cookies in batches using 2 medium baking sheets.

2. In a medium bowl, whisk together the flour and cream of tartar.

3. In a large bowl, use a hand mixer to beat the coconut sugar, vegan butter, applesauce, vanilla extract, and flaxseed eggs until creamy.

4. Gradually add the dry mixture to the wet mixture while stirring; continue stirring until the mixtures are well combined and you have a thick and sticky dough.

5. Use a 1½-tablespoon cookie scoop to form the dough into 20 balls and place on the prepared baking sheet, about 1½ inches apart. (If you don't have a medium cookie scoop, scoop up heaping tablespoons of the dough and form the portions of dough into balls between your hands.)

6. Using the back of a spoon, lightly press each dough ball until flattened to about ½ inch thick.

7. Bake for 12 to 15 minutes, until the cookies are lightly golden. Remove from the oven and let cool for 15 minutes before removing from the pan and transferring to a rack to cool completely.

8. While the cookies are cooling, stir the frosting with the food coloring; set aside.

9. When the cookies are completely cool, spread 2 tablespoons of the colored frosting on top of each cookie. Top with the sprinkles. Store in an airtight container at room temperature for up to 5 days or in the refrigerator for up to a week.

Chocolate Peppermint Cookies

OPTION

YIELD: 20 cookies   **PREP TIME:** 10 minutes   **COOK TIME:** 15 minutes

The perfect holiday treat, these cookies are bursting with fresh mint and rich chocolatey flavors. Don't tell him I told you, but I hear they're Santa's favorite! These cookies aren't just for holiday baking, however; the cool thing about mint is that it gets another season to shine on St. Patrick's Day. I highly recommend making a double batch of these cookies, because they will be gone in the blink of an eye! If you don't need them cookies to be gluten-free, you can substitute all-purpose flour for the gluten-free baking flour. Both options work fabulously.

1⅓ cups gluten-free 1-to-1 baking flour

⅔ cup raw cacao powder

¾ cup coconut sugar

½ cup vegan butter, softened (see Notes)

⅓ cup unsweetened applesauce

1 teaspoon pure vanilla extract

1 teaspoon espresso powder (optional; see Notes)

2 tablespoons unsweetened dairy-free milk (if needed)

½ cup crushed vegan peppermint candies (see Notes)

½ cup vegan dark chocolate chips (55% to 70% cacao)

1. Place an oven rack in the middle position and preheat the oven to 350°F. Line a large baking sheet (at least 17 by 14 inches) with parchment paper. Alternatively, you can bake the cookies in batches using 2 medium baking sheets.

2. In a medium bowl, whisk together the flour and cacao powder.

3. In a large bowl, use a hand mixer to beat the coconut sugar, vegan butter, applesauce, vanilla extract, and espresso powder, if using, until creamy.

4. Gradually add the dry mixture to the wet mixture while stirring; continue stirring until the mixtures are well combined and you have a thick and sticky dough. Add the dairy-free milk if needed to help the dough form. Then fold in the peppermint candies and chocolate chips.

5. Use a 1½-tablespoon cookie scoop to form the dough into 20 balls and place on the prepared baking sheet, about 1 inch apart. (If you don't have a medium cookie scoop, scoop up heaping tablespoons of the dough and form the portions of dough into balls between your hands.)

6. Bake for 12 to 15 minutes, until the cookies have spread slightly.

7. Remove from the oven and let the cookies cool for 15 minutes before removing from the pan. Store in an airtight container at room temperature for up to 5 days or in the refrigerator for up to a week.

Notes

You can swap coconut oil for the vegan butter, but I prefer the taste of vegan butter in these cookies. It makes them fudgier.

The espresso powder is optional, but I really do recommend it. It makes these cookies all the more chocolatey!

For a nut-free dairy-free milk, I recommend coconut or oat milk. (If using oat milk and you require it to be gluten-free, be sure to buy a brand labeled as such.)

There are a few options for vegan peppermint candies in stores and online. If you prefer, you can replace the candies with 1 teaspoon of peppermint extract, adding it in Step 3, and increase the amount of chocolate chips to 1 cup.

Monster Cookies

OPTION OPTION OPTION

YIELD: 20 cookies   **PREP TIME:** 10 minutes   **COOK TIME:** 15 minutes

I feel like monster cookies are supposed to be a kid version of chocolate chip cookies, but let's be honest: these cookies aren't just for the kids' table. Whether you're six or sixty, who doesn't love eating cookies filled with candy-coated chocolates in all kinds of fun colors? I make a batch of these every other weekend for a treat to have throughout the week. We all deserve a little extra sweetness in our lives, and who says you can't meal prep desserts?

1½ cups gluten-free 1-to-1 baking flour or all-purpose flour

½ cup gluten-free rolled oats, ground into a rustic flour (see Notes)

¾ cup coconut sugar

⅓ cup creamy unsalted peanut butter or sunflower seed butter

⅓ cup coconut oil, softened

⅓ cup unsweetened applesauce

1 teaspoon pure vanilla extract

2 tablespoons unsweetened dairy-free milk (if needed)

¾ cup UnReal Dark Chocolate Crispy Gems (see Notes)

1. Place an oven rack in the middle position and preheat the oven to 350°F. Line a large baking sheet (at least 17 by 14 inches) with parchment paper. Alternatively, you can bake the cookies in batches using 2 medium baking sheets.

2. In a medium bowl, whisk together the flour and ground oats.

3. In a large bowl, use a hand mixer to beat the coconut sugar, peanut butter, coconut oil, applesauce, and vanilla extract until creamy.

4. Gradually add the dry mixture to the wet mixture while stirring; continue stirring until the mixtures are well combined and you have a thick and sticky dough. Add the dairy-free milk if needed to help the dough form. Then fold in the chocolate gems.

5. Use a 1½-tablespoon cookie scoop to form the dough into 20 balls and place on the prepared baking sheet, about 1 inch apart. (If you don't have a medium cookie scoop, scoop up heaping tablespoons of the dough and form into balls between your hands.)

6. Bake for 12 to 15 minutes, until the cookies are lightly golden and have spread slightly.

7. Remove from the oven and let cool for 15 minutes before removing the cookies from the pan. Store in an airtight container at room temperature for up to 5 days or in the refrigerator for up to a week.

Notes

To grind the rolled oats into a rustic flour, place them in a food processor or high-powered blender and pulse until most of the oats have been pulverized into a fine flour but some larger pieces remain, about 5 seconds. There should not be any whole pieces of oats remaining.

UnReal is the only brand I know of that makes vegan candy-coated chocolate gems. They are available in supermarkets and online. However, you can absolutely make your own; there are a plethora of recipes online!

Chocolate-Topped Shortbread Cookies

OPTION

YIELD: 36 cookies   **PREP TIME:** 15 minutes, plus 30 minutes to chill dough
COOK TIME: 20 minutes

Some people may think shortbread cookies lack the pizazz of some of their more decorated cookie cousins, but honestly, sometimes it's the simplest things that bring the greatest joy. And once you drizzle them with (or dunk them in) chocolate, who could possibly find them plain? These simple Paleo vegan cookies are an elegant and flavorful treat that's very easy to eat. You think 36 cookies is a lot? Just wait until you try your first bite. You might need to make an extra batch!

2 cups super-fine blanched almond flour

1¾ cups cassava flour, plus more for the work surface

1 cup vegan butter, softened

½ cup maple syrup

¼ cup coconut sugar

1 tablespoon pure vanilla extract

8 ounces vegan dark chocolate (80% cacao), chopped, for dipping and/or drizzling

1. Sift the flours into a medium bowl.

2. In a large bowl, use a hand mixer to beat the vegan butter, maple syrup, coconut sugar, and vanilla extract until smooth.

3. Sift the flour mixture into the wet mixture, stirring to combine the mixtures until a sticky dough has formed.

4. Split the dough in half and form each half into a ball, then flatten into a disc. Wrap each cookie dough disc with plastic wrap and place in the refrigerator to chill for 30 minutes.

5. Place an oven rack in the middle position and preheat the oven to 350°F. Line 2 baking sheets with parchment paper.

6. Remove a chilled cookie dough disc from the refrigerator. Lightly flour a clean work surface and place the chilled dough on the surface, then lightly flour the top of the dough and a clean rolling pin.

7. Gently roll out the dough until it is ½ inch thick. Press a round cookie cutter into the rolled-out dough, creating as many cookies as can fit. Gently peel away the dough scraps from around the sides of the cut-out cookies and set aside. Form the scraps into a dough ball for rerolling.

8. Use a spatula to carefully transfer the cookie cutouts to one of the prepared baking sheets, placing them about ½ inch apart. Lightly reflour the surface and rolling pin, then reroll the remaining dough and use the cookie cutter to cut more cookies. Transfer the cut-out cookies to the baking sheet.

9. Bake for 10 minutes, or until lightly golden. After removing the cookies from the oven, allow them to cool for 15 minutes before removing from the pan.

10. While the first batch of cookies is baking, repeat Steps 6 through 8 using the second chilled cookie dough disc and second prepared baking sheet. As soon as the first batch of cookies is done, bake the second batch, following Step 9.

11. While the baked cookies are cooling, melt the chocolate in the microwave or on the stovetop, following the instructions on pages 14 and 15.

12. Once the cookies are cool, lightly dip half of a cookie into the melted chocolate or lightly drizzle the chocolate over the cookies using a spoon or butter knife to create a free-form design.

13. Allow the chocolate to set for 10 minutes. Store the cookies in an airtight container in the refrigerator for up to a week or in the freezer for up to 3 months.

Notes —————————————————————————————

You can swap the cassava flour with gluten-free 1-to-1 baking flour or all-purpose flour.

To make these cookies Paleo, use Miyoko's vegan butter. You can replace the vegan butter with coconut oil, but they won't have the classic shortbread cookie taste.

Chocolate Chip Cookie Cups

OPTION OPTION

YIELD: 12 cookie cups   **PREP TIME:** 10 minutes   **COOK TIME:** 15 minutes

These cookie cups are almost like eating a mini edible cookie bowl. Think of a bread bowl for soup…only miniaturized and for a dessert! They're incredibly easy to make and perfect for cookie exchanges or parties. Plus, they can easily be made allergy friendly.

1¾ cups all-purpose flour or gluten-free 1-to-1 baking flour

1 teaspoon baking soda

¼ teaspoon finely ground sea salt

1 cup coconut sugar

½ cup coconut oil, softened

⅓ cup unsweetened applesauce, room temperature

1 teaspoon pure vanilla extract

2 tablespoons unsweetened dairy-free milk, room temperature (if needed)

1½ cups vegan dark chocolate chips (55% to 70% cacao), divided

1. Place an oven rack in the middle position and preheat the oven to 350°F. Grease a standard-sized muffin tin generously with coconut oil.

2. In a medium bowl, whisk together the flour, baking soda, and salt.

3. In a large bowl, use a hand mixer to beat the coconut sugar, coconut oil, applesauce, and vanilla extract until creamy.

4. Gradually add the dry mixture to the wet mixture while stirring; continue stirring until the mixtures are well combined. You should have a sticky and thick dough. Add 2 tablespoons of dairy-free milk if needed to help the dough form.

5. Fold in ⅔ cup of the chocolate chips.

6. Use a 3-tablespoon cookie scoop to scoop a dough ball and roll it between your hands. (If you don't have a large cookie scoop, scoop up 3 tablespoons of the dough and form it into a ball between your hands.) Gently press the ball of dough into a well of the prepared muffin tin and work it up the sides. Repeat with the remaining dough.

7. Bake for 12 to 15 minutes, until lightly golden and slightly firm to the touch.

8. Remove from the oven and immediately fill the cookie cups with the remaining chocolate chips. Allow the chocolate to melt and the cookies to cool completely before removing from the pan. Use a knife to detach the cookie cups, gently moving it around the edges of the cups. Store in an airtight container at room temperature for up to 5 days or in the refrigerator for up to a week.

Note

For a nut-free dairy-free milk, I recommend coconut or oat milk. (If using oat milk and you require it to be gluten-free, be sure to buy a brand labeled as such.)

Peanut Butter Raspberry

THUMBPRINT COOKIES

OPTION OPTION OPTION

YIELD: 18 cookies   **PREP TIME:** 15 minutes   **COOK TIME:** 15 minutes

As a kid, I was notorious for bringing a peanut butter and jelly sandwich for lunch every day all the way from kindergarten until eighth grade. Anyone else? There's a reason why this duo is so famous! The pairing of creamy peanut butter and sweet, fresh fruit jam in these cookies is out of this world. Plus, thumbprint cookies are so fun to make! Easily one of my favorite cookies just for the joy of making them.

1½ cups gluten-free 1-to-1 baking flour or all-purpose flour

½ teaspoon baking soda

¼ teaspoon finely ground sea salt

¾ cup coconut sugar

½ cup creamy unsalted peanut butter or sunflower seed butter

½ cup coconut oil, softened

¼ cup unsweetened applesauce

1 teaspoon pure vanilla extract

2 tablespoons unsweetened dairy-free milk (if needed)

6 tablespoons Berry Jam (page 48), made with raspberries

1. Preheat the oven to 350°F. Line a large baking sheet (at least 17 by 14 inches) with parchment paper. Alternatively, you can divide the cookies between 2 regular-size baking sheets and bake them in batches.

2. In a medium bowl, whisk together the flour, baking soda, and salt.

3. In a large bowl, use a hand mixer to beat the coconut sugar, peanut butter, coconut oil, applesauce, and vanilla extract until creamy.

4. Gradually add the dry mixture to the wet mixture while stirring; continue stirring until the mixtures are well combined and you have a thick and sticky dough. Add the dairy-free milk if needed to help the dough form.

5. Use a 1½-tablespoon cookie scoop to form the dough into 18 balls. (If you don't have a medium cookie scoop, scoop up heaping tablespoons of the dough and form the portions of dough into balls between your hands.) Press your thumb lightly into the middle of each dough ball. If the dough cracks, just smooth it over with your fingers. Place the cookies an inch apart on the prepared baking sheet.

6. Spoon 1 teaspoon of jam into the middle of each cookie where you made the thumbprint.

7. Bake for 12 to 15 minutes, until the cookies are lightly golden.

8. Remove from the oven and let cool for 15 minutes before removing the cookies from the pan. Store in an airtight container at room temperature for up to 5 days or in the refrigerator for up to a week.

Note ───────────────────

For a nut-free dairy-free milk, I recommend coconut or oat milk. (If using oat milk and you require it to be gluten-free, be sure to buy a brand labeled as such.)

Chocolate & Vanilla Linzer Cookies

OPTION OPTION

YIELD: 18 to 20 sandwich cookies   **PREP TIME:** 15 minutes, plus 45 minutes to chill dough and cut out cookies   **COOK TIME:** 20 minutes

I do love fruit-filled Linzer cookies, but of course, chocolate beats out everything else for me. This easy recipe makes a mix of chocolate and vanilla Linzer cookies with a melted chocolate filling. That way, you please the hardcore chocolate lovers in the crowd as well as those who just like a bit of chocolate. (Personally, I cannot speak for those people, as I fall into the former category—ha!)

2 cups gluten-free 1-to-1 baking flour

1¾ cups cassava flour, plus more for the work surface

1 cup vegan butter, softened

½ cup maple syrup

¼ cup coconut sugar

1 tablespoon pure vanilla extract

¼ cup raw cacao powder

2 tablespoons unsweetened dairy-free milk

9 ounces vegan dark chocolate (80% cacao), chopped

1. Sift the flours into a medium bowl.

2. In a large bowl, use a hand mixer to beat the vegan butter, maple syrup, coconut sugar, and vanilla extract until creamy.

3. Sift the flour mixture into the wet mixture, stirring to combine the mixtures until a sticky dough has formed.

4. Split the dough in half and place one half in a separate bowl. Add the cacao powder and dairy-free milk to one of the bowls and use your hands to mix them into the dough until the cacao powder is evenly distributed. Form each half of the dough into a ball, then flatten into a disc. Wrap each disc with plastic wrap and place in the refrigerator to chill for 30 minutes.

5. Place an oven rack in the middle position and preheat the oven to 350°F. Line 2 baking sheets with parchment paper.

6. Remove one chilled cookie dough disc from the refrigerator. Lightly flour a clean work surface and place the dough on the surface, then lightly flour the top of the dough and a rolling pin.

7. Gently roll out the dough until it is ½ inch thick. Press a round Linzer cookie cutter (without the middle insert) into the rolled-out dough, creating 9 whole cookies. Then secure the middle piece into the cookie cutter and create 9 cookies with their centers removed. Gently peel away the dough scraps from the sides of the cut out cookies and set aside. Form the scraps into a ball for rerolling.

8. Use a spatula to carefully transfer the cookie cutouts to one of the prepared baking sheets, spacing them about ½ inch apart. Lightly reflour the surface and rolling pin, then reroll the remaining dough and use the cookie cutter to cut out more cookies. Transfer the cookie cutouts to the baking sheet.

9. Place the cookies in the refrigerator to chill for 15 minutes, then bake for 10 minutes; the vanilla cookies will be lightly golden when done. After removing the cookies from the oven, allow them to cool for 15 minutes before removing from the pan.

10. While the first batch of cookies is baking, repeat Steps 6 through 8 using the second chilled cookie dough disc and second prepared baking sheet. As soon as the first batch of cookies is done, bake the second batch, following Step 9.

11. While the cookies are cooling, melt the chocolate in the microwave or on the stovetop, following the instructions on pages 14 and 15.

12. Once the cookies are cool, spread about 1 teaspoon of melted chocolate onto each whole cookie (without the middle missing). Set a cookie with its center cut out on top of the chocolate filling, then press down gently. Allow the chocolate to set for 10 minutes.

13. Store the cookies in an airtight container in the refrigerator for up to a week or in the freezer for up to 3 months.

Notes

You can swap the cassava flour with more gluten-free baking flour or all-purpose flour.

To make these cookies Paleo, use all cassava flour and Miyoko's vegan butter. You can also replace the vegan butter with coconut oil, but the cookies won't have the classic Linzer cookie taste.

Mini Teddy Bear Cookies

OPTION OPTION

YIELD: 50 mini cookies   **PREP TIME:** 15 minutes, plus 45 minutes to chill dough and cut out cookies   **COOK TIME:** 20 minutes

Teddy Grahams were one of my favorite snacks as a kid. Unfortunately, those mini golden cookies don't have the best ingredients, but rest assured, this recipe is nearly identical in taste to the childhood classic—only made with much simpler and entirely plant-based ingredients!

¾ cup vegan butter, softened (see Notes)

⅓ cup maple syrup

1 tablespoon pure vanilla extract

2 cups cassava flour, plus more for the work surface

¼ cup raw cacao powder

1 tablespoon unsweetened dairy-free milk

1. In a large bowl, use a hand mixer to beat the vegan butter, maple syrup, and vanilla extract until smooth.

2. Sift the flour into the wet mixture, stirring until a sticky dough has formed.

3. Split the dough in half and place one half in a separate bowl. Add the cacao powder and dairy-free milk to one of the bowls and use your hands to mix the cacao powder into the dough until it's evenly distributed. Form each half of the dough into a ball and then flatten into a disc. Wrap each disc with plastic wrap and place in the refrigerator to chill for 30 minutes.

4. Place an oven rack in the middle position and preheat the oven to 350°F. Line 2 baking sheets with parchment paper.

5. Remove one chilled cookie dough disc from the refrigerator. Lightly flour a clean work surface and place the chilled dough on the surface, then lightly flour the top of the dough and a clean rolling pin.

6. Gently roll out the dough until it is ½ inch thick. Press a mini teddy bear cookie cutter into the rolled-out dough, creating as many cookies as possible. Gently peel away the dough scraps from around the sides of the cut out cookies and set aside. Form the scraps into a dough ball for rerolling.

7. Use a spatula to carefully transfer the cookie cutouts to one of the prepared baking sheets, spacing them about ½ inch apart. Lightly reflour the surface and rolling pin, then reroll the remaining dough and use the cookie cutter to cut more cookies. Transfer the cut out cookies to the baking sheet.

8. Place the cookies in the refrigerator to chill for 15 minutes, then bake for 10 minutes; the vanilla cookies will be lightly golden when done. After removing the cookies from the oven, allow them to cool for 15 minutes before removing from the pan.

9. While the first batch of cookies is baking, repeat Steps 6 through 8 using the second chilled cookie dough disc and second prepared baking sheet. As soon as

the first batch of cookies is done, place the second batch in the oven and bake for 10 minutes, allowing the cookies to cool for 15 minutes before removing from the pan.

10. Store the cookies in an airtight container in the refrigerator for up to a week or in the freezer for up to 3 months.

Notes ————————————————————————————

To make these cookies Paleo, use Miyoko's vegan butter. You can also replace the vegan butter with coconut oil, but the cookies won't have the classic shortbread taste.

You can swap the cassava flour with gluten-free 1-to-1 baking flour or all-purpose flour.

Sugar Cookie Cutouts

OPTION OPTION

YIELD: 36 large cookies   **PREP TIME:** 20 minutes, plus 1 hour to chill dough and cut out cookies   **COOK TIME:** 12 minutes

Cutout sugar cookies are great—not only are they perfect for the winter holidays, but they can easily be used for spring, summer, and fall holidays as well. All you need to do is find a cookie cutter for the theme of your choice. These cookies are absolutely delicious with a simple royal icing, as shown, but they're also wonderful with a smear of Vegan Buttercream Frosting (page 38). I give the option for both a Paleo icing and a regular vegan icing. Use whichever you prefer! I like to add the almond extract so that the flavor is reminiscent of an Italian tricolore cookie, but that is completely up to you.

SUGAR COOKIE DOUGH:

½ cup vegan butter or coconut oil, softened

½ cup coconut sugar

2 Flaxseed Eggs (page 34)

2 teaspoons pure vanilla extract

1 teaspoon almond extract (optional)

1¼ cups super-fine blanched almond flour

¾ cup cassava flour or gluten-free 1-to-1 baking flour, plus more for the work surface

REGULAR ICING (NOT PALEO):

2 cups powdered sugar

2 tablespoons unsweetened dairy-free milk

PALEO ICING:

½ cup coconut butter, melted

1 tablespoon maple syrup

1. Line a large baking sheet (at least 17 by 14 inches) with parchment paper. If you don't have a large baking sheet, you can bake the cookies in batches using 2 medium baking sheets.

2. To make the cookies, place the vegan butter and sugar in a large bowl and beat them using a hand mixer until creamy and smooth.

3. Add the flaxseed eggs, vanilla extract, and almond extract, if using, and mix to combine. Then sift in the flours. Continue to beat all of the ingredients until you have a sticky dough.

4. Form the dough into a ball, then flatten it into a disc and wrap it in plastic wrap. Place the dough disc in the refrigerator to chill for 30 minutes.

5. When the dough is ready, lightly flour a clean work surface with cassava flour (or almond flour) and place the chilled dough on the surface, then lightly flour the top of the dough and a clean rolling pin.

6. Roll out the dough until it is about ¼ inch thick. Press your favorite cookie cutters into the dough. (For a yield of 36 large cookies, use cookie cutters about 2¼ inches in diameter.) Peel away the scraps, then reroll and cut out the remaining dough. Place the cutouts on the lined baking sheet.

7. Place the cookies in the refrigerator to chill for 30 minutes. While the cookies are chilling, place an oven rack in the middle position and preheat the oven to 350°F.

8. Bake the cookies for 10 to 12 minutes, until slightly puffy and golden. Remove from the oven and let cool completely before removing from the baking sheet and icing.

9. When the cookies are cool, make the icing: Either mix together the powdered sugar and dairy-free milk or melt together the coconut butter and maple syrup for a Paleo icing. Place the icing in a piping bag or spread it directly onto the cookies.

10. Store in an airtight container at room temperature for up to 5 days or in the refrigerator for up to a week.

Notes

To make these cookies Paleo, use cassava flour rather than gluten-free baking flour. If you don't need them to be gluten-free, you can also use all-purpose flour in place of both flours.

For a nut-free dairy-free milk, I recommend coconut or oat milk. (If using oat milk and you require it to be gluten-free, be sure to buy a brand labeled as such.)

Ginger Molasses Cookies

OPTION OPTION

YIELD: 20 cookies   **PREP TIME:** 10 minutes, plus 10 minutes to chill dough
COOK TIME: 15 minutes

While I find molasses on its own to be a bit too strong for my liking, ginger molasses cookies are another story. I could easily go back for seconds and thirds of these chewy, spicy cookies, which are not only rich with warming ginger but also not so overwhelmingly sweet that you get a headache (the kind of cookie we need in our holiday cookie arsenal!). I give the option for rolling these cookies in granulated sugar, but keep in mind that doing so will make them not Paleo. If you choose to omit the sugar, not to worry—these cookies will still be a hit!

½ cup coconut oil or vegan butter, softened

⅓ cup coconut sugar

⅓ cup molasses

¼ cup unsweetened applesauce, room temperature

4 teaspoons Paleo Baking Powder (page 37)

3 Flaxseed Eggs (page 34)

¾ cup cassava flour

¼ cup coconut flour

2 teaspoons ginger powder

½ cup granulated sugar or coconut sugar, for rolling (optional)

1. Place an oven rack in the middle position and preheat the oven to 350°F. Line a large baking sheet (at least 17 by 14 inches) with parchment paper. If you don't have a large baking sheet, you can bake the cookies in batches using 2 medium baking sheets.

2. In a large bowl, cream the coconut oil and coconut sugar together using a hand mixer. Add the molasses, applesauce, and baking powder and continue to beat until smooth.

3. Fold in the flaxseed eggs until well combined.

4. Sift in the cassava flour, coconut flour, and ginger and stir until you have a sticky dough.

5. Chill the dough for 10 minutes, then use a 1½-tablespoon cookie scoop to form a dough ball. Lightly roll the ball in the sugar, if desired, and repeat with the remaining dough to create 20 cookies, placing them on the prepared baking sheet, about 1½ inches apart. (If you don't have a medium cookie scoop, scoop up heaping tablespoons of the dough and form the portions of dough into balls between your hands.)

6. Bake for 12 to 15 minutes, until the cookies have spread and the edges are set.

7. Remove from the oven and let cool for 15 minutes before removing the cookies from the pan. Store in an airtight container at room temperature for up to 5 days or in the refrigerator for up to a week.

Flourless Peanut Butter

CHOCOLATE CHIP COOKIES

OPTION OPTION

YIELD: 20 cookies   **PREP TIME:** 10 minutes, plus 30 minutes to chill dough
COOK TIME: 15 minutes

Flourless recipes should be more popular than they are! They're less of a mess to clean up and perfect for kids to help out. These one-bowl cookies are incredibly easy to whip together. The key to success is allowing the cookies to rest at the end. I know so many who want to skip the resting time and eat cookies fresh out of the oven, but these cookies do require that crucial setting period.

1 cup creamy unsalted peanut butter

2 Flaxseed Eggs (page 34)

1 cup coconut sugar or granulated sugar

1 teaspoon baking soda

1 teaspoon pure vanilla extract

¼ teaspoon finely ground sea salt

⅔ cup vegan dark chocolate chunks (55% to 70% cacao)

1. In a medium bowl, mix together the peanut butter, flaxseed eggs, sugar, baking soda, vanilla extract, and salt. Fold in the chocolate chunks.

2. Place the bowl in the refrigerator to chill for 30 minutes. While the dough is chilling, place an oven rack in the middle position and preheat the oven to 350°F. Line a large baking sheet (at least 17 by 14 inches) with parchment paper. If you don't have a large baking sheet, you can bake the cookies in batches using 2 medium baking sheets.

3. Remove the dough from the refrigerator and use a 1½-tablespoon cookie scoop to form dough balls. Place about 2 inches apart on the prepared baking sheet to ensure that they have room to spread without touching. (If you don't have a medium cookie scoop, scoop up heaping tablespoons of the dough and form the portions of dough into balls between your hands.)

4. Bake for 15 minutes, or until the edges and almost all of the middle is set.

5. Remove from the oven and allow the cookies to cool and set for 15 minutes before removing from the pan. Store in an airtight container at room temperature for up to 5 days or in the refrigerator for up to a week.

Note

To make these cookies Paleo and peanut-free, swap in almond butter or sunflower seed butter for the peanut butter. For Paleo, also use coconut sugar.

Chapter 7
CUPCAKES

Caramel-Filled Cupcakes

OPTION   OPTION

YIELD: 12 cupcakes   **PREP TIME:** 15 minutes   **COOK TIME:** 35 minutes

I think I developed a love for filled cupcakes when I was a packer at Georgetown Cupcakes while attending college. Yep, I worked at the Georgetown Cupcakes, a celebrated cupcake shop in Washington, D.C. (To get a sneak peek of what I did, check out their TV show, DC Cupcakes, on TLC!) It was a great way not only to get outside the college world for a bit, but also to learn some fun baking (and frosting!) hacks. One of those hacks was stuffing cupcakes with a delicious and fun filling. It's like a surprise in the middle that complements the rest of the flavors in the cupcake. Because I'm obsessed with my Coconut Caramel Sauce, I thought, why not dedicate an entire cupcake to it? Now, you can frost them plain as I did or get a little fancy and drizzle some caramel sauce on top as well. Either way, you'll have an absolute showstopper of a cupcake with a beautiful caramel surprise in the middle!

2½ cups cake flour or sifted gluten-free 1-to-1 baking flour

1 cup granulated sugar or coconut sugar (see Notes)

1 tablespoon baking powder

2 teaspoons baking soda

1 cup Vegan Buttermilk (page 35), room temperature

½ cup coconut oil, melted

⅓ cup unsweetened applesauce, room temperature

1 tablespoon pure vanilla extract

½ cup Coconut Caramel Sauce (page 46), plus more for garnish if desired

1 batch Vegan Buttercream Frosting (page 38)

1. Preheat the oven to 350°F. Place 12 cupcake liners in a standard-size muffin tin.

2. In a large bowl, whisk together the flour, sugar, baking powder, and baking soda.

3. In a medium bowl, mix together the vegan buttermilk, coconut oil, applesauce, and vanilla extract.

4. Pour the wet mixture into the dry mixture and mix just enough to combine the ingredients and remove any remaining clumps of flour. Be careful not to overmix.

5. Using a ⅓-cup measuring scoop or a 3-tablespoon cookie scoop, fill each cupcake liner three-quarters of the way full.

6. Bake for 30 to 35 minutes, until a toothpick comes out clean when inserted in the middle of a cupcake. The cupcakes should be lightly golden and bounce back at a light touch.

7. Remove from the oven and let cool for 5 minutes. Carefully invert the cupcakes onto a cooling rack and turn them right side up to cool completely, about 30 minutes.

8. Once cool, use a paring knife to carefully carve a 1-inch circle into the top of each cupcake that goes halfway down the cupcake. Carefully remove the carved cores and slice them in half crosswise. You will use the top half of the cores as plugs to seal the filling in the cupcakes.

9. Place 2 teaspoons of caramel sauce in the cavity in a cupcake. Place a cupcake "plug" in the hole to cover the caramel sauce, pressing down lightly until the top of the plug is fairly even with the top of the cupcake. Repeat with the rest of the cupcakes, cupcake "plugs," and caramel sauce.

10. When ready to frost, scoop the buttercream into a piping bag fitted with a frosting tip or into a plastic bag with a corner snipped off. Pipe the frosting onto each cupcake and drizzle with extra caramel sauce, if desired. To bake one day ahead, follow the steps through Step 7, then cover the cooled cupcakes with plastic wrap and store at room temperature. Fill and frost the next day. To store after frosting, keep them in an airtight container in the refrigerator for up to 3 days.

Notes —————————————————————————

Using coconut sugar makes cakes and cupcakes slightly darker, but they'll still be delicious! As you can see in the photo, if used in vegan buttercream, coconut sugar also adds flecks of tan color to the frosting.

To make these cupcakes nut-free, follow the nut-free options for the Vegan Buttermilk, Coconut Caramel Sauce, and Vegan Buttercream Frosting.

Chocolate Chip Banana Cupcakes

OPTION   OPTION

YIELD: 12 cupcakes   **PREP TIME:** 15 minutes   **COOK TIME:** 35 minutes

It wouldn't be a cupcake chapter without a banana recipe in here somewhere! These cupcakes remind me of my gluten-free vegan banana cake, but with chocolate, of course. I'm frequently asked what's the difference between banana bread and banana cake (or cupcakes, in this case). When it comes to more standard baking, there are quite a few differences, but with gluten-free vegan baking, I often find that the cake and cupcake versions are much lighter, whereas banana bread is quite dense. I want you to feel refreshed after eating this cupcake, even with a bit of deliciously melty chocolate in every bite!

2¾ cups cake flour or sifted gluten-free 1-to-1 baking flour

1 cup granulated sugar or coconut sugar (see Notes)

1 tablespoon baking powder

2 teaspoons baking soda

1 teaspoon ground cinnamon, plus more for garnish if desired

1 cup Vegan Buttermilk (page 35), room temperature

¾ cup mashed bananas (about 2 large ripe bananas)

½ cup coconut oil, melted

¼ cup unsweetened applesauce, room temperature

1 tablespoon pure vanilla extract

½ cup vegan dark chocolate chips (55% to 70% cacao)

1 batch Vegan Buttercream Frosting (page 38)

1. Preheat the oven to 350°F. Place 12 cupcake liners in a standard-size muffin tin.

2. In a large bowl, whisk together the flour, sugar, baking powder, baking soda, and cinnamon.

3. In a medium bowl, use a wooden spoon to mix together the vegan buttermilk, mashed bananas, coconut oil, applesauce, and vanilla extract.

4. Pour the wet mixture into the dry mixture and mix just enough to combine the ingredients and remove any remaining clumps of flour. Be careful not to overmix.

5. Fold in the chocolate chips.

6. Using a ⅓-cup measuring scoop or a 3-tablespoon cookie scoop, fill each cupcake liner three-quarters of the way full.

7. Bake for 30 to 35 minutes, until a toothpick comes out clean when inserted in the middle of a cupcake. The cupcakes should be lightly golden and bounce back at a light touch.

8. Remove from the oven and let cool for 5 minutes. Carefully invert the cupcakes onto a cooling rack and turn them right side up to cool completely, about 30 minutes.

9. When ready to frost, scoop the buttercream into a piping bag fitted with a frosting tip or into a plastic bag with a corner snipped off. Pipe the frosting onto each cupcake and sprinkle with extra cinnamon, if desired. To bake one day ahead,

follow the steps through Step 7, then cover the cooled cupcakes with plastic wrap and store at room temperature. Frost the next day. To store after frosting, keep them in an airtight container in the refrigerator for up to 3 days.

Notes

Using coconut sugar makes cakes and cupcakes slightly darker, but they'll still be delicious!

To make these cupcakes nut-free, follow the nut-free options for the Vegan Buttermilk and Vegan Buttercream Frosting.

Carrot Cake Cupcakes

OPTION

YIELD: 12 cupcakes   **PREP TIME:** 20 minutes   **COOK TIME:** 40 minutes

As a kid, I was disgusted by the idea of putting vegetables in something sweet and calling it dessert. It used to baffle me how my dad loved having a slice of carrot cake (or a cupcake!) over chocolate or vanilla. Now? I'm proud to say that I finally see the light! I like to think I've finally learned how to appreciate the subtle flavors and natural sweetness of produce that I normally would have consumed only alongside something savory. One thing I specifically love about carrot cake cupcakes is that they can be enjoyed nearly year-round. Make a batch to celebrate the winter with the warming spices, or decorate them with flowers as spring approaches!

2½ cups gluten-free rolled oats, ground into a rustic flour (see Notes, page 117)

¾ cup coconut sugar

½ cup cassava flour

1 tablespoon baking powder

2 teaspoons baking soda

2 teaspoons ground cinnamon, plus more for garnish if desired

1 teaspoon ground nutmeg

½ teaspoon ginger powder

1 cup Vegan Buttermilk (page 35), room temperature

½ cup maple syrup, room temperature

½ cup coconut oil, melted

3 Flaxseed Eggs (page 34)

1 tablespoon pure vanilla extract

2 cups shredded carrots

1 batch Vegan Cream Cheese Frosting (page 42)

1. Preheat the oven to 350°F. Place 12 cupcake liners in a standard-size muffin tin.

2. In a large bowl, whisk together the oat flour, sugar, cassava flour, baking powder, baking soda, cinnamon, nutmeg, and ginger.

3. In a medium bowl, use a wooden spoon to mix together the vegan buttermilk, maple syrup, coconut oil, flaxseed eggs, and vanilla extract.

4. Fold the wet mixture into the dry mixture just until the mixtures are combined and there are no remaining clumps of flour. The batter will be thick.

5. Fold in the carrots.

6. Using a ⅓-cup measuring scoop or a 3-tablespoon cookie scoop, fill each cupcake liner three-quarters of the way full.

7. Bake for 35 to 40 minutes, until a toothpick comes out clean when inserted in the middle of a cupcake. The cupcakes should be lightly golden.

8. Remove from the oven and let cool for 5 minutes. Carefully invert the cupcakes onto a cooling rack and turn them right side up to cool completely, about 30 minutes.

9. When ready to frost, scoop the frosting into a piping bag fitted with a frosting tip or into a plastic bag with a corner snipped off. Pipe the frosting onto each cupcake and sprinkle with extra cinnamon, if desired. To bake one day ahead, follow the

steps through Step 7, then cover the cooled cupcakes with plastic wrap and store at room temperature. Frost the next day. To store after frosting, keep them in an airtight container in the refrigerator for up to 3 days.

Note

To make these cupcakes nut-free, follow the nut-free options for the Vegan Buttermilk and Vegan Cream Cheese Frosting.

Boston Cream Pie Cupcakes

OPTION OPTION

YIELD: 12 cupcakes   **PREP TIME:** 15 minutes   **COOK TIME:** 35 minutes

The first time I had Boston cream pie (prior to my plant-based days) was at the Omni Parker House in Boston, said to be the original founding place of the Boston cream pie. While Boston cream pie is technically more of a cake than a traditional pie, it's still a favorite dessert for many. I mean, you can't beat the chocolate and vanilla cream pudding filling. This easy plant-based version, turned into cupcakes, is like having individually portioned Boston cream pies—they're perfect for parties and undetectably vegan, with gluten-free and nut-free options!

2½ cups cake flour or sifted gluten-free 1-to-1 baking flour

1 cup granulated sugar or coconut sugar (see Notes, page 139)

1 tablespoon baking powder

2 teaspoons baking soda

1 cup Vegan Buttermilk (page 35)

½ cup coconut oil, melted

⅓ cup unsweetened applesauce

1 tablespoon pure vanilla extract

½ cup coconut butter, melted (see Notes)

1 batch Paleo Vegan Chocolate Buttercream Frosting (page 40)

1. Preheat the oven to 350°F. Place 12 cupcake liners in a standard-size muffin tin.

2. In a large bowl, whisk together the flour, sugar, baking powder, and baking soda.

3. In a medium bowl, use a wooden spoon to mix together the vegan buttermilk, coconut oil, applesauce, and vanilla extract.

4. Pour the wet mixture into the dry mixture and mix just enough to combine the ingredients and remove any remaining clumps of flour. Be careful not to overmix.

5. Using a ⅓-cup measuring scoop or a 3-tablespoon cookie scoop, fill each cupcake liner three-quarters of the way full.

6. Bake for 30 to 35 minutes, until a toothpick comes out clean when inserted in the middle of a cupcake. The cupcakes should be lightly golden and bounce back at a light touch.

7. Remove from the oven and let cool for 5 minutes. Carefully invert the cupcakes onto a cooling rack and turn them right side up to cool completely, about 30 minutes.

8. Once cool, use a paring knife to carefully carve a 1-inch circle into the top of each cupcake that goes halfway down the cupcake. Carefully remove the carved cores.

9. Place 2 teaspoons of coconut butter in the cavity of each cupcake.

10. When ready to frost, scoop the buttercream into a piping bag fitted with a frosting tip or into a plastic bag with a corner snipped off. Pipe the frosting onto each cupcake. To bake the cupcakes one day ahead, complete Steps 1 through 7, then cover the cooled cupcakes with plastic wrap and store at room temperature. Fill and frost the next day. After frosting, store them in an airtight container in the refrigerator for up to 3 days.

Notes ————————————

To make these cupcakes nut-free, follow the nut-free options for the Vegan Buttermilk and Paleo Vegan Chocolate Buttercream Frosting.

If you want a vanilla-flavored filling rather than coconut, you can swap in dairy-free vanilla yogurt or dairy-free frozen whipped topping for the coconut butter.

Funfetti Cupcakes

OPTION OPTION

YIELD: 12 cupcakes   **PREP TIME:** 15 minutes   **COOK TIME:** 35 minutes

You want to know the truth? I am head-over-heels for these cupcakes and my Birthday Cake (page 204). I know what you're thinking: it's vanilla, though. Believe me, vanilla is far from flavorless. It's the base of every flavor, if you've noticed! Vanilla also adds a subtle sweetness with a rich and bold punch of an absolutely delicious aroma. Plus, don't the sprinkles give these cupcakes such a fun pop of color? I mean, how could you not be happy enjoying one (or two!) of these? Perfect for birthdays or any occasion when you need a little extra sunshine!

2½ cups cake flour or sifted gluten-free 1-to-1 baking flour

1 cup granulated sugar or coconut sugar (see Notes, page 139)

1 tablespoon baking powder

2 teaspoons baking soda

1 cup Vegan Buttermilk (page 35), room temperature

½ cup coconut oil, melted

⅓ cup unsweetened applesauce, room temperature

1½ tablespoons pure vanilla extract

½ cup vegan sprinkles, plus more for garnish if desired

1 batch Vegan Buttercream Frosting (page 38)

1. Preheat the oven to 350°F. Place 12 cupcake liners in a standard-size muffin tin.

2. In a large bowl, whisk together the flour, sugar, baking powder, and baking soda.

3. In a medium bowl, use a wooden spoon to mix together the vegan buttermilk, coconut oil, applesauce, and vanilla extract.

4. Pour the wet mixture into the dry mixture and mix just enough to combine the ingredients and remove any remaining clumps of flour. Be careful not to overmix.

5. Fold in the sprinkles.

6. Using a ⅓-cup measuring scoop or a 3-tablespoon cookie scoop, fill each cupcake liner three-quarters of the way full.

7. Bake for 30 to 35 minutes, until a toothpick comes out clean when inserted in the middle of a cupcake. The cupcakes should be lightly golden and bounce back at a light touch.

8. Remove from the oven and let cool for 5 minutes. Carefully invert the cupcakes onto a cooling rack and turn them right side up to cool completely, about 30 minutes.

9. When ready to frost, scoop the buttercream into a piping bag fitted with a frosting tip or into a plastic bag with a corner snipped off. Pipe the frosting onto each cupcake and sprinkle with extra sprinkles, if desired. To bake one day ahead, follow the steps through Step 7, then cover the cooled cupcakes with plastic wrap and store at room temperature. Frost the next day. To store after frosting, keep them in an airtight container in the refrigerator for up to 3 days.

Notes —————————————————————

To make these cupcakes nut-free, follow the nut-free options for the Vegan Buttermilk and Vegan Buttercream Frosting.

To make them Paleo, use cassava flour in lieu of the cake flour and use the Paleo versions of the Vegan Buttermilk and Vegan Buttercream Frosting.

Hot Chocolate Cupcakes

OPTION

YIELD: 12 cupcakes   **PREP TIME:** 15 minutes   **COOK TIME:** 35 minutes

Who says you have to drink your hot chocolate? These cupcakes are basically like having a cup of hot chocolate in mini cake form. This might be chocolate overload, but why not make a cup of hot cocoa to go alongside these Hot Chocolate Cupcakes? Just the thought of that combo makes me want to cuddle up on the couch with a blanket while watching snow fall! What's unique about these cupcakes is the filling and topping: a homemade vegan marshmallow fluff. Traditionally, marshmallow fluff is made from egg whites, but this version uses vegan marshmallows and maple syrup. There are a few brands of vegan marshmallows on the market, so choose whichever you prefer! I highly recommend using a light-colored maple syrup for the fluff if you don't want too much of a maple flavor.

CHOCOLATE CUPCAKES:

1¼ cups cassava flour

1 cup coconut sugar

½ cup raw cacao powder

1 tablespoon baking powder

2 teaspoons baking soda

1 cup Vegan Buttermilk (page 35)

½ cup olive oil

⅓ cup unsweetened applesauce

1 teaspoon pure vanilla extract

MARSHMALLOW FLUFF:

2 cups vegan marshmallows

½ cup maple syrup

½ cup vegan dark chocolate chips (55% to 70% cacao)

Note ———————————————————————

To make these cupcakes nut-free, follow the nut-free option for the Vegan Buttermilk.

1. Preheat the oven to 350°F. Place 12 cupcake liners in a standard-size muffin tin.

2. In a large bowl, whisk together the flour, sugar, cacao powder, baking powder, and baking soda.

3. In a medium bowl, use a wooden spoon to mix together the vegan buttermilk, olive oil, applesauce, and vanilla extract.

4. Pour the wet mixture into the dry mixture and mix just enough to combine the ingredients and remove any remaining clumps of flour. Be careful not to overmix.

5. Using a ⅓-cup measuring scoop or a 3-tablespoon cookie scoop, fill each cupcake liner three-quarters of the way full.

6. Bake for 30 to 35 minutes, until a toothpick comes out clean when inserted in the middle of a cupcake. The cupcakes should be set and bounce back at a light touch.

7. Remove from the oven and let cool for 5 minutes. Carefully invert the cupcakes onto a cooling rack and turn them right side up. Allow them to cool at room temperature for 15 minutes, then place the cooling rack in the refrigerator for 30 minutes to chill the cupcakes. They will be cool to the touch and firm.

8. About 5 minutes before the cupcakes are done cooling, prepare the marshmallow fluff. Put the marshmallows and maple syrup in a microwave-safe bowl. Microwave in 30-second increments at a time, using a spoon to gently mix the marshmallows after each increment. After about 2 or 3 rounds of microwaving, the marshmallows should be soft enough to combine completely with the maple syrup. Continue to mix until it resembles marshmallow fluff.

9. Remove the cupcakes from the refrigerator and use a paring knife to carefully carve a 1-inch circle into the top of each cupcake that goes halfway down the cupcake. Carefully remove the carved cores and slice them in half crosswise. You will use the top halves of the cores as plugs to seal the filling in the cupcakes.

10. Place 2 teaspoons of the marshmallow fluff in the cavity in a cupcake. Place a cupcake "plug" in the hole to cover the filling, pressing down lightly until the top of the plug is fairly even with the top of the cupcake. Repeat with the rest of cupcakes, cupcake "plugs," and marshmallow fluff.

11. Top the cupcakes with the remaining marshmallow fluff, using about 2 tablespoons per cupcake.

12. Melt the chocolate chips in the microwave or on the stovetop, following the instructions on pages 14 and 15.

13. Drizzle the chocolate over each cupcake and serve. To bake one day ahead, follow the steps through Step 7, then cover the cooled cupcakes with plastic wrap and store at room temperature. The next day, fill and top with the marshmallow fluff and melted chocolate. To store after filling and topping, keep them in an airtight container in the refrigerator for up to 3 days,

Vanilla & Chocolate

MARBLED CUPCAKES

OPTION OPTION

YIELD: 12 cupcakes   **PREP TIME:** 15 minutes   **COOK TIME:** 35 minutes

The best of both worlds, these mesmerizing cupcakes are a mix of a beautifully "buttery" vanilla cake swirl paired with a rich chocolate cake. Plus, they are topped with a swirl of vanilla and chocolate vegan buttercream frosting. The trick to these cupcakes is adopting the notion that less is more: just a bit of a gentle swirl of the batter and the frosting gives you the perfect swirl that still shows the vanilla and chocolate as stand-alone flavors.

2¼ cups cake flour or sifted gluten-free 1-to-1 baking flour

1 cup granulated sugar or coconut sugar (see Notes, page 139)

1 tablespoon baking powder

2 teaspoons baking soda

1 cup plus 2 tablespoons Vegan Buttermilk (page 35), divided

½ cup coconut oil, melted

⅓ cup unsweetened applesauce

1 tablespoon pure vanilla extract

¾ cup raw cacao powder, divided

1 batch Vegan Buttercream Frosting (page 38)

2 tablespoons unsweetened dairy-free milk

1. Preheat the oven to 350°F. Place 12 cupcake liners in a standard-size muffin tin.

2. In a large bowl, whisk together the flour, sugar, baking powder, and baking soda.

3. In a medium bowl, use a wooden spoon to mix together 1 cup of the vegan buttermilk, the coconut oil, applesauce, and vanilla extract.

4. Pour the wet mixture into the dry mixture and mix just enough to combine the ingredients and remove any remaining clumps of flour. Be careful not to overmix.

5. Divide the batter between 2 bowls. Add ¼ cup of the cacao powder to one bowl, along with the remaining 2 tablespoons of buttermilk. Gently mix to evenly distribute the cacao powder.

6. Evenly divide the chocolate batter among the cupcake liners, filling each about one-third full. Top the chocolate batter with the vanilla batter, dividing it evenly among the liners until they are about two-thirds full of batter. Using a butter knife, gently swirl the batter. Less is more—just enough to get the vanilla to go toward the bottom and the chocolate toward the top.

7. Bake for 30 to 35 minutes, until a toothpick comes out clean when inserted in the middle of a cupcake. The cupcakes should bounce back at a light touch and the vanilla parts should be lightly golden.

8. Remove from the oven and let cool for 5 minutes. Carefully invert the cupcakes onto a cooling rack and turn them right side up to cool completely, about 30 minutes.

9. When ready to frost, divide the buttercream frosting between 2 bowls. To one bowl, add the remaining ½ cup of cacao powder and the dairy-free milk. Beat until

the cacao powder is evenly distributed. Use a rubber spatula to scoop the vanilla buttercream into a piping bag fitted with a frosting tip or into a plastic bag with a corner snipped off. Then add the chocolate buttercream and use the spatula to gently mix the frostings. Again, less is more! Pipe the frosting onto each cupcake. To bake the cupcakes one day ahead, complete Steps 1 through 8, then cover the cooled cupcakes with plastic wrap and store at room temperature. Frost the next day. After frosting, store them in an airtight container in the refrigerator for up to 3 days.

Note ————————————————————————————

To make these cupcakes nut-free, follow the nut-free options for the Vegan Buttermilk and Vegan Buttercream Frosting.

Ice Cream Sundae Cupcakes

OPTION OPTION

YIELD: 12 cupcakes   **PREP TIME:** 15 minutes   **COOK TIME:** 35 minutes

Don't be fooled! These cupcakes are not ice cream sundaes, but they look pretty similar. Filled with melted chocolate and topped with sprinkles, they are a fun summer treat on the days when you're not in need of a dairy-free ice cream sundae to cool you down. Or maybe you're dreaming of summer in the middle of winter…in which case, these are your cupcakes! To make them even more like ice cream sundaes, melt extra chocolate for drizzling on top.

2 cups cake flour or sifted gluten-free 1-to-1 baking flour

1 cup granulated sugar or coconut sugar

½ cup raw cacao powder

1 tablespoon baking powder

2 teaspoons baking soda

1 cup Vegan Buttermilk (page 35)

½ cup coconut oil, melted

⅓ cup unsweetened applesauce

1 tablespoon pure vanilla extract

½ cup vegan dark chocolate chips (55% to 70% cacao), plus more for drizzling if desired

1 batch Vegan Buttercream Frosting (page 38)

Vegan sprinkles, for garnish

1. Preheat the oven to 350°F. Place 12 cupcake liners in a standard-size muffin tin.

2. In a large bowl, whisk together the flour, sugar, cacao powder, baking powder, and baking soda.

3. In a medium bowl, use a wooden spoon to mix together the vegan buttermilk, coconut oil, applesauce, and vanilla extract.

4. Pour the wet mixture into the dry mixture and mix just enough to combine the ingredients and remove any remaining clumps of flour. Be careful not to overmix.

5. Using a ⅓-cup measuring scoop or a 3-tablespoon cookie scoop, fill each cupcake liner three-quarters of the way full.

6. Bake for 30 to 35 minutes, until a toothpick comes out clean when inserted in the middle of a cupcake. The cupcakes should be lightly golden and bounce back at a light touch.

7. Remove from the oven and let cool for 5 minutes. Carefully invert the cupcakes onto a cooling rack and turn them right side up to cool completely, about 30 minutes.

8. Once cool, use a paring knife to carefully carve a 1-inch circle into the top of each cupcake that goes halfway down the cupcake. Carefully remove the carved cores.

9. Melt the chocolate, following the instructions on pages 14 and 15.

10. Place 2 teaspoons of melted chocolate in the cavity of each cupcake and replace the core.

11. When ready to frost, scoop the buttercream into a piping bag fitted with a frosting tip or into a plastic bag with a corner snipped off. Pipe the frosting onto

each cupcake and top each cupcake with sprinkles and extra melted chocolate, if desired. To bake the cupcakes one day ahead, complete Steps 1 through 7, then cover the cooled cupcakes with plastic wrap and store at room temperature. Fill and frost the next day. After frosting, store them in an airtight container in the refrigerator for up to 3 days.

Note ——————————————————————————————

To make these cupcakes nut-free, follow the nut-free options for the Vegan Buttermilk and Vegan Buttercream Frosting.

Zesty Lemon Cupcakes

OPTION OPTION

YIELD: 12 cupcakes   **PREP TIME:** 15 minutes   **COOK TIME:** 35 minutes

*If you ever need to brighten your day, these cupcakes will surely do the trick. They're quite literally bursting with zesty flavor, but just sweet enough not to overwhelm you. Now, if you've never made a citrus-flavored baked treat or dessert, let me tell you that the zest is key. Learn from my mistakes: you'll end up with a **good** cupcake if you forget or leave out the zest. But you'll end up with a fantastic cupcake when the zest is in there. A little extra effort goes a long way! Now, the lemon wedges on top are totally optional, but I do love a little decoration.*

2½ cups cake flour or sifted gluten-free 1-to-1 baking flour

1 cup granulated sugar or coconut sugar (see Notes, page 139)

1 tablespoon baking powder

2 teaspoons baking soda

1 cup Vegan Buttermilk (page 35)

½ cup coconut oil, melted

½ cup unsweetened applesauce

1 tablespoon grated lemon zest (about 1 lemon)

3 tablespoons freshly squeezed lemon juice (about 1 lemon)

1 tablespoon pure vanilla extract

1 batch Vegan Buttercream Frosting (page 38)

12 thin lemon wedges, for garnish (optional)

1. Preheat the oven to 350°F. Place 12 cupcake liners in a standard-size muffin tin.

2. In a large bowl, whisk together the flour, sugar, baking powder, and baking soda.

3. In a medium bowl, use a wooden spoon to mix together the vegan buttermilk, coconut oil, applesauce, lemon zest, lemon juice, and vanilla extract.

4. Pour the wet mixture into the dry mixture and mix just enough to combine the ingredients and remove any remaining clumps of flour. Be careful not to overmix.

5. Using a ⅓-cup measuring scoop or a 3-tablespoon cookie scoop, fill each cupcake liner three-quarters of the way full.

6. Bake for 30 to 35 minutes, until a toothpick comes out clean when inserted in the middle of a cupcake. The cupcakes should be lightly golden and bounce back at a light touch.

7. Remove from the oven and let cool for 5 minutes. Carefully invert the cupcakes onto a cooling rack and turn them right side up to cool completely, about 30 minutes.

8. When ready to frost, scoop the buttercream into a piping bag fitted with a frosting tip or into a plastic bag with a corner snipped off. Pipe the frosting onto each cupcake and top with a lemon wedge, if desired. To bake one day ahead, follow the steps through Step 7, then cover the cooled cupcakes with plastic wrap and store at room temperature. Frost the next day. To store after frosting, keep them in an airtight container in the refrigerator for up to 3 days.

Note

To make these cupcakes nut-free, follow the nut-free options for the
Vegan Buttermilk and Vegan Buttercream Frosting.

Raspberry Coconut Cupcakes

OPTION OPTION

YIELD: 12 cupcakes   **PREP TIME:** 15 minutes   **COOK TIME:** 35 minutes

I think the fruit and coconut combination is so underrated. Coconut is amazing on its own, but let's be real: the addition of a berry brings a burst of brightness to keep the overall feeling of the cupcake light (because I'll be the first to admit: coconut is heavy!). These light coconut cupcakes filled with a fresh raspberry jam and topped with a coconut raspberry frosting are a delight to make and to eat. Absolutely delicious and refreshing for a picnic or summer holiday get-together!

2 cups cake flour or sifted gluten-free 1-to-1 baking flour

1 cup granulated sugar or coconut sugar (see Notes, page 139)

1 cup unsweetened shredded coconut, divided

1 tablespoon baking powder

2 teaspoons baking soda

1 cup Vegan Buttermilk (page 35), room temperature

½ cup olive oil

⅓ cup unsweetened applesauce, room temperature

1 tablespoon pure vanilla extract

1 cup Berry Jam (page 48), made with raspberries, divided

1 batch Vegan Buttercream Frosting (page 38)

1. Preheat the oven to 350°F. Place 12 cupcake liners in a standard-size muffin tin.

2. In a large bowl, whisk together the flour, sugar, ½ cup of the shredded coconut, baking powder, and baking soda.

3. In a medium bowl, use a wooden spoon to mix together the vegan buttermilk, olive oil, applesauce, and vanilla extract.

4. Pour the wet mixture into the dry mixture and mix just enough to combine the ingredients and remove any remaining clumps of flour. Be careful not to overmix.

5. Using a ⅓-cup measuring scoop or a 3-tablespoon cookie scoop, fill each cupcake liner three-quarters of the way full.

6. Bake for 30 to 35 minutes, until a toothpick comes out clean when inserted in the middle of a cupcake. The cupcakes should be lightly golden and bounce back at a light touch.

7. Remove from the oven and let cool for 5 minutes. Carefully invert the cupcakes onto a cooling rack and turn them right side up to cool completely, about 30 minutes.

8. Once cool, use a paring knife to carefully carve a 1-inch circle into the top of each cupcake that goes halfway down the cupcake. Carefully remove the carved cores and slice them in half crosswise. You will use the top half of the cores as plugs to seal the filling in the cupcakes.

9. Place 2 teaspoons of raspberry jam in the cavity in a cupcake. Place a cupcake "plug" in the hole to cover the raspberry jam, pressing down lightly until the top

of the plug is fairly even with the top of the cupcake. Repeat with the rest of the cupcakes, cupcake "plugs," and raspberry jam.

10. To prepare the frosting, use a hand mixer to beat the buttercream and remaining ½ cup of raspberry jam until well combined.

11. When ready to frost, scoop the buttercream into a piping bag fitted with a frosting tip or into a plastic bag with a corner snipped off. Place the remaining ½ cup of shredded coconut in a small bowl. Pipe the frosting onto each cupcake, then carefully dip the frosted cupcakes into the shredded coconut or sprinkle it on top. To bake one day ahead, follow the steps through Step 7, then cover the cooled cupcakes with plastic wrap and store at room temperature. Fill and frost the next day. To store after frosting, keep them in an airtight container in the refrigerator for up to 3 days.

Note ───────────────────────────────

To make these cupcakes nut-free, follow the nut-free options for the Vegan Buttermilk and Vegan Buttercream Frosting.

Peanut Butter–Filled Cupcakes

OPTION OPTION OPTION

YIELD: 12 cupcakes   **PREP TIME:** 15 minutes   **COOK TIME:** 35 minutes

What's better than a Reese's peanut butter cup? A gluten-free, vegan version in cupcake form, of course! Basically, this is an extra-large chocolate cup stuffed with creamy peanut butter, but as cake. As you've probably figured out by now, my love for peanut butter and chocolate runs deep. It's what my partner, Jared, and I really bonded over: we both were obsessed with peanut butter and chocolate! What I love most about these cupcakes is that there's a Paleo option, as well as an option for nut-free and peanut-free.

1¼ cups cassava flour

1 cup coconut sugar

½ cup raw cacao powder

1 tablespoon baking powder

2 teaspoons baking soda

1 cup Vegan Buttermilk (page 35)

½ cup olive oil

⅓ cup unsweetened applesauce

1 teaspoon pure vanilla extract

½ cup creamy unsalted peanut butter

1 batch Paleo Vegan Chocolate Buttercream Frosting (page 40)

1. Preheat the oven to 350°F. Place 12 cupcake liners in a standard-size muffin tin.

2. In a large bowl, whisk together the flour, sugar, cacao powder, baking powder, and baking soda.

3. In a medium bowl, use a wooden spoon to mix together the vegan buttermilk, olive oil, applesauce, and vanilla extract.

4. Pour the wet mixture into the dry mixture and mix just enough to combine the ingredients and remove any remaining clumps of flour. Be careful not to overmix.

5. Using a ⅓-cup measuring scoop or a 3-tablespoon cookie scoop, fill each cupcake liner three-quarters of the way full.

6. Bake for 30 to 35 minutes, until a toothpick comes out clean when inserted in the middle of a cupcake. The cupcakes should be set and bounce back at a light touch.

7. Remove from the oven and let cool for 5 minutes. Carefully invert the cupcakes onto a cooling rack and turn them right side up. Allow them to cool for 15 minutes, then place the cooling rack in the refrigerator to chill the cupcakes for 30 minutes. They will be cool to the touch and firm.

8. Once cool, use a paring knife to carefully carve a 1-inch circle into the top of each cupcake that goes halfway down the cupcake. Carefully remove the carved cores and slice them in half crosswise. You will use the top half of the cores as plugs to seal the filling in the cupcakes.

9. Place 2 teaspoons of peanut butter in the cavity in a cupcake. Place a cupcake "plug" in the hole to cover the peanut butter, pressing down lightly until the top of the plug is fairly even with the top of the cupcake. Repeat with the rest of the cupcakes, cupcake "plugs," and peanut butter.

10. When ready to frost, scoop the buttercream into a piping bag fitted with a frosting tip or into a plastic bag with a corner snipped off. Pipe the frosting onto each cupcake. To bake one day ahead, follow the steps through Step 7, then cover the cooled cupcakes with plastic wrap and store at room temperature. Fill and frost the next day. To store after frosting, keep them in an airtight container in the refrigerator for up to 3 days.

Notes

To make these cupcakes nut-free, follow the nut-free options for the Vegan Buttermilk and Paleo Vegan Chocolate Buttercream Frosting.

To make them Paleo, swap almond butter for the peanut butter and use the Paleo baking powder on page 37, but add it to the wet ingredients in Step 3.

To make them peanut-free, swap almond butter for the peanut butter.

Pecan Cupcakes

OPTION

YIELD: 12 cupcakes   **PREP TIME:** 15 minutes   **COOK TIME:** 35 minutes

One of my favorite parts of mid-to-late fall is the sweet aroma of nuts roasting in the kitchen. While I love a good pumpkin or apple pie, pecan pie is my favorite, and these cupcakes remind me of it. However, while pecan pie is rather heavy, these cupcakes are quite light. Plus, I like to think that the pecans add some nutritional benefit to an otherwise indulgent dessert! The trick to these cupcakes is to candy the pecans so that they're nice and sweet before going into the batter. Just a touch of maple syrup, and it is quite literally autumn in a bite!

1 tablespoon vegan butter

1 cup chopped raw pecans, divided

1 tablespoon maple syrup

2½ cups cake flour or sifted gluten-free 1-to-1 baking flour

1 cup granulated sugar or coconut sugar (see Notes, page 139)

1 tablespoon baking powder

2 teaspoons baking soda

1 cup Vegan Buttermilk (page 35), room temperature

½ cup coconut oil, melted

½ cup unsweetened applesauce, room temperature

1½ tablespoons pure vanilla extract

1 batch Vegan Buttercream Frosting (page 38)

1. Preheat the oven to 350°F. Place 12 cupcake liners in a standard-size muffin tin.

2. In a small saucepan, melt the vegan butter over medium-low heat. Add ½ cup of the pecans and the maple syrup and reduce the heat to low. Lightly stir for 5 minutes, or until aromatic. Transfer the pecans to a small bowl and let cool while you prepare the batter.

3. In a large bowl, whisk together the flour, sugar, baking powder, and baking soda.

4. In a medium bowl, use a wooden spoon to mix together the vegan buttermilk, coconut oil, applesauce, and vanilla extract.

5. Pour the wet mixture into the dry mixture and mix just enough to combine the ingredients and remove any remaining clumps of flour. Be careful not to overmix. Fold in the candied pecans.

6. Using a ⅓-cup measuring scoop or a 3-tablespoon cookie scoop, fill each cupcake liner three-quarters of the way full.

7. Bake for 30 to 35 minutes, until a toothpick comes out clean when inserted in the middle of a cupcake. The cupcakes should be lightly golden and bounce back at a light touch.

8. Remove from the oven and let cool for 5 minutes. Carefully invert the cupcakes onto a cooling rack and turn them right side up to cool completely, about 30 minutes.

9. When ready to frost, scoop the buttercream into a piping bag fitted with a frosting tip or into a plastic bag with a corner snipped off. Pipe the frosting onto the cupcakes and sprinkle with the remaining ½ cup of pecans. To store after frosting, keep them in an airtight container in the refrigerator for up to 3 days.

Red Velvet Cupcakes

OPTION OPTION

YIELD: 12 cupcakes   **PREP TIME:** 15 minutes   **COOK TIME:** 35 minutes

Did you know that when red velvet cake was first invented, it contained way more cocoa powder than it does today? Its origins point to the 1800s, when either almond flour or cornstarch was used with a touch of cacao powder in combination with wheat flour. When everything was baked together, it yielded a beautiful velvety texture that differentiated itself from its other cake counterparts. Now, traditionally, red velvet cake contains some brown sugar, originally called red sugar (hence the name red velvet!). Slowly, people started adding red food coloring to give the cake that reddish hue that we now associate with red velvet. History lesson aside, this vegan version of a classic—with a gluten-free option!—will not disappoint. Every bite is as rich, tangy, and velvety as a more traditional red velvet cupcake.

1½ cups cake flour or sifted gluten-free 1-to-1 baking flour

¾ cup granulated sugar or coconut sugar (see Notes)

3 tablespoons beet powder

1 tablespoon raw cacao powder

1 tablespoon baking powder

2 teaspoons baking soda

½ teaspoon finely ground sea salt

1¼ cups Vegan Buttermilk (page 35), room temperature

½ cup coconut oil, melted

⅓ cup unsweetened applesauce, room temperature

3 tablespoons plain unsweetened coconut or cashew yogurt, room temperature (see Notes)

1 tablespoon pure vanilla extract

1 batch Vegan Cream Cheese Frosting (page 42)

1. Preheat the oven to 350°F. Place 12 cupcake liners in a standard-size muffin tin.

2. In a large bowl, whisk together the flour, sugar, beet powder, cacao powder, baking powder, baking soda, and salt.

3. In a medium bowl, use a wooden spoon to mix together the vegan buttermilk, coconut oil, applesauce, yogurt, and vanilla extract.

4. Pour the wet mixture into the dry mixture and mix just enough to combine the ingredients and remove any remaining clumps of flour. Be careful not to overmix.

5. Using a ⅓-cup measuring scoop or a 3-tablespoon cookie scoop, fill each cupcake liner three-quarters of the way full.

6. Bake for 30 to 35 minutes, until a toothpick comes out clean when inserted in the middle of a cupcake. The cupcakes should be lightly golden and bounce back at a light touch.

7. Remove from the oven and let cool for 5 minutes. Carefully invert the cupcakes onto a cooling rack and turn them right side up to cool completely, about 30 minutes.

8. When ready to frost, scoop the cream cheese frosting into a piping bag fitted with a frosting tip or into a plastic bag with a corner snipped off. Pipe the frosting onto each cupcake. To bake one day ahead, follow the steps through Step 7, then cover the cooled cupcakes with plastic wrap and store at room temperature. Frost the next day. To store after frosting, keep them in an airtight container in the refrigerator for up to 3 days.

Notes ___

If you use coconut sugar in the batter, the cupcakes will have a slightly brown-red color, but they'll still be delicious!

For the best taste and texture, coconut or cashew milk yogurt is preferred here; however, you can use almond milk yogurt if desired.

To make these cupcakes nut-free, use coconut milk yogurt and follow the nut-free options for the Vegan Buttermilk and Vegan Cream Cheese Frosting.

Mocha Cupcakes

OPTION OPTION

YIELD: 12 cupcakes   **PREP TIME:** 15 minutes   **COOK TIME:** 35 minutes

Every morning, without fail, I make myself a large Americano (at least two shots) with a tablespoon of cacao powder. I can't remember a morning when I didn't have this combination, so, needless to say, the pairing of chocolate and espresso is near and dear to my heart. Here, the ground espresso not only complements the chocolate but also cuts the sugar a bit so you don't get a rush of sweetness in your mouth. If you're making these cupcakes for an evening party, I recommend using decaf espresso—you want to be able to go to sleep afterward! But if you're making these for the daytime, the espresso will give you a nice energy boost.

2¼ cups cake flour or sifted gluten-free 1-to-1 baking flour

1 cup granulated sugar or coconut sugar

¼ cup raw cacao powder

1 tablespoon ground espresso, plus more for topping if desired

1 tablespoon baking powder

2 teaspoons baking soda

1 cup Vegan Buttermilk (page 35)

½ cup coconut oil, melted

⅓ cup unsweetened applesauce

1 tablespoon pure vanilla extract

1 batch Paleo Vegan Chocolate Buttercream Frosting (page 40)

1. Preheat the oven to 350°F. Place 12 cupcake liners in a standard-size muffin tin.

2. In a large bowl, whisk together the flour, sugar, cacao powder, ground espresso, baking powder, and baking soda.

3. In a medium bowl, use a wooden spoon to mix together the vegan buttermilk, coconut oil, applesauce, and vanilla extract.

4. Pour the wet mixture into the dry mixture and mix just enough to combine the ingredients and remove any remaining clumps of flour. Be careful not to overmix.

5. Using a ⅓-cup measuring scoop or a 3-tablespoon cookie scoop, fill each cupcake liner three-quarters of the way full.

6. Bake for 30 to 35 minutes, until a toothpick comes out clean when inserted in the middle of a cupcake. The cupcakes should be lightly golden and bounce back at a light touch.

7. Remove from the oven and let cool for 5 minutes. Carefully invert the cupcakes onto a cooling rack and turn them right side up to cool completely, about 30 minutes.

8. When ready to frost, scoop the buttercream into a piping bag fitted with a frosting tip or into a plastic bag with a corner snipped off. Pipe the frosting onto each cupcake and top each cupcake with a sprinkle of ground espresso, if desired. To bake the cupcakes one day ahead, complete Steps 1 through 7, then cover the cooled cupcakes with plastic wrap and store at room temperature. Frost the next day. After frosting, store them in an airtight container in the refrigerator for up to 3 days.

Note —————————————————————————————————————

To make these cupcakes nut-free, follow the nut-free options for the
Vegan Buttermilk and Paleo Vegan Chocolate Buttercream Frosting.

Strawberry Vanilla Cupcakes

OPTION OPTION

YIELD: 12 cupcakes   **PREP TIME:** 15 minutes   **COOK TIME:** 35 minutes

This might seem odd, but I really dislike chocolate and strawberries together. Chocolate and raspberries, totally fine. Chocolate and banana? Would never turn it down. But chocolate and strawberries is a no-go. Vanilla and strawberries, however, is a different story. One of my favorite treats in the late spring and summer is a little bowl of coconut whipped cream with freshly sliced strawberries. Absolutely heavenly. These cupcakes echo that deliciously light and refreshing flavor. The strawberry cake is my favorite part: it's packed with vanilla and fresh jam. Top it with vanilla buttercream and a fresh strawberry, and you have the perfect warm-weather treat!

2¾ cups cake flour or sifted gluten-free 1-to-1 baking flour

1 cup granulated sugar or coconut sugar (see Notes, page 139)

1 tablespoon baking powder

2 teaspoons baking soda

1 cup Vegan Buttermilk (page 35), room temperature

½ cup coconut oil, melted

½ cup Berry Jam (page 48), made with strawberries

⅓ cup unsweetened applesauce, room temperature

1½ tablespoons pure vanilla extract

1 batch Vegan Buttercream Frosting (page 38)

6 fresh strawberries, sliced in half, for garnish (optional)

1. Preheat the oven to 350°F. Place 12 cupcake liners in a standard-size muffin tin.

2. In a large bowl, whisk together the flour, sugar, baking powder, and baking soda.

3. In a medium bowl, use a wooden spoon to mix together the vegan buttermilk, coconut oil, strawberry jam, applesauce, and vanilla extract.

4. Pour the wet mixture into the dry mixture and mix just enough to combine the ingredients and remove any remaining clumps of flour. Be careful not to overmix.

5. Using a ⅓-cup measuring scoop or a 3-tablespoon cookie scoop, fill each cupcake liner three-quarters of the way full.

6. Bake for 30 to 35 minutes, until a toothpick comes out clean when inserted in the middle of a cupcake. The cupcakes should be lightly golden and bounce back at a light touch.

7. Remove from the oven and let cool for 5 minutes. Carefully invert the cupcakes onto a cooling rack and turn them right side up to cool completely, about 30 minutes.

8. When ready to frost, scoop the buttercream into a piping bag fitted with a frosting tip or into a plastic bag with a corner snipped off. Pipe the frosting onto each cupcake and garnish with a strawberry half, if desired. To bake one day ahead, follow the steps through Step 7, then cover the cooled cupcakes with plastic wrap and store at room temperature. Frost the next day. To store after frosting, keep them in an airtight container in the refrigerator for up to 3 days.

Note ——————————————————

To make these cupcakes nut-free, follow the nut-free options for the
Vegan Buttermilk and Vegan Buttercream Frosting.

Cookies 'n' Cream Cupcakes

OPTION OPTION

YIELD: 12 cupcakes   **PREP TIME:** 15 minutes   **COOK TIME:** 35 minutes

Combining two of my favorite loves into one, these cookie-filled cupcakes are an easy and decadent dessert to make for all ages. With a cookie-speckled cake and chunks of creme-filled chocolate sandwich cookie frosting, these cupcakes are very easy to eat. There are options for making them both gluten-free and nut-free, but please note: when making the frosting, it is essential that all of the cookie pieces are small enough to fit through the piping tip! Otherwise, a piece will get stuck, and trying to fix it is a messy process.

2½ cups cake flour or sifted gluten-free 1-to-1 baking flour

1 cup granulated sugar or coconut sugar (see Notes, page 139)

1 tablespoon baking powder

2 teaspoons baking soda

1 cup Vegan Buttermilk (page 35)

½ cup coconut oil, melted

⅓ cup unsweetened applesauce

1 tablespoon pure vanilla extract

1½ cups crushed vegan creme-filled chocolate sandwich cookies, divided

1 batch Vegan Buttercream Frosting (page 38)

12 whole vegan creme-filled chocolate sandwich cookies, for topping (optional)

1. Preheat the oven to 350°F. Place 12 cupcake liners in a standard-size muffin tin.

2. In a large bowl, whisk together the flour, sugar, baking powder, and baking soda.

3. In a medium bowl, use a wooden spoon to mix together the vegan buttermilk, coconut oil, applesauce, and vanilla extract.

4. Pour the wet mixture into the dry mixture and mix just enough to combine the ingredients and remove any remaining clumps of flour. Be careful not to overmix.

5. Gently fold 1 cup of the crushed chocolate cookies into the batter.

6. Using a ⅓-cup measuring scoop or a 3-tablespoon cookie scoop, fill each cupcake liner three-quarters of the way full.

7. Bake for 30 to 35 minutes, until a toothpick comes out clean when inserted in the middle of a cupcake. The cupcakes should be lightly golden and bounce back at a light touch.

8. Remove from the oven and let cool for 5 minutes. Carefully invert the cupcakes onto a cooling rack and turn them right side up to cool completely, about 30 minutes.

9. When ready to frost, prepare the frosting by beating together the Vegan Buttercream and the remaining ½ cup of crushed cookies until almost smooth. You don't want any large chunks of cookie that won't fit through the piping tip.

10. Scoop the buttercream into a piping bag fitted with a frosting tip or into a plastic bag with a corner snipped off. Pipe the frosting onto each cupcake and top each cupcake with a whole sandwich cookie, if desired. To bake the cupcakes one

day ahead, complete Steps 1 through 8, then cover the cooled cupcakes with plastic wrap and store at room temperature. Frost the next day. After frosting, store them in an airtight container in the refrigerator for up to 3 days.

Notes

To make these cupcakes gluten-free, use gluten-free 1-to-1 baking flour and gluten-free creme-filled chocolate cookie sandwiches.

To make them nut-free, follow the nut-free options for the Vegan Buttermilk and Vegan Buttercream Frosting.

Pumpkin Cupcakes

OPTION   OPTION

YIELD: 12 cupcakes   **PREP TIME:** 15 minutes   **COOK TIME:** 35 minutes

Surprisingly, this recipe was hard for me to figure out—I think because pumpkin can be a tricky ingredient to work with. (It adds a lot of moisture, which is a good thing, but it can lead to a dense and gooey cupcake.) But never fear: this recipe has been tested nearly ten times to ensure that it comes out perfect every time, whether you've baked with pumpkin or not. These cupcakes are truly an ode to fall; packed with pumpkin pie spice and frosted with a vegan cream cheese frosting, they're the perfect fall treat after apple picking or even pumpkin picking. Bonus points if you make your own homemade pumpkin puree!

1¾ cups cake flour or sifted gluten-free 1-to-1 baking flour

⅔ cup granulated sugar or coconut sugar (see Notes, page 139)

1 tablespoon pumpkin pie spice, store-bought or homemade (see Notes)

1 tablespoon ground cinnamon

2 teaspoons baking powder

1 teaspoon baking soda

¼ teaspoon finely ground sea salt

1 cup pumpkin puree

½ cup Vegan Buttermilk (page 35)

2 Flaxseed Eggs (page 34)

¼ cup olive, avocado, or coconut oil

1 tablespoon maple syrup

1 teaspoon pure vanilla extract

1 batch Vegan Cream Cheese Frosting (page 42)

12 vegan sugared pumpkin candies (optional)

1. Preheat the oven to 350°F. Place 12 cupcake liners in a standard-size muffin tin.

2. In a large bowl, whisk together the flour, sugar, pumpkin pie spice, cinnamon, baking powder, baking soda, and salt.

3. In a medium bowl, use a wooden spoon to mix together the pumpkin puree, vegan buttermilk, flaxseed eggs, olive oil, maple syrup, and vanilla extract.

4. Pour the wet mixture into the dry mixture and mix just enough to combine the ingredients and remove any remaining clumps of flour. Be careful not to overmix.

5. Using a ⅓-cup measuring scoop or a 3-tablespoon cookie scoop, fill each cupcake liner three-quarters of the way full.

6. Bake for 30 to 35 minutes, until a toothpick comes out clean when inserted in the middle of a cupcake. The cupcakes should be golden and bounce back at a light touch.

7. Remove from the oven and let cool for 5 minutes. Carefully invert the cupcakes onto a cooling rack and turn them right side up to cool completely, about 30 minutes.

8. When ready to frost, scoop the cream cheese frosting into a piping bag fitted with a frosting tip or into a plastic bag with a corner snipped off. Pipe the frosting onto each cupcake and top each cupcake with a pumpkin candy, if desired. To bake

the cupcakes one day ahead, complete Steps 1 through 7, then cover the cooled cupcakes with plastic wrap and store at room temperature. Frost the next day. After frosting, store them in an airtight container in the refrigerator for up to 3 days.

Notes

To make your own pumpkin pie spice for this recipe, combine 2 teaspoons ground cinnamon, 1 teaspoon ginger powder, ½ teaspoon ground cloves, and ½ teaspoon ground nutmeg.

To make these cupcakes nut-free, follow the nut-free options for the Vegan Buttermilk and Vegan Cream Cheese Frosting.

Chapter 8

CAKES

Chocolate Hazelnut Cake

YIELD: One 3-layer, 6-inch cake, or one 2-layer, 8-inch cake
PREP TIME: 25 minutes **COOK TIME:** 30 to 39 minutes, depending on size

The only combination that rivals my love of chocolate and peanut butter very closely is my love of chocolate and hazelnuts. There is something about hazelnuts that makes me want to keep going back for more—it must be the Italian in me! I adore this dessert because it's basically like taking big bites of Nutella in cake form. Layers of decadently rich buttercream and crunchy hazelnuts nestled between unbelievably moist chocolate cake layers make this particular dessert an ultimate indulgence. Not to mention it's completely Paleo and gluten-free as is—no modifications needed.

CAKE:

3 cups cassava flour

1 cup raw cacao powder

1 cup coconut sugar

1 tablespoon baking soda

3¼ cups unsweetened coconut milk, room temperature

½ cup maple syrup

4 Flaxseed Eggs (page 34)

1½ tablespoons Paleo Baking Powder (page 37) (see Note)

1 tablespoon pure vanilla extract

1 cup vegan dark chocolate chips (55% to 70% cacao), melted (see pages 14 and 15)

1 batch Paleo Vegan Chocolate Buttercream Frosting (page 40)

1 cup raw hazelnut pieces and/or halves

Note

If you do not need the cake to be 100 percent Paleo, you can use any store-bought baking powder in place of the homemade version. Add it to the dry ingredients in Step 2, along with the baking soda.

1. Preheat the oven to 350°F. Line three 6-inch or two 8-inch nonstick cake pans with parchment paper. (If you don't have nonstick pans, grease the pans with cooking spray or coconut oil, then use about 1 tablespoon of extra flour per pan to lightly flour them.)

2. In a large bowl, whisk together the flour, cacao powder, coconut sugar, and baking soda.

3. In a medium bowl, use a wooden spoon to mix together the coconut milk, maple syrup, flaxseed eggs, baking powder, and vanilla extract.

4. Add the melted chocolate to the wet mixture and mix thoroughly until well combined.

5. Fold the wet mixture into the dry until combined, making sure there are no clumps of the dry mixture left.

6. Evenly divide the batter among the prepared cake pans. Bake for 30 to 35 minutes for 6-inch cakes or 36 to 39 minutes for 8-inch cakes. When done, a toothpick will come out clean when inserted in the middle and the cakes will be completely set and bounce back at a light touch.

7. Remove the cakes from the oven and carefully invert them onto a cooling rack, then turn them right side up. Let the cakes cool completely; this should take about 30 minutes.

8. When ready to frost, place one cake on a cake plate or stand. Spread about one-third of the chocolate buttercream frosting on top and sprinkle with ⅓ cup of the hazelnuts. Place the second cake on top and repeat. Then place the last cake on top and repeat with the remaining buttercream and hazelnuts. (If making a two-layer 8-inch cake, use half of the frosting and ½ cup of the hazelnuts for the first layer and the remaining frosting and hazelnuts for the top layer.)

9. Slice and serve. Store in an airtight container in the refrigerator for up to 5 days or in the freezer for up to a month. To prepare this cake a day ahead, complete Steps 1 through 7. Then place the cooled cakes on separate plates, cover them with plastic wrap, and store at room temperature until you're ready to frost the next day.

Lemon Blueberry Cake

OPTION OPTION

YIELD: One 2-layer, 8-inch cake   **PREP TIME:** 15 minutes
COOK TIME: 35 minutes

I kid you not, once I finished photographing this cake, I had to stop everything and enjoy a slice. With over a hundred recipes in this book, I had a lot to do, but this cake was so enticing that I needed to give myself a minute to enjoy it. From the vibrant purple hue of the frosting to the texture and flavor of the cake, it tastes like the joy of spring in a bite. And it was a welcome reprieve, as I was creating these recipes in the middle of winter! Yes, most people love chocolate, but I truly believe that when this zesty yet sweet cake is served at a party, both kids and adults will fall in love with it.

LEMON BLUEBERRY CAKE:

3⅔ cups cake flour or sifted gluten-free 1-to-1 baking flour

1½ cups coconut sugar or granulated sugar (see Notes, page 139)

1 tablespoon baking powder

1 teaspoon baking soda

1½ cups unsweetened dairy-free milk, room temperature

½ cup coconut oil, melted

½ cup unsweetened applesauce, room temperature

1 tablespoon grated lemon zest (about 1 lemon)

3 tablespoons freshly squeezed lemon juice (about 1 lemon)

1 tablespoon pure vanilla extract

½ cup fresh blueberries

BLUEBERRY FROSTING:

1 batch Vegan Buttercream Frosting (page 38)

½ cup Berry Jam (page 48), made with blueberries

FOR GARNISH:

Fresh blueberries

Thinly sliced lemon wedges

Note

To make this cake nut-free, use a nut-free dairy-free milk (coconut and oat milk are good choices) and follow the nut-free option for the Vegan Buttercream Frosting. (If using oat milk and you require it to be gluten-free, be sure to buy a brand labeled as such.)

To make the cake:

1. Preheat the oven to 350°F. Line two 8-inch nonstick cake pans with parchment paper. (If you don't have nonstick pans, grease the pans with cooking spray or coconut oil, then use about 1 tablespoon of extra flour per pan to lightly flour them.)

2. In a large bowl, whisk together the flour, sugar, baking powder, and baking soda.

3. In a medium bowl, use a wooden spoon to mix together the dairy-free milk, coconut oil, applesauce, lemon zest, lemon juice, and vanilla extract.

4. Fold the wet mixture into the dry until combined, making sure there are no clumps of the dry mixture left.

5. Fold in the blueberries.

6. Evenly divide the batter between the prepared cake pans. Bake for 33 to 35 minutes, until a toothpick comes out clean when inserted in the middle. The cakes should be completely set and bounce back at a light touch.

7. Remove the cakes from the oven and carefully invert them onto a cooling rack, then turn them right side up. Let the cakes cool completely; this should take about 30 minutes.

To make the frosting:

8. Use a hand mixer to mix the buttercream with the blueberry jam until well combined.

9. When ready to frost, place one cake on a cake plate or stand. Evenly spread about ⅔ cup of the blueberry frosting on the top of the first layer. Place the second cake on top and frost the top with about ½ cup of the blueberry frosting. Use the remaining frosting to generously frost the edges and sides of the cake (you may have some frosting left over). Garnish with fresh blueberries and lemon wedges.

10. Slice and serve. Store the cake in an airtight container in the refrigerator for up to 5 days or in the freezer for up to a month; store any leftover frosting in an airtight container in the refrigerator for up to a week.

11. To prepare this cake a day ahead, complete Steps 1 through 7. Then place the cooled cakes on separate plates, cover them with plastic wrap, and store at room temperature until you're ready to frost the next day.

Chocolate Mousse Cake

OPTION

YIELD: One 9 by 12-inch sheet cake   **PREP TIME:** 25 minutes
COOK TIME: 35 minutes

Funny story: Jared told me that when he was a kid, he refused to eat mousse cake because he thought it had moose in it. Then one day he realized it was just chocolate, and he fell madly in love with this classic delight. I had my own confusion surrounding this dessert—how it could achieve both the fluffy texture of cake and the silky smooth feel of mousse is some magic I will never quite understand. And yet here it is! The cake melts into a soft mousse and, coupled with the fudgy avocado chocolate frosting, the experience is out of this world. Not only that, but it's also incredibly simple to make. If layer cakes aren't your thing, rest assured that this sheet cake is definitely up your alley! And yes, it's 100 percent vegan—no moose involved.

CHOCOLATE MOUSSE CAKE:

1 cup cassava flour

1¼ cups gluten-free rolled oats, ground into a rustic flour (see Notes, page 117)

¾ cup raw cacao powder

¾ cup coconut sugar

1 tablespoon baking powder

1 teaspoon baking soda

1½ cups Vegan Buttermilk (page 35), room temperature

1 cup vegan butter, melted

2 Flaxseed Eggs (page 34)

1 teaspoon pure vanilla extract

AVOCADO CHOCOLATE FROSTING:

2 large ripe avocados, pitted and skin removed

½ cup maple syrup

½ cup raw cacao powder

Note

To make this cake nut-free, follow the nut-free option for the Vegan Buttermilk and use Earth Balance's vegan buttery sticks.

To make the cake:

1. Preheat the oven to 350°F. Line 9 by 12-inch nonstick baking pan with parchment paper. (If your cake pan isn't nonstick, grease it with cooking spray or coconut oil, then use about 1 tablespoon of flour to lightly flour it.)

2. In a large bowl, whisk together the flours, cacao powder, sugar, baking powder, and baking soda.

3. In a medium bowl, use a wooden spoon to mix together the vegan buttermilk, vegan butter, flaxseed eggs, and vanilla extract.

4. Fold the wet mixture into the dry until combined, making sure there are no clumps of the dry mixture left.

5. Pour the batter into the prepared pan. Bake for 30 to 35 minutes, until a toothpick comes out clean when inserted in the middle. The cake should be completely set and bounce back at a light touch.

6. Remove the cake from the oven and carefully invert it onto a cooling rack, then turn it right side up. Let the cake cool completely; this should take about 30 minutes. Alternatively, you can leave the cake in the pan to cool completely before frosting and serving from the pan.

To make the frosting:

7. Place the avocados into a food processor and puree until smooth and creamy, about 2 minutes.

8. Add the maple syrup and cacao powder and puree again until smooth.

9. Frost the cake before slicing and serving.

10. Store in an airtight container in the refrigerator for up to 5 days or in the freezer for up to a month. To prepare this cake a day ahead, complete Steps 1 through 6. Then place the cooled cake on a tray, cover it with plastic wrap, and store at room temperature until you're ready to frost the next day.

Molten Lava Cakes

YIELD: 4 small cakes   **PREP TIME:** 5 minutes   **COOK TIME:** 18 minutes

This recipe is my go-to for my anniversary with my partner, Jared, as well as for Valentine's Day, birthday celebrations for hardcore chocolate lovers, and small dinner parties. It's so easy to prepare, yet so elegant and decadent. I love to top the cakes with a little homemade coconut whipped cream and fresh raspberries, but you can also serve them à la mode.

½ cup plus 1 tablespoon vegan butter or coconut oil, divided

½ cup plus 1 tablespoon cassava flour, divided

⅔ cup plus ½ scant cup unsweetened chocolate chips (100% cacao), divided

½ cup unsweetened applesauce, room temperature

½ cup coconut sugar

Coconut whipped cream, store-bought or homemade (page 49), for topping (optional)

Fresh raspberries, for garnish (optional)

1. Preheat the oven to 425°F. Melt 1 tablespoon of the vegan butter and use it to grease four 5.4-ounce ramekins, then dust the ramekins with 1 tablespoon of cassava flour.

2. In a microwave-safe bowl, heat the remaining ½ cup of vegan butter until melted and hot to the touch. Add ⅔ cup of the chocolate chips and stir until melted. Set aside.

3. In a large bowl, use a hand mixer to beat the applesauce and coconut sugar until well combined.

4. Pour in the melted vegan butter and chocolate mixture and fold it into the applesauce mixture.

5. Add the remaining ½ cup of cassava flour and mix until there are no clumps.

6. Fill each ramekin three-quarters of the way full with batter. (There will be batter remaining in the bowl.) Add 1 heaping tablespoon of chocolate chips to the middle of each ramekin.

7. Top with the remaining batter. Place the ramekins on a rimmed baking sheet and bake for 16 to 18 minutes, until the middle just begins to set.

8. Remove from the oven and let cool and set for 10 minutes.

9. Run a knife around the edges of the cakes (use oven mitts if the ramekins are hot) and flip over gently onto serving plates.

10. Serve warm, topped with the coconut whipped cream and raspberries, if desired.

Peanut Butter Banana Cake

OPTION   OPTION   OPTION

YIELD: One 9 by 12-inch sheet cake   **PREP TIME:** 25 minutes
COOK TIME: 35 minutes

This snack cake is irresistible. Topped with a creamy peanut butter frosting and sweetened with both bananas and just a little maple syrup, each slice is pure bliss. Plus, it's incredibly easy to make. The gluten-free and non-gluten-free versions taste nearly identical, so rest assured, you can serve this cake to everyone, and no one will complain! Top it with some more crushed peanuts, if desired.

BANANA CAKE:

3 cups cake flour or sifted gluten-free 1-to-1 baking flour

1 tablespoon baking powder

1 teaspoon baking soda

¼ teaspoon finely ground sea salt

1 cup mashed bananas (about 3 large ripe bananas)

1 cup Vegan Buttermilk (page 35)

¾ cup maple syrup, room temperature

2 teaspoons pure vanilla extract

PEANUT BUTTER FROSTING:

1 batch Vegan Buttercream Frosting (page 38)

½ cup creamy unsalted peanut butter

⅓ cup crushed raw unsalted peanuts, for topping (optional)

To make the cake:

1. Preheat the oven to 350°F. Line a 9 by 12-inch nonstick baking pan with parchment paper. (If your pan isn't nonstick, grease it with cooking spray or coconut oil, then use about 1 tablespoon of flour to lightly flour it.)

2. In a large bowl, whisk together the flour, baking powder, and baking soda.

3. In a medium bowl, stir the mashed bananas, vegan buttermilk, maple syrup, and vanilla extract until combined.

4. Fold the wet mixture into the dry until combined, making sure there are no clumps of the dry mixture left.

5. Pour the batter into the prepared pan and bake for 30 to 35 minutes, until a toothpick comes out clean when inserted in the middle. The cake should be completely set and bounce back at a light touch.

6. Remove from the oven and carefully invert the cake onto a cooling rack, then turn it right side up. Let the cake cool completely; this should take about 30 minutes. Alternatively, you can leave the cake in the pan to cool completely before frosting and serving from the pan.

To make the frosting:

7. In a large bowl, use a hand mixer to beat the buttercream and peanut butter until completely combined. Frost the cake and top with crushed peanuts, if desired.

8. Store in an airtight container in the refrigerator for up to 5 days or the freezer for up to a month. To prepare this cake a day ahead, complete Steps 1 through 6. Then cover the cooled cake with plastic wrap and store at room temperature until you're ready to frost it the next day.

Notes

To make this cake nut-free, follow the nut-free options for the Vegan Buttermilk and Vegan Buttercream Frosting.

To make it peanut-free, swap in a nut butter or sunflower seed butter for the peanut butter in the frosting and omit the crushed peanut topping.

Chai Pumpkin Cake

OPTION OPTION

YIELD: One 8-inch square sheet cake **PREP TIME:** 25 minutes
COOK TIME: 37 minutes

When fall hits, I start turning every recipe into a pumpkin recipe—brownies, cupcakes, cookies, and, of course, cakes. This pumpkin cake is so light and refreshing that it could be served as either a dessert or a snack. I gave it a bit of a twist, though: instead of using pumpkin pie spice, we're using chai spices! You'd never know that this pumpkin cake topped with a cream cheese frosting is vegan and can easily be made gluten-free and nut-free.

2 cups cake flour or sifted gluten-free 1-to-1 baking flour

1 cup coconut sugar

1 tablespoon chai spice blend, plus 1 teaspoon for topping if desired

1 tablespoon baking powder

1 teaspoon baking soda

1 (15-ounce) can pumpkin puree

1 cup vegan butter, melted

3 Flaxseed Eggs (page 34)

½ cup Vegan Buttermilk (page 35)

1 teaspoon pure vanilla extract

1 batch Vegan Cream Cheese Frosting (page 42)

1. Preheat the oven to 350°F. Line an 8-inch square nonstick baking pan with parchment paper. (If your pan isn't nonstick, grease it with cooking spray or coconut oil, then use about 1 tablespoon of flour to lightly flour it.)

2. In a large bowl, whisk together the flour, sugar, chai spice blend, baking powder, and baking soda.

3. In a medium bowl, use a wooden spoon to mix together the pumpkin puree, vegan butter, flaxseed eggs, vegan buttermilk, and vanilla extract.

4. Fold the wet mixture into the dry until combined, making sure there are no clumps of the dry mixture left.

5. Pour the batter into the prepared pan and bake for 35 to 37 minutes, until a toothpick comes out clean when inserted in the middle. The cake should be completely set and bounce back at a light touch.

6. Remove the cake from the oven and carefully invert it onto a cooling rack, then turn it right side up. Let the cake cool completely; this should take about 30 minutes. Alternatively, you can leave the cake in the pan to cool completely before frosting and serve it from the pan.

7. Frost the cake before slicing and serving. Sprinkle with 1 teaspoon chai spice blend, if desired.

8. Store in an airtight container in the refrigerator for up to 5 days or the freezer for up to a month. To prepare this cake a day ahead, complete Steps 1 through 6. Cover the cooled cake with plastic wrap and store at room temperature until you're ready to frost the next day.

Coconut Lemon Cake

OPTION OPTION

YIELD: One 2-layer, 8-inch cake **PREP TIME:** 15 minutes
COOK TIME: 35 minutes

Typically, sweet and sour brings to mind a sauce that accompanies Asian cuisine, but this cake proves that sweet and sour is a winning formula for more than just stir-fry. Lemon pairs perfectly with coconut, making this cake not too sweet, yet not sour enough to make your lips pucker. I do love coconut cake, but sometimes I find it a bit too heavy and sweet, so if you're in the mood for something slightly lighter (I mean, it is still coconut!), this is the cake for you. If you'd like, you can toast the coconut flakes used to top the cake. Of course, you want to let them cool first, or you'll end up with melted vegan buttercream everywhere. Through my many trials and errors of cake making, I now fully understand the importance of letting a cake cool completely in order to save the kitchen floors from yet another scrubbing!

COCONUT LEMON CAKE:

3 cups cake flour or sifted gluten-free 1-to-1 baking flour

1 cup unsweetened shredded coconut

1½ cups granulated sugar or coconut sugar (see Notes, page 139)

1 tablespoon baking powder

1½ teaspoons baking soda

1 (13.5-ounce) can unsweetened coconut cream, room temperature

1 cup coconut oil, melted

3 Flaxseed Eggs (page 34)

3 tablespoons freshly squeezed lemon juice (about 1 lemon)

1 tablespoon pure vanilla extract

COCONUT FROSTING:

1 batch Vegan Buttercream Frosting (page 38)

1½ cups unsweetened shredded coconut

Thin lemon slices, for garnish (optional)

Note

To make this cake nut-free, follow the nut-free option for the Vegan Buttercream Frosting.

1. Preheat the oven to 350°F. Line two 8-inch nonstick cake pans with parchment paper. (If you don't have nonstick pans, grease the pans with cooking spray or coconut oil, then use about 1 tablespoon of extra flour per pan to lightly flour them.)

2. In a large bowl, whisk together the flour, shredded coconut, sugar, baking powder, and baking soda.

3. In a medium bowl, use a wooden spoon to mix together the coconut cream, coconut oil, flaxseed eggs, lemon juice, and vanilla extract.

4. Fold the wet mixture into the dry until combined, making sure there are no clumps of the dry mixture left.

5. Evenly divide the batter between the prepared pans. Bake for 33 to 35 minutes, until a toothpick comes out clean when inserted in the middle. The cakes should be completely set and bounce back at a light touch.

6. Remove the cakes from the oven and carefully invert them onto a cooling rack, then turn them right side up. Let the cakes cool completely; this should take about 30 minutes.

7. When ready to frost, place one cake on a cake plate or stand. Evenly spread about ⅔ cup of buttercream on the top of the first layer. Sprinkle with ½ cup of the shredded coconut. Place the second cake on top and frost the top with about ½ cup of the buttercream. Sprinkle with another ½ cup of the shredded coconut. Use the remaining frosting to generously frost the edges and sides of the cake (you may have some frosting left over) and gently press the remaining ½ cup of shredded coconut onto the frosting. Garnish with lemon slices, if desired.

8. Slice and serve. Store the cake in an airtight container in the refrigerator for up to 5 days or in the freezer for up to a month; store any leftover frosting in an airtight container in the refrigerator for up to a week. To prepare this cake a day ahead, complete Steps 1 through 6. Then place the cooled cakes on separate plates, cover them with plastic wrap, and store at room temperature until you're ready to frost the next day.

Paleo Chocolate Cake

YIELD: One 3-layer, 6-inch cake or one 2-layer, 8-inch cake
PREP TIME: 25 minutes   **COOK TIME:** 30 to 39 minutes, depending on size

If you're a chocolate lover, look no further. This ultra-rich, ultra-moist, and ultra-tender Paleo chocolate cake is a dream, whether or not you eat Paleo or vegan. In fact, I've had both Ghirardelli devotees and those who follow a plant-based diet say that this is one of the best chocolate cakes they've had. (Not to brag or anything, but I'm just saying, you need to try this recipe if you love chocolate!) Plus, this cake is entirely nut-free, making it a wonderful option for those who are allergic to any of the top eight allergens.

CHOCOLATE CAKE:

3 cups cassava flour

1 cup raw cacao powder

1 cup coconut sugar

1 tablespoon baking soda

3¼ cups unsweetened coconut milk

½ cup maple syrup

⅔ cup plain unsweetened dairy-free yogurt

1½ tablespoons Paleo Baking Powder (page 37) (see Note)

1 tablespoon pure vanilla extract

1 cup vegan dark chocolate chips (55% to 70% cacao), melted

1 batch Paleo Vegan Chocolate Buttercream Frosting (page 40)

1. Preheat the oven to 350°F. Line three 6-inch or two 8-inch nonstick cake pans with parchment paper. (If you don't have nonstick pans, grease the pans with cooking spray or coconut oil, then use about 1 tablespoon of extra flour per pan to lightly flour them.)

2. In a large bowl, whisk together the flour, cacao powder, coconut sugar, and baking soda.

3. In a medium bowl, use a wooden spoon to mix together the coconut milk, maple syrup, dairy-free yogurt, baking powder, and vanilla extract.

4. Add the melted chocolate to the wet mixture and mix thoroughly until well combined.

5. Fold the wet mixture into the dry until combined, making sure there are no clumps of the dry mixture left.

6. Divide the batter evenly among the prepared cake pans and bake for 30 to 35 minutes for 6-inch cakes or 36 to 39 minutes for 8-inch cakes, until a toothpick comes out clean when inserted in the middle of a cake. The cakes should be completely set and bounce back at a light touch.

7. Remove the cakes from the oven and carefully invert them onto a cooling rack, then turn them right side up. Let the cakes cool completely; this should take about 30 minutes.

8. When ready to frost, place one cake on a cake plate or stand. Spread one-third of the chocolate buttercream on top. Place the second cake on top and repeat. Then place the last cake on top and repeat with the remaining buttercream. (If making a two-layer 8-inch cake, use half of the frosting for the first layer and the remaining frosting for the top layer.)

9. Slice and serve. Store in an airtight container in the refrigerator for up to 5 days or in the freezer for up to a month. To prepare this cake a day ahead, complete Steps 1 through 7. Then place the cooled cakes on separate plates, cover with plastic wrap, and store at room temperature until you're ready to frost the next day.

Note —————————————————

If you do not need the cake to be 100 percent Paleo, you can use any store-bought baking powder in place of the homemade version. Add it to the dry ingredients in Step 2, along with the baking soda.

Chocolate Peanut Butter

FUDGE CAKE

OPTION OPTION

YIELD: One 2-layer, 8-inch cake **PREP TIME:** 15 minutes
COOK TIME: 35 minutes

The batter I developed for this recipe creates a cake that is more like fudge, especially when paired with peanut butter (hence its name!). In my opinion, if there's one food pairing that reminds us all that we're kids at heart, it is chocolate and peanut butter. This cake definitely speaks to that. It's like an adult version of an extra-large peanut butter cup. Who wouldn't enjoy a massive slice of this cake with a tall glass of coconut or almond milk?

CHOCOLATE CAKE:

2½ cups cassava flour

1½ cups coconut sugar

1 cup raw cacao powder

1 tablespoon baking powder

2 teaspoons baking soda

1½ cups Vegan Buttermilk (page 35), room temperature

½ cup olive oil

½ cup unsweetened applesauce, room temperature

⅓ cup maple syrup

1 teaspoon pure vanilla extract

PEANUT BUTTER FROSTING:

1 batch Vegan Buttercream Frosting (page 38)

½ cup creamy unsalted peanut butter

CHOCOLATE TOPPING:

5 ounces unsweetened baking chocolate (100% cacao), chopped (about ½ cup)

Notes

To make this cake nut-free, Paleo, or both, follow the nut-free and/or Paleo options for the Vegan Buttermilk and Vegan Buttercream Frosting. For Paleo, also swap almond butter or sunflower seed butter for the peanut butter in the frosting.

To make the cake peanut-free, swap your favorite nut or seed butter for the peanut butter.

To make the cake:

1. Preheat the oven to 350°F. Line two 8-inch nonstick cake pans with parchment paper. (If you don't have nonstick pans, grease the pans with cooking spray or coconut oil, then use about 1 tablespoon of extra flour per pan to lightly flour them.)

2. In a large bowl, whisk together the flour, sugar, cacao powder, baking powder, and baking soda.

3. In a medium bowl, use a wooden spoon to mix together the vegan buttermilk, olive oil, applesauce, maple syrup, and vanilla extract.

4. Fold the wet mixture into the dry until combined, making sure there are no clumps of the dry mixture left.

5. Evenly divide the batter between the prepared pans. Bake for 30 to 35 minutes, until a toothpick comes out clean when inserted in the middle. The cakes should be completely set and bounce back at a light touch.

6. Remove the cakes from the oven and carefully invert them onto a cooling rack, then turn them right side up. Let the cakes cool completely; this should take about 30 minutes.

To make the frosting:

7. Use a hand mixer to beat the buttercream with the peanut butter until smooth.

8. When ready to frost, place one cake on a cake plate or stand. Spread about ⅔ cup of the buttercream frosting on top. Place the second cake on top and repeat. Using half to two-thirds of the remaining frosting, apply a thin layer of frosting around the sides of the cake.

To make the chocolate topping:

9. Melt the chocolate in the microwave or on the stovetop, following the instructions on pages 14 and 15. Allow the melted chocolate to cool for 5 minutes, then pour it on top of the cake.

10. Slice and serve. Store the cake in an airtight container in the refrigerator for up to 5 days or in the freezer for up to a month; store leftover frosting in an airtight container in the refrigerator for up to a week. To prepare this cake a day ahead, complete Steps 1 through 6. Then place the cooled cakes on separate plates, cover them with plastic wrap, and store at room temperature until you're ready to frost the next day.

Flourless Chocolate Cake

YIELD: One 8-inch cake   **PREP TIME:** 5 minutes   **COOK TIME:** 40 minutes

It honestly does not get any simpler than the ingredients found in this flourless chocolate cake. Yet the taste is so rich and decadent, you'd think it took a whole lot of effort to prepare (when in all honesty, it's the easiest cake in this book!). Sprinkle it with a little extra cacao powder and serve it with a scoop of coconut milk ice cream or a dollop of Coconut Whipped Cream (page 49). Enjoy!

6 Flaxseed Eggs (page 34)

1 cup coconut oil, melted

½ cup maple syrup, room temperature

¼ cup unsweetened applesauce, room temperature

2 teaspoons Paleo Baking Powder (page 37) (see Notes)

1 cup plus 2 tablespoons raw cacao powder, divided

¼ cup coconut sugar

½ cup unsweetened baking chips (100% cacao)

1. Preheat the oven to 350°F. Line an 8-inch springform pan with parchment paper.

2. In a large bowl, mix together the flaxseed eggs, coconut oil, maple syrup, and applesauce. The oil should be completely mixed into the flaxseed mixture, which will take a few minutes. If you're using the Paleo baking powder, mix it into the batter here.

3. Sift in 1 cup of the cacao powder, then add the coconut sugar. Stir the dry ingredients into the wet mixture until the ingredients are well combined.

4. Melt the chocolate in the microwave or on the stovetop, following the instructions on pages 14 and 15.

5. Add the melted chocolate to the bowl and fold it into the batter.

6. Spoon the batter into the prepared pan and bake for 35 to 40 minutes, until a toothpick inserted in the middle comes out clean.

7. Remove from the oven and allow to cool in the pan for 30 minutes. Then remove the cake from the pan and sprinkle with the remaining 2 tablespoons of cacao powder.

8. Store on a plate wrapped in plastic wrap in the refrigerator for up to 5 days or at room temperature for up to 2 days.

Notes

If you don't need this cake to be 100 percent Paleo, you can omit the Paleo baking powder and sift in 2 teaspoons regular baking powder along with the cacao powder in Step 3.

If you would prefer to use dark chocolate chips, I recommend using chips that have a higher cacao content, since this cake is already quite sweet.

Birthday Cake

OPTION   OPTION

YIELD: One 3-layer, 6-inch cake, or one 2-layer, 8-inch cake
PREP TIME: 15 minutes   **COOK TIME:** 35 minutes

I've always loved making birthday cakes, even as a kid. I think I was inspired by a children's book my mom always used to read to us: It's My Birthday, *by Helen Oxenbury. Of course, this birthday cake is completely vegan, with an option of being gluten-free as well, but that children's story is still a major source of inspiration. Whenever appropriate, I top my cakes with sprinkles because I believe we all could use a little more color and joy in our lives! And don't worry, you can make this cake even if it's not someone's birthday, because, truly, every day deserves to be celebrated.*

CAKE:

3⅔ cups cake flour or sifted gluten-free 1-to-1 baking flour

1½ cups coconut sugar or granulated sugar (see Notes, page 139)

1 tablespoon baking powder

1 teaspoon baking soda

1½ cups unsweetened dairy-free milk, room temperature

½ cup vegan butter or coconut oil, melted

½ cup unsweetened applesauce, room temperature

1½ tablespoons pure vanilla extract

1 batch Paleo Vegan Chocolate Buttercream Frosting (page 40)

½ cup vegan sprinkles

1. Preheat the oven to 350°F. Line three 6-inch or two 8-inch nonstick cake pans with parchment paper. (If you don't have nonstick pans, grease the pans with cooking spray or coconut oil, then use about 1 tablespoon of extra flour per pan to lightly flour them.)

2. In a large bowl, whisk together the flour, sugar, baking powder, and baking soda.

3. In a medium bowl, use a wooden spoon to mix together the dairy-free milk, vegan butter, applesauce, and vanilla extract.

4. Fold the wet mixture into the dry until combined, making sure there are no clumps of the dry mixture left.

5. Evenly divide the batter among the prepared pans. Bake for 30 to 35 minutes for 6-inch cakes or 36 to 39 minutes for 8-inch cakes. When done, a toothpick will come out clean when inserted in the middle and the cakes will be completely set and bounce back at a light touch.

6. Remove the cakes from the oven and carefully invert them onto a cooling rack, then turn them right side up. Let the cakes cool completely; this should take about 30 minutes.

7. When ready to frost, place one cake on a cake plate or stand. Evenly spread about ½ cup of the buttercream on the top of the first layer. Repeat with the remaining layers. (If making a two-layer 8-inch cake, frost the top of each layer with ¾ cup

of frosting.) Generously frost the edges and sides of the cake with the remaining frosting (you may have some frosting left over). Decorate the top with the sprinkles.

8. Slice and serve. Store the cake in an airtight container in the refrigerator for up to 5 days or in the freezer for up to a month; store any leftover frosting in the refrigerator for up to a week. To prepare this cake a day ahead, complete Steps 1 through 6. Then place the cooled cakes on separate plates, cover them with plastic wrap, and store at room temperature until you're ready to frost the next day.

Note ——————————————————

To make this cake nut-free, use a nut-free dairy-free milk (coconut and oat milk are good options), use Earth Balance's vegan buttery sticks, and follow the nut-free option for the Paleo Vegan Chocolate Buttercream Frosting.

Eton Mess

YIELD: Eight ¾-cup servings, or twelve ½-cup servings
PREP TIME: 25 minutes, plus 1 hour to rest in oven   **COOK TIME:** 1 hour

I discovered this dessert a few years back, when family friends who are British brought over Eton Mess for a barbecue we were hosting. It was first noted in 1893 and is believed to have been created at Eton College, located in Berkshire, England. I thought it was the most elegant dessert I had ever seen, and it tasted out-of-this-world refreshing, light, creamy, and smooth. It's the perfect dessert, really, because guests can take as much or as little as they'd like, and it's not too heavy to have after a large meal. Traditional Eton Mess uses meringue made from egg whites, but seeing as this is a vegan baking book, I decided, why not veganize it? Now, making meringue in general is a process, but trust me, it is well worth it. It's not complicated, but it requires a little patience to get the perfect crunch to go along with the creamy and delicious coconut whipped cream!

VEGAN MERINGUES:

¾ cup aquafaba (see Notes)

¼ teaspoon cream of tartar

1 cup granulated sugar

1 teaspoon pure vanilla extract

TOPPINGS:

3 cups frozen coconut whipped topping, divided (see Notes)

3 cups sliced strawberries, divided

To make the meringues:

1. In a stand mixer, beat the aquafaba on high speed for 5 to 7 minutes, until stiff white peaks form (it's similar to whipping egg whites). Alternatively, you can whip the aquafaba in a large glass or metal bowl using a hand mixer.

2. Add the cream of tartar, then whip for 1 minute more to incorporate.

3. Gradually add the granulated sugar, about ¼ cup at a time, continuing to beat until the mixture becomes glossy. The meringue should be very stiff now.

4. Add the vanilla extract and beat for 1 minute to fully incorporate.

5. Preheat the oven to 225°F. Line a large baking sheet (at least 17 by 14 inches) with parchment paper.

6. Scoop the meringue into a piping bag fitted with a decorating tip (a #32 star tip is ideal) or into a plastic bag with a corner snipped off. Pipe the meringue onto the baking sheet in 2-inch circles, about 2 inches apart. You should get 20 to 24 meringue cookies, depending how much meringue was created.

7. Bake the meringues for 1 hour, turning the pan every 15 minutes to allow even baking.

8. Turn off the oven and allow the meringues to rest in the oven for 1 hour.

9. Remove the meringues from the oven and allow them to cool for 15 minutes before removing from the pan.

To assemble:

10. Scoop 1 cup of coconut whipped topping into a large serving dish. Top with 1 cup of sliced strawberries and one-third of the meringues (8 if you made 24 meringues).

11. Repeat the layers with the remaining coconut whipped topping, strawberries, and meringues. Serve immediately.

Notes ───────────────────────────────

Aquafaba is the liquid found in cans of chickpeas. When whipped, it acts much like egg whites. For this recipe, make sure to purchase unsalted canned chickpeas. Aquafaba that contains salt will not work here. One 15-ounce can of chickpeas will yield about ½ cup aquafaba, so you'll need two cans for this recipe.

For the frozen coconut whipped topping, I purchase Cocowhip, a So Delicious product that is available in the freezer section at most grocery stores. It comes in a 9-ounce container, which is equivalent to just over 1 cup of topping. If you'd like to make your own coconut whipped cream from scratch, see my recipe on page 49.

Cookie Dough Cake

OPTION OPTION

YIELD: One 3-layer, 6-inch cake, or one 2-layer, 8-inch cake
PREP TIME: 15 minutes   **COOK TIME:** 35 minutes

Do you love dipping chocolate chip cookies into a tall glass of (plant-based) milk? Me too, but the milk always drips away so fast that I end up having to bring my mouth as close as humanly possible to the glass to maximize the amount of cookie and milk in each bite. Tell me I'm not the only one, please? For all you cookie dippers out there, I have excellent news: this cake is like a glass of milk and freshly baked chocolate chip cookies all in one bite—no dipping or dripping required! The soft cake layers are speckled with chocolate chips and, when topped with vegan buttercream frosting…well, it's just like eating cookie dough! You can decorate the cake however your heart desires. I like to mix a portion of the chocolate chips into the frosting and decorate the top of the cake with a combination of crushed and whole store-bought gluten-free vegan chocolate chip cookies. But you can also keep the buttercream plain and use the remaining chocolate chips to decorate the top of the cake, sans cookies.

3½ cups cake flour or sifted gluten-free 1-to-1 baking flour

1½ cups coconut sugar or granulated sugar (see Notes, page 139)

1 tablespoon baking powder

1 teaspoon baking soda

1⅓ cups unsweetened dairy-free milk, room temperature

½ cup vegan butter, melted

½ cup unsweetened applesauce, room temperature

1½ tablespoons pure vanilla extract

1¼ cups vegan dark chocolate chips (55% to 70% cacao), divided

1 batch Vegan Buttercream Frosting (page 38)

½ cup crushed plus a few whole gluten-free vegan chocolate chip cookies, for garnish (optional; see Notes)

Notes

To make this cake nut-free, use a nut-free dairy-free milk (coconut and oat milk are good options), use Earth Balance's vegan buttery sticks, and follow the nut-free option for the Vegan Buttercream Frosting. If using oat milk and you require it to be gluten-free, be sure to buy a brand labeled as such.

My favorite brands of gluten-free vegan chocolate chip cookies are Simple Mills and Enjoy Life. However, you can absolutely bake your own!

1. Preheat the oven to 350°F. Line three 6-inch or two 8-inch nonstick cake pans with parchment paper. (If you don't have nonstick pans, grease the pans with cooking spray or coconut oil, then use about 1 tablespoon of extra flour per pan to lightly flour them.)

2. In a large bowl, whisk together the flour, sugar, baking powder, and baking soda.

3. In a medium bowl, use a wooden spoon to mix together the dairy-free milk, vegan butter, applesauce, and vanilla extract.

4. Fold the wet mixture into the dry until combined, making sure there are no clumps of the dry mixture left.

5. Fold in ⅔ cup of the chocolate chips.

6. Evenly divide the batter among the prepared pans. Bake for 30 to 35 minutes for 6-inch cakes or 36 to 39 minutes for 8-inch cakes. When done, a toothpick will come out clean when inserted in the middle and the cakes will be completely set and bounce back at a light touch.

7. Remove the cakes from the oven and carefully invert them onto a cooling rack, then turn them right side up. Let the cakes cool completely; this should take about 30 minutes.

8. When the cakes are ready to be frosted, fold the remaining chocolate chips into the buttercream.

9. When ready to frost, place one cake on a cake plate or stand. Evenly spread about ½ cup of the frosting on the top of the first layer. Repeat with the 2 remaining layers. (If making a two-layer 8-inch cake, frost the top of each layer with ¾ cup of frosting.) Generously frost the edges and sides of the cake with the remaining frosting (you may have some frosting left over). Decorate the top with crushed and whole chocolate chip cookies, if desired.

10. Slice and serve. Store in an airtight container in the refrigerator for up to 5 days or in the freezer for up to a month. To prepare this cake a day ahead, complete Steps 1 through 7. Then place the cooled cakes on separate plates, cover with plastic wrap, and store at room temperature until you're ready to frost the next day.

Chocolate Chip Banana
BUNDT CAKE

OPTION

YIELD: One Bundt cake   **PREP TIME:** 15 minutes   **COOK TIME:** 37 minutes

I'm pretty sure there's at least one banana recipe in almost every chapter of this cookbook, which seems fitting, as my blog is The Banana Diaries. *This particular banana recipe is neither as dense and chewy as banana bread nor as light and fluffy as a typical banana cake. It's more like the Goldilocks of the two—a perfect blending of bread and cake into one satisfying treat, featuring all of the delicious and warming flavors that we associate with any banana dessert. I highly recommend serving this cake with a drizzle of melted chocolate, because you can, and why not?*

1 teaspoon olive oil, for greasing

2½ cups gluten-free rolled oats, ground into a rustic flour (see Notes, page 117)

¾ cup cassava flour

⅔ cup coconut sugar

1 tablespoon ground cinnamon

1 tablespoon baking powder

1 teaspoon baking soda

1 cup mashed bananas (about 3 large ripe bananas)

1 cup unsweetened dairy-free milk

¾ cup coconut oil, softened

3 Flaxseed Eggs (page 34)

1 teaspoon pure vanilla extract

1 cup vegan dark chocolate chips (55% to 70% cacao), plus ½ cup more for topping if desired

1. Preheat the oven to 350°F. Grease a 10-cup Bundt pan with the olive oil.

2. In a large bowl, whisk together the oat flour, cassava flour, coconut sugar, cinnamon, baking powder, and baking soda.

3. In a medium bowl, use a wooden spoon to mix together the mashed bananas, dairy-free milk, coconut oil, flaxseed eggs, and vanilla extract.

4. Fold the wet mixture into the dry until combined, making sure there are no clumps of the dry mixture left.

5. Fold in 1 cup of chocolate chips until completely incorporated.

6. Pour the batter into the prepared pan and bake for 35 to 37 minutes, until a toothpick comes out clean when inserted in the middle. The cake should be completely set and bounce back at a light touch.

7. Remove the cake from the oven and allow to cool completely in the pan before serving, about 30 minutes.

8. If desired, melt ½ cup of chocolate chips following the instructions on pages 14 and 15 and drizzle the melted chocolate over the cake.

9. Store in an airtight container in the refrigerator for up to 5 days or in the freezer for up to a month.

Notes ————————————————

Rolled oats and oat products are sometimes subject to gluten contamination depending on how they are processed. To be sure the oats you use for this recipe are gluten-free, purchase a product that is certified gluten-free.

To make this cake nut-free, use a nut-free dairy-free milk (coconut and oat milk are good choices). If using oat milk and you require it to be gluten-free, be sure to buy a brand labeled as such.

Sweet Potato Cake

WITH MAPLE CREAM CHEESE FROSTING

OPTION

YIELD: One 2-layer, 8-inch cake   **PREP TIME:** 15 minutes
COOK TIME: 40 minutes

Fun fact: I despised sweet potatoes as a kid. Only baked potatoes for me, please! My mom would always have a sweet potato with dinner, and I always gawked at her—how could she choose that over a baked potato?! Needless to say, I'm grateful I outgrew that taste preference. These days, you could even say I'm sweet potato obsessed. When I started my blog, it featured quite the compilation of recipes using sweet potatoes. I made ice cream, toast, bagels, and cake. This sweet potato cake is an ode to some of the first recipes I ever put on the blog. It's completely Paleo and vegan, yet incredibly moist, rich, and full of flavor. This cake in particular reminds me so much of the peak of fall on the East Coast, when all of the leaves have fallen and everything smells so crisp and cozy. (Can you tell autumn is my favorite season?) And just wait until you try this frosting!

SWEET POTATO CAKE:

3 cups cassava flour

½ cup coconut sugar

1 tablespoon ground cinnamon

1 teaspoon baking soda

2 cups Vegan Buttermilk (page 35)

1½ cups mashed cooked sweet potato (about 2 large sweet potatoes)

½ cup maple syrup

3 Flaxseed Eggs (page 34)

1 tablespoon Paleo Baking Powder (page 37) (see Notes)

1 tablespoon pure vanilla extract

MAPLE CREAM CHEESE FROSTING:

1 batch Vegan Cream Cheese Frosting (page 42)

¼ cup maple syrup

Notes

To make this cake nut-free, follow the nut-free options for the Vegan Buttermilk and Vegan Cream Cheese Frosting.

If you do not need the cake to be 100 percent Paleo, you can use any store-bought baking powder in place of the homemade version. Add it to the dry ingredients in Step 2, along with the baking soda.

To make the cake:

1. Preheat the oven to 375°F. Line two 8-inch nonstick cake pans with parchment paper. (If you don't have nonstick pans, grease the pans with cooking spray or coconut oil, then use about 1 tablespoon of extra flour per pan to lightly flour them.)

2. In a large bowl, whisk together the cassava flour, coconut sugar, cinnamon, and baking soda.

3. In a medium bowl, use a wooden spoon to mix together the vegan buttermilk, sweet potato, maple syrup, flaxseed eggs, baking powder, and vanilla extract.

4. Fold the wet mixture into the dry until combined, making sure there are no clumps of the dry mixture left.

5. Evenly divide the batter between the prepared pans, then bake for 40 minutes, or until a toothpick comes out clean when inserted in the middle. The cakes should be completely set and bounce back at a light touch.

6. Remove the cakes from the oven and carefully invert them onto a cooling rack, then turn them right side up. Let the cakes cool completely; this should take about 30 minutes.

To make the frosting:

7. Use a hand mixer to beat together the cream cheese frosting and maple syrup.

8. When ready to frost, place one cake on a cake plate or stand. Evenly spread about ¾ cup of the buttercream frosting on top. Repeat with the remaining layer. Use the remaining frosting to generously frost the edges and sides of the cake (you may have some frosting left over).

9. Slice and serve. Store the cake in an airtight container in the refrigerator for up to 5 days or in the freezer for up to a month; store any leftover frosting in an airtight container in the refrigerator for up to a week. To prepare this cake a day ahead, complete Steps 1 through 6. Then place the cooled cakes on separate plates, cover them with plastic wrap, and store at room temperature until you're ready to frost the next day.

Blueberry Coffee Cake

OPTION

YIELD: One 8-inch cake   **PREP TIME:** 15 minutes   **COOK TIME:** 37 minutes

The first time my mom offered me coffee cake, I was at the ripe age of six, and I was baffled that she'd offer me something containing coffee. I said, "But Mommy, coffee isn't good for kids my age! I won't grow!" She laughed and told me coffee cake doesn't actually contain coffee; it's usually eaten with coffee. While I probably should still avoid caffeine, I do love a good cup of strong black coffee paired with this cake. It has just the right amount of sweetness, and the fresh blueberries take it up another level. What's great about this cake is that it's easily made not only nut-free (just use a nut-free milk in the vegan buttermilk) but also gluten-free and gum-free. The combination of oat flour and cassava flour gives it the taste and texture of any gluten-filled coffee cake, without the need for xanthan gum.

BLUEBERRY CAKE:

2½ cups rolled oats, ground into a rustic flour (see Notes, page 117)

½ cup cassava flour

¾ cup coconut sugar

2 teaspoons baking powder

1 teaspoon baking soda

¾ cup Vegan Buttermilk (page 35), room temperature

½ cup coconut oil, melted

¼ cup unsweetened applesauce, room temperature

2 Flaxseed Eggs (page 34)

1 tablespoon pure vanilla extract

½ cup fresh blueberries, plus more for garnish if desired

CINNAMON CRUMBLE:

½ cup cassava flour

3 tablespoons ground cinnamon

¼ cup coconut oil, melted

2 tablespoons maple syrup

Notes

To make this cake nut-free, follow the nut-free option for the Vegan Buttermilk.

Rolled oats and oat products are sometimes subject to gluten contamination, depending on how they are processed. To be sure the oats you use for this recipe are gluten-free, purchase a product that is certified gluten-free.

To make the cake:

1. Preheat the oven to 350°F. Line the bottom and sides of an 8-inch springform pan with parchment paper.

2. In a large bowl, whisk together the oat flour, cassava flour, coconut sugar, baking powder, and baking soda.

3. In a medium bowl, use a wooden spoon to mix together the vegan buttermilk, coconut oil, applesauce, flaxseed eggs, and vanilla extract.

4. Fold the wet mixture into the dry until combined, making sure there are no clumps of the dry mixture left.

5. Fold in the blueberries.

6. Pour the batter into the prepared pan and set aside while you make the cinnamon crumble.

To make the crumble:

7. In a medium bowl, whisk together the cassava flour and cinnamon.

8. Add the coconut oil and maple syrup and stir vigorously to combine.

9. Sprinkle the crumble over the blueberry cake batter and place the pan in the oven.

10. Bake for 35 to 37 minutes, until a toothpick comes out clean when inserted in the middle. The crumble should be golden brown.

11. Remove the cake from the oven and allow to cool completely in the pan before removing, about 30 minutes. When ready to serve, garnish with fresh blueberries, if desired.

12. Store in an airtight container in the refrigerator for up to 5 days or in the freezer for up to a month.

German Chocolate Cake

YIELD: One 3-layer, 6-inch cake, or one 2-layer, 8-inch cake
PREP TIME: 25 minutes   **COOK TIME:** 30 to 39 minutes, depending on size

Did you know that German chocolate cake isn't actually from Germany? Nope! This mid-century American cake gets its name from the brand of chocolate used in its making. We have Mrs. George Clay to thank for the cake recipe and Samuel German to thank for the chocolate, which dates back to the mid-nineteenth century. German developed a baking chocolate to go into cakes, yielding a more moist and decadent taste and texture. See, history lessons can be fun…at least when they're about chocolate! Naturally, I altered the recipe a bit (I don't think Mr. German or Mrs. Clay ever could have imagined it would be crafted into a Paleo and vegan version!), swapping out the traditional custard for my Coconut Caramel Sauce to be mixed with the requisite pecans and coconut. The result is an absolute dream! The layers of chocolate cake with the creamy and sweet nut and coconut filling meld so perfectly. My grandma said that out of every creation in this book, this cake is her favorite!

COCONUT PECAN FILLING:

1 teaspoon coconut oil

1 cup raw pecan halves and/or pieces

1 batch Coconut Caramel Sauce (page 46)

2 cups unsweetened shredded coconut

CHOCOLATE CAKE:

3 cups cassava flour

1 cup raw cacao powder

1 cup coconut sugar

1 tablespoon baking soda

3¼ cups unsweetened coconut milk, room temperature

½ cup maple syrup

4 Flaxseed Eggs (page 34)

1½ tablespoons Paleo Baking Powder (page 37) (see Note)

1 tablespoon pure vanilla extract

1 cup vegan dark chocolate chips (55% to 70% cacao), melted (see pages 14 and 15)

1 batch Paleo Vegan Chocolate Buttercream Frosting (page 40)

Note

If you do not need the cake to be 100 percent Paleo, you can use any store-bought baking powder in place of the homemade version. Add it to the dry ingredients in Step 6, along with the baking soda.

To make the filling:

1. In a medium saucepan, heat the coconut oil over medium-low heat.

2. Toast the pecans in the oil for 4 to 5 minutes, until the nuts are aromatic and slightly browned.

3. Reduce the heat to low and stir in the caramel sauce and shredded coconut.

4. Remove the pan from the heat and set aside to cool for 5 minutes, then transfer the filling to a container. Place the filling in the refrigerator to chill as you prepare the cakes.

To make the cake:

5. Preheat the oven to 350°F. Line three 6-inch or two 8-inch nonstick cake pans with parchment paper. (If you don't have nonstick pans, grease the pans with cooking spray or coconut oil, then use about 1 tablespoon of extra flour per pan to lightly flour them.)

6. In a large bowl, whisk together the flour, cacao powder, coconut sugar, and baking soda.

7. In a medium bowl, use a wooden spoon to mix together the coconut milk, maple syrup, flaxseed eggs, baking powder, and vanilla extract.

8. Add the melted chocolate to the wet mixture and mix thoroughly until well combined.

9. Fold the wet mixture into the dry until combined, making sure there are no clumps of the dry mixture left.

10. Evenly divide the batter among the prepared cake pans. Bake for 30 to 35 minutes for 6-inch cakes or 36 to 39 minutes for 8-inch cakes. When done, a toothpick will come out clean when inserted in the middle and the cakes will be completely set and bounce back at a light touch.

11. Remove the cakes from the oven and let them cool completely by carefully placing them on a cooling rack and flipping them right side up. This should take about 30 minutes.

To assemble the cake:

12. When ready to frost, place one cake on a cake plate or stand. Spread about one-third of the chocolate buttercream frosting on top and evenly sprinkle with ⅓ cup of the coconut pecan filling. Place the second cake on top and repeat. Then place the last cake on top and repeat with the remaining buttercream and coconut pecan filling. (If making a two-layer 8-inch cake, use half of the frosting and ½ cup of the coconut pecan filling for the first layer and the remaining frosting and filling for the top layer.)

13. Slice and serve. Store in an airtight container in the refrigerator for up to 5 days or in the freezer for up to a month. To prepare this cake a day ahead, prep the cake part first. Then wrap the cakes on separate plates and store at room temperature until you're ready to frost the next day.

Strawberry Shortcake Cake

YIELD: One 2-layer, 6-inch cake **PREP TIME:** 25 minutes
COOK TIME: 35 minutes

Strawberry shortcake is one of those desserts that you might think takes a lot more effort to put together than it actually does. This cake is thoughtful and elegant in appearance, but the recipe is so easy, and it's made with simple plant-based and Paleo ingredients that will please both healthy and not-so-healthy dessert lovers. Typically, strawberry shortcake is prepared with split biscuits as an individual-sized dessert, but for large summer parties, it's so much fun to serve as a whole cake!

2 cups cassava flour

¾ cup coconut sugar

1 tablespoon baking soda

1¼ cups unsweetened coconut milk

¼ cup maple syrup

2 Flaxseed Eggs (page 34)

1½ tablespoons Paleo Baking Powder (page 37) (see Note)

1 tablespoon pure vanilla extract

2½ cups coconut whipped cream, store-bought or homemade (page 49)

2 cups sliced fresh strawberries

1. Preheat the oven to 350°F. Line two 6-inch nonstick cake pans with parchment paper. (If you don't have nonstick pans, grease the pans with cooking spray or coconut oil, then use about 1 tablespoon of extra flour per pan to lightly flour them.)

2. In a large bowl, whisk together the flour, coconut sugar, and baking soda.

3. In a medium bowl, use a wooden spoon to mix together the coconut milk, maple syrup, flaxseed eggs, baking powder, and vanilla extract.

4. Fold the wet mixture into the dry until combined, making sure there are no clumps of the dry mixture left.

5. Divide the batter evenly between the prepared cake pans and bake for 30 to 35 minutes, until a toothpick comes out clean when inserted in the middle. The cakes should be completely set and bounce back at a light touch.

6. Remove the cakes from the oven and carefully invert them onto a cooling rack, then turn them right side up. Let the cakes cool completely; this should take about 30 minutes.

7. When ready to layer, place one cake on a cake plate or stand. Spread half of the coconut whipped cream on top and layer with 1 cup of sliced strawberries. Place the second cake on top and repeat.

8. Slice and serve. Store in an airtight container in the refrigerator for up to 2 days; the unfrosted cakes can be refrigerated for up to 5 days or frozen for up to a month. To prepare this cake a day ahead, complete Steps 1 through 6, then place the cooled cakes on separate plates, cover with plastic wrap, and store at room temperature until you're ready to layer the next day.

Mini Blueberry Mug Cake

OPTION   OPTION

YIELD: 1 mug cake   **PREP TIME:** 2 minutes   **COOK TIME:** 3 minutes

Sometimes you just don't want to turn on your oven, but you still want cake. I get it. I've been there. (Actually, given that I bake so much, I often have that mentality a lot come the weekend!) Enter the easiest microwave blueberry mug cake. In fact, it's so easy, you mix the ingredients in the same bowl in which you "bake" it. (I also give an oven method if you prefer that over the microwave.) The result is a deliciously light vanilla cake that's bursting with warm berries. This is a single serving, so go ahead and eat the entire thing!

1 teaspoon olive oil or coconut oil, for greasing

3 tablespoons cake flour or sifted gluten-free 1-to-1 baking flour

1½ tablespoons granulated sugar or coconut sugar (see Notes, page 139)

½ teaspoon baking powder

¼ teaspoon baking soda

3 tablespoons unsweetened dairy-free milk

1 Flaxseed Egg (page 34)

1 teaspoon pure vanilla extract

¼ cup fresh blueberries

1. Grease a 5.4-ounce ramekin or microwave-safe mug with the oil. (If using the oven, see below.)

2. In the ramekin, use a fork to gently whisk together the flour, sugar, baking powder, and baking soda. Add the dairy-free milk, flaxseed egg, vanilla extract, and blueberries and mix until there are no clumps of dry mixture.

3. Place the ramekin in the microwave and heat on high power for 45 seconds. Allow the cake to rest for 30 seconds, then do another interval of 60 seconds. The cake should be set on top and bounce back at a light touch. Additionally, you can test doneness by inserting a toothpick in the middle; it should come out with a few crumbs. If it needs more cooking, do another interval of 15 seconds.

4. Carefully remove from the microwave using oven mitts. Allow to cool for 5 minutes before enjoying.

Oven Method

Preheat the oven to 350°F and prepare a large ramekin or oven-safe dish. Follow Step 2, then place the ramekin in the preheated oven to bake for 5 to 7 minutes, until the top of the cake is set and bounces back at a light touch.

Note —————————————————————————

To make this cake nut-free, use a nut-free dairy-free milk (coconut and oat milk are good choices). If using oat milk and you require it to be gluten-free, be sure to buy a brand labeled as such.

Chapter 9

PIES, TARTS & CHEESECAKES

Chocolate Peanut Butter

CHEESECAKE

OPTION

YIELD: One 8-inch cheesecake   **PREP TIME:** 15 minutes, plus 2 to 3 hours to soak dates and cashews and 2¼ hours to chill   **COOK TIME:** 45 minutes

If you knew me as a kid, you'd know how deep my love for chocolate and peanut butter runs. As a classy seven-year-old, I would take a big spoonful of peanut butter, top it with a handful of chocolate chips, and call it dessert. That was the level of "cooking" expertise I was working with back in the day, but I'd like to think my skills have improved, and this cheesecake speaks to that progress. With a deliciously rich oat crust and the creamiest, slightly tangy peanut butter filling, it tastes like a childhood treat for grown-ups. What I love most about this recipe is the crust: it's sweetened just with dates! You'll need to presoak both the dates and the cashews, which, conveniently, you can do at the same time. Sprinkle the cake with some organic raw peanuts and drizzle it with your favorite chocolate for a classy yet dangerously easy-to-make treat!

CHOCOLATE OAT CRUST

2 cups gluten-free rolled oats

1 cup raw cacao powder

1 cup pitted medjool dates, soaked in water for 2 hours and drained

⅓ cup gluten-free oat milk or water

TOPPINGS:

¼ cup raw peanuts

½ cup chopped vegan dark chocolate (80% cacao), melted (see pages 14 and 15)

PEANUT BUTTER FILLING:

16 ounces raw cashews, soaked in water for 2 to 3 hours and drained

1 cup plain unsweetened dairy-free yogurt

⅓ cup creamy unsalted peanut butter

⅓ cup maple syrup

3 tablespoons arrowroot powder

To make the crust:

1. Line an 8-inch springform pan with parchment paper.

2. In a food processor, pulse the oats and cacao powder to almost a fine powder.

3. Add the soaked dates and oat milk or water and blend until it forms a thick and sticky dough, 2 to 3 minutes.

4. Press the dough into the bottom and about three-quarters of the way up the sides of the prepared springform pan. Place the pan in the freezer to chill while you prepare the peanut butter filling.

To make the filling:

5. Preheat the oven to 350°F.

6. In a food processor, blend the cashews until smooth, 3 to 4 minutes.

7. Add the yogurt, peanut butter, maple syrup, and arrowroot powder and blend until smooth. There should be no visible pieces of cashew.

8. Remove the pan from the freezer and pour the filling into the crust.

9. Bake for 45 minutes, or until the cheesecake is set around the edges but not at the center. (The center of the cake will appear slightly glossy, whereas the rest of the cake will look set when the cake is ready to come out of the oven.)

10. Remove the cheesecake from the oven and let it cool on the countertop for 15 minutes, then place the cake in the freezer to chill for 2 hours.

11. When ready to serve, allow the cheesecake to sit at room temperature for 15 minutes, then top with the peanuts and drizzle with the melted chocolate. Remove the sides of the springform pan and carefully place the cake on a plate to serve. Store covered in the refrigerator for up to 5 days or in the freezer for up to a month.

Note _____

To make this cake peanut-free, swap in a nut butter or sunflower seed butter for the peanut butter and omit the peanut topping.

Banoffee Tart

OPTION   OPTION

YIELD: One 9-inch tart   **PREP TIME:** 15 minutes, plus 30 minutes to chill crust
COOK TIME: 15 minutes

Seeing as I blog over at The Banana Diaries, I felt it was fitting to include a few banana recipes in this book. This pie definitely fits the bill. It's one of those desserts that looks elegant but is actually quite straightforward and easy to assemble: all you need to do is layer caramel, sliced bananas, and coconut whipped cream! Now, traditionally, banoffee pie is made with a toffee sauce, but I feel that my Paleo and vegan Coconut Caramel Sauce more than fits the bill (it's really a cross between a caramel and toffee sauce) and definitely makes this pie rich in flavor and sweetness.

1 teaspoon coconut oil, for greasing
1 batch Vegan Oat Crust (page 50)

BANOFFEE FILLING:
1 cup Coconut Caramel Sauce (page 46)
2 large ripe bananas, sliced
2 cups coconut whipped cream, store-bought or homemade (page 49)

1. Grease a 9-inch ceramic tart pan with the coconut oil.

2. Press the dough for the oat crust into the bottom and up the sides of the prepared tart pan; be sure to press the dough firmly into the fluted shapes around the sides of the pan. Place in the refrigerator to chill for 30 minutes.

3. Preheat the oven to 375°F.

4. Remove the crust from the refrigerator and poke the bottom of the crust 5 or 6 times with a fork. Blind bake the crust for 12 to 15 minutes, until cooked and lightly golden but not browned.

5. Remove from the oven and let cool for 15 minutes before filling.

6. Once the crust is cool, spoon the caramel sauce into the prebaked crust. Top with sliced bananas and finish with coconut whipped cream, either piped or spooned on top of the bananas.

7. Store covered in the refrigerator for up to 5 days.

Notes

To make this tart nut-free, follow the nut-free option for the Coconut Caramel Sauce.

To make it Paleo, swap the Paleo Vegan Pie Crust (page 52) for the Vegan Oat Crust. Complete the instructions for a prebaked Paleo crust, using a 9-inch ceramic tart pan, then pick up with this recipe at Step 6.

Salted Caramel Pear Tart

OPTION

YIELD: One 9-inch tart **PREP TIME:** 15 minutes, plus 30 minutes to chill crust
COOK TIME: 50 minutes

If apple isn't your thing but you still want that start-of-fall feeling with a seasonal fruit dessert, then this salted caramel pear tart is most definitely for you. The sweetness from the pears and gooey caramel sauce combined with a touch of salt from the caramel makes this sweet enough to want a second bite, but not so sweet that you get a sugar rush! I personally love the oat crust as well—it makes this tart look and taste more like a rustic autumn dessert than other fruit pies, which stand out in the summer.

1 teaspoon coconut oil, for greasing

1 batch Vegan Oat Crust (page 50)

PEAR FILLING:

1 cup sliced pears (about 2 medium pears)

½ batch Coconut Caramel Sauce (page 46)

1. Grease a 9-inch ceramic tart pan with the coconut oil.

2. Press the dough for the oat crust into the bottom and up the sides of the prepared tart pan; be sure to press the dough firmly into the fluted shapes around the sides of the pan. Place the crust in the refrigerator to chill for 30 minutes.

3. Preheat the oven to 375°F.

4. Remove the crust from the refrigerator and poke the bottom of the crust 5 or 6 times with a fork. Blind bake the crust for 10 minutes, until cooked and just beginning to turn lightly golden.

5. Remove from the oven and let cool for 15 minutes before filling. Reduce the oven temperature to 350°F.

6. When ready to fill the crust, place the pear slices in a large bowl, top with the caramel sauce, saving 1 tablespoon of sauce for drizzling on top, and toss to coat.

7. Arrange the pears in the middle of the par-baked crust and drizzle with the remaining caramel sauce.

8. Bake the tart for 40 minutes, or until the caramel sauce begins to bubble. Remove from the oven and let cool for 45 minutes before serving.

9. Store covered in the refrigerator for up to 5 days or in the freezer for up to a month.

Note

To make this tart Paleo, swap the Paleo Vegan Pie Crust (page 52) for the Vegan Oat Crust. Follow the instructions for a par-baked Paleo crust, using a 9-inch ceramic tart pan. Preheat the oven to 350°F and pick up with this recipe at Step 6.

Cookies 'n' Cream Cheesecake

YIELD: One 8-inch cheesecake   **PREP TIME:** 15 minutes, plus 2 to 3 hours to soak cashews and 2 hours to chill   **COOK TIME:** 45 minutes

Though it is rich and decadent, there's something about this cheesecake that makes it easy for me to go back for bite after bite. I blame it on the chocolate creme-filled cookies. They're so deliciously sweet that you can't help but want another taste. For this recipe, you can use your favorite vegan and gluten-free chocolate creme-filled cookies. I also have a recipe on The Banana Diaries *for a homemade version (see Note below) if you prefer to make this a fully from-scratch recipe.*

CHOCOLATE COOKIE CRUST:

2 cups gluten-free rolled oats

2 cups vegan gluten-free chocolate creme-filled sandwich cookies

⅓ cup maple syrup

⅓ cup gluten-free oat milk or water

COOKIES 'N' CREAM FILLING:

16 ounces raw cashews, soaked in water for 2 to 3 hours and drained

1 cup plain unsweetened dairy-free yogurt

⅓ cup maple syrup

1 tablespoon pure vanilla extract

3 tablespoons arrowroot powder

1 cup vegan gluten-free chocolate creme-filled sandwich cookies, crushed (see Note)

⅔ cup crushed gluten-free vegan chocolate creme-filled cookies, for topping (optional)

Note

Looking for a recipe for homemade chocolate creme-filled sandwich cookies? Visit my blog, The Banana Diaries, *and type "Paleo vegan oreo cookies" in the search field. Though there is not a Paleo option for this cheesecake—the crust requires oats to work—my faux Oreo recipe can be enjoyed by vegans and Paleo folks alike.*

To make the crust:

1. Line an 8-inch springform pan with parchment paper.

2. In a food processor, pulse the oats and sandwich cookies to almost a fine powder.

3. Add the maple syrup and oat milk or water and blend for 2 to 3 minutes, until a thick and sticky dough forms.

4. Press the dough into the bottom and about three-quarters of the way up the sides of the prepared springform pan. Place the pan in the freezer to chill while you prepare the cookies 'n' cream filling.

To make the filling:

5. Preheat the oven to 350°F.

6. In a food processor, blend the cashews until smooth, 3 to 4 minutes.

7. Add the yogurt, maple syrup, vanilla extract, and arrowroot powder and blend until smooth. There should be no visible pieces of cashew.

8. Add the crushed sandwich cookies to the filling in the food processor and use a spoon to mix the cookie sandwich pieces into the filling by hand, until evenly distributed.

9. Remove the springform pan from the freezer and pour the filling into the pan.

10. Bake for 45 minutes, or until the cheesecake is set around the edges but not at the very center. (The center of the cake will appear slightly glossy while the outer edges will be set when the cake is ready to come out of the oven.)

11. Remove the cheesecake from the oven and let it cool on the countertop for 15 minutes, then place it in the freezer to chill for 2 hours.

12. When ready to serve, allow the cheesecake to sit at room temperature for 15 minutes. Remove the sides of the springform pan and carefully place the cheesecake on a plate to serve. Top with crushed chocolate creme-filled cookies, if desired. Store covered in the refrigerator for up to 5 days or in the freezer for up to a month.

Cannoli Tart

OPTION

YIELD: One 9-inch tart   **PREP TIME:** 15 minutes, plus 4½ hours to chill
COOK TIME: 35 minutes

As much as I'd love to take credit for this beautiful, tangy tart, my Italian grandmother gave me the idea about a year ago, and it quickly rose to become the top recipe on The Banana Diaries. *Thanks, Grandma! She was over for a visit one day and saw me struggling to make vegan and gluten-free cannoli . (I'm still working on it!) She looked over at my mess and said, "Why not try a pie? It looks more like a pie filling anyway, and who's made a vegan and gluten-free cannoli pie?" I have to say, she's really on top of her baking game, especially for being seventy-nine years old. I quickly threw together a crust, pressed it into a tart pan, and filled it with my remaining filling experiment, and this recipe was born. It took me a few more tries to perfect the consistency, but I've made this tart as it is today nearly twenty times, and it's perfect every time.*

1 teaspoon coconut oil, for greasing

1 batch Vegan Oat Crust (page 50)

TOPPINGS (OPTIONAL):

½ cup mini dark chocolate chips

¼ cup powdered sugar

CANNOLI FILLING:

8 ounces full-fat plain coconut milk yogurt (see Notes)

4 ounces Miyoko's vegan butter, softened (see Notes)

½ cup maple syrup

½ cup unsweetened coconut cream

¼ cup arrowroot powder

2 teaspoons pure vanilla extract

½ cup vegan dark chocolate chips (55% to 70% cacao)

Notes

To make this tart Paleo, swap the Paleo Vegan Pie Crust (page 52) for the Vegan Oat Crust. Follow the instructions for a par-baked Paleo crust, using a 9-inch ceramic tart pan. Preheat the oven to 375°F and pick up with this recipe at Step 6. You can also use Paleo vegan chocolate chips if needed.

For this recipe, coconut milk yogurt is the best choice. It must be full-fat, and the ingredient list should include just coconut cream, water, and live active cultures. Not using a full-fat coconut yogurt will result in a runny tart. My recommended brands are Anita's, Culina, and CoYo, all of which I've tried with great success.

For the vegan butter, I strongly recommend using Miyoko's. I purchase it at Trader Joe's and Whole Foods. If it is not available in your area, you can use coconut oil–based vegan butter, but the results may vary, and the tart may require additional setting time.

1. Grease a 9-inch ceramic tart pan with the coconut oil.

2. Press the dough for the oat crust into the bottom and up the sides of the prepared tart pan; be sure to press the dough firmly into the fluted shapes around the sides of the pan. Place the crust in the refrigerator to chill for 30 minutes.

3. Preheat the oven to 375°F.

4. Remove the crust from the refrigerator and poke the bottom of the crust 5 or 6 times with a fork. Blind bake the crust for 10 minutes, until cooked and just beginning to turn golden.

5. Remove from the oven and let cool for 15 minutes before filling. Keep the oven at 375°F.

To make the filling:

6. In a large bowl, use a hand mixer to beat the coconut yogurt, vegan butter, maple syrup, coconut cream, arrowroot powder, and vanilla extract until well combined.

7. Fold in the chocolate chips.

8. Pour the cannoli filling into the par-baked crust. Cover the edges with either a pie-crust saver or aluminum foil, but leave the filling uncovered. Bake for 15 to 20 minutes, until the filling begins to set along the outside but is a little wobbly at the center.

9. Carefully remove the tart from the oven and let it cool for 15 minutes. Then place the tart in the refrigerator for about 4 hours, or overnight.

10. Remove the tart from the refrigerator and top with chocolate chips and powdered sugar, if desired. Serve.

11. Store covered in the refrigerator for up to 5 days or in the freezer for up to a month.

Neapolitan Cheesecake

YIELD: One 8-inch cheesecake   PREP TIME: 15 minutes, plus 2 to 3 hours to soak dates and cashews and 2 hours to freeze   COOK TIME: 45 minutes

Of all the recipes in this chapter, this one is probably my favorite in terms of presentation. I love the beautiful layers of chocolate, vanilla, and strawberry. It's quite the crowd-pleaser and perfect for dinner parties and celebrations! Plus, the combination of the creamy cashews with the traditional Neapolitan flavors makes it taste like you're eating ice cream in cheesecake form.

OAT CRUST:

3 cups gluten-free rolled oats

1 cup pitted medjool dates, soaked in water for 2 hours and drained

⅓ cup gluten-free oat milk or water

½ teaspoon finely ground sea salt

Coconut whipped cream, store-bought or homemade (page 49), for topping

NEAPOLITAN FILLING:

16 ounces raw cashews, soaked in water for 2 to 3 hours and drained

1 cup plain unsweetened dairy-free yogurt

⅓ cup maple syrup

1 tablespoon pure vanilla extract

3 tablespoons arrowroot powder

⅓ cup raw cacao powder, for the chocolate layer

1 cup fresh strawberries, sliced, for the strawberry layer

To make the crust:

1. Line an 8-inch springform pan with parchment paper.

2. In a food processor, pulse the oats to almost a fine powder.

3. Add the dates, oat milk or water, and salt and blend until it forms a thick and sticky dough, 2 to 3 minutes.

4. Press the dough into the bottom and about three-quarters of the way up the sides of the prepared springform pan. Place the pan in the freezer to chill while you prepare the filling.

To make the filling layers:

5. Preheat the oven to 350°F.

6. In a food processor, blend the cashews until smooth, 3 to 4 minutes.

7. Add the yogurt, maple syrup, vanilla extract, and arrowroot powder and blend until smooth. There should be no visible pieces of cashew.

8. Divide the filling among 3 small bowls. One of these bowls will be the vanilla flavor, while the other two will be used to create the chocolate layer and the strawberry layer.

9. Prepare the chocolate filling layer: Pour the filling in one of the bowls back into the food processor, then add the cacao powder. Blend until smooth.

10. Remove the pan from the freezer and pour in the chocolate filling. Smooth out the filling so that it is flat and evenly covers the crust. Pour the vanilla filling from one of the remaining bowls on top of the chocolate and carefully smooth the vanilla layer so as not to mix the chocolate and vanilla together.

11. Prepare the strawberry filling layer: Rinse out the food processor, then pour in the filling from the third bowl. Add the strawberries and blend until smooth.

12. Pour the strawberry layer on top of the vanilla layer and carefully smooth the strawberry layer so as not to mix the vanilla in with the strawberry.

13. Bake for 45 minutes, or until the cheesecake is set around the edges but not at the very center. (When the cake is ready to come out of the oven, the center will appear slightly glossy, but the edges will be entirely set.)

14. Remove the cheesecake from the oven and let cool on the countertop for 15 minutes, then place in the freezer to chill for 2 hours.

15. When ready to serve, allow the cheesecake to sit at room temperature for 15 minutes. Remove the sides of the springform pan and carefully place the cake on a plate. Top with coconut whipped cream and serve. Store covered in the refrigerator for up to 5 days or in the freezer for up to a month.

Raspberry Tart

OPTION

YIELD: One 9-inch tart   **PREP TIME:** 15 minutes, plus 2½ hours to chill
COOK TIME: 25 minutes

A fresh berry tart is one of my favorite treats for summertime. The flavor combination of coconut and raspberries is so refreshing and light, you could easily say this tart serves only five because you'll want another slice! Now, if you have another berry that's your favorite, not a problem. You can make the Berry Jam with blueberries or strawberries and replace the ½ cup of fresh raspberries to match. Make sure you top this tart with some fresh berries, though, because there's nothing like fresh fruit on a hot summer day!

1 teaspoon coconut oil, for greasing
1 batch Vegan Oat Crust (page 50)

RASPBERRY FILLING:

1 (13.5-ounce) can unsweetened coconut cream

¼ cup maple syrup

1 tablespoon pure vanilla extract

¼ cup arrowroot powder

½ cup Berry Jam (page 48), made with raspberries

½ cup fresh raspberries, for garnish

1. Preheat the oven to 375°F and use the coconut oil to grease a 9-inch tart pan with a removable bottom.

2. Press the dough for the oat crust into the bottom and up the sides of the prepared tart pan; be sure to press the dough firmly into the fluted shapes around the sides of the pan. Place the crust in the refrigerator to chill for 30 minutes while the oven continues to preheat.

3. Remove the crust from the refrigerator and poke the bottom of the crust 5 or 6 times with a fork. Blind bake the crust for 12 to 15 minutes, until cooked and lightly golden but not browned.

4. Remove from the oven and let cool for 15 minutes.

To make the filling:

5. In a large saucepan, bring the coconut cream to a boil.

6. Once boiling, reduce the heat to medium-low and add the maple syrup and vanilla extract, whisking to combine.

7. Sift in the arrowroot powder and stir until it dissolves. Reduce the heat to maintain a simmer and continue to stir until the coconut cream begins to thicken, about 7 minutes.

8. Once thickened, pour the coconut milk mixture into the prebaked crust. Top with the raspberry jam, then lightly stir the jam into the coconut milk mixture to create a swirl. Be careful not to overmix the jam and coconut mixture.

9. Place the tart in the refrigerator to set for at least 2 hours. When ready to serve, remove from the refrigerator and top with the fresh raspberries. Carefully remove the sides of the tart pan by holding the bottom of the pan and allowing the side to fall over your arm. Carefully place the tart on a plate to serve.

10. Store covered in the refrigerator for up to 5 days.

Note ───────────────────────────────

To make this tart Paleo, swap the Paleo Vegan Pie Crust (page 52) for the Vegan Oat Crust. Follow the instructions for a prebaked Paleo crust, using a 9-inch tart pan with a removable bottom, then pick up with this recipe at Step 5.

Chocolate Caramel Pretzel Tart

OPTION

YIELD: One 9-inch tart   **PREP TIME:** 25 minutes, plus 1 hour 20 minutes to chill
COOK TIME: 15 minutes

There's nothing like a salty-sweet combo. This rich tart is definitely sweet but also slightly salty to balance it out. It is surprisingly easy to make, yet it looks like it took a lot of effort (which means you get the praise, but there's no need to break a sweat in the kitchen!). It has a delicious gluten-free pretzel crust that is filled with layers of chocolate ganache and caramel, then finished with coconut whipped cream and pretzels for garnish. That way, you get just the right amount of pretzel, chocolate, caramel, and whipped cream in every decadent bite!

PRETZEL CRUST:

3 cups gluten-free pretzels

½ cup coconut oil, softened, plus 1 teaspoon for greasing

¼ cup maple syrup

1 teaspoon arrowroot powder

1 teaspoon baking soda

1 teaspoon pure vanilla extract

4 to 6 tablespoons chilled water

CHOCOLATE GANACHE CARAMEL FILLING:

1 cup vegan butter

8 ounces vegan dark chocolate (80% cacao), chopped (about 1 cup)

1 cup Coconut Caramel Sauce (page 46)

FOR GARNISH:

Coconut whipped cream, store-bought or homemade (page 49)

Gluten-free pretzels

To make the crust:

1. In a food processor, pulse the pretzels to almost a fine powder.

2. Add the coconut oil, maple syrup, arrowroot powder, baking soda, and vanilla extract and blend until you have a thick and sticky dough.

3. Add the chilled water to the dough, starting with 4 tablespoons, and blend again, adding the remaining 2 tablespoons a little bit at a time if the dough is not yet a consistent sticky dough.

4. Preheat the oven to 375°F. Grease a 9-inch ceramic tart pan with 1 teaspoon of coconut oil.

5. Press the dough into the bottom and up the sides of the prepared tart pan; be sure to press the dough firmly into the fluted shapes around the sides of the pan. Place the crust in the refrigerator to chill for 30 minutes while the oven continues to preheat.

6. Remove the crust from the refrigerator and poke the bottom 5 or 6 times with a fork. Blind bake the crust for 12 to 15 minutes, until just beginning to turn golden.

7. Remove from the oven and let cool for 15 minutes.

To make the filling:

8. In a microwave-safe bowl, heat the vegan butter until melted, 1 to 2 minutes, depending on the microwave.

9. Add the chocolate to the bowl and stir until the chocolate has completely melted.

10. Pour the melted chocolate mixture into the prebaked crust and place in the refrigerator to set for 15 to 20 minutes.

11. Once the ganache is set, remove the tart from the refrigerator and pour the caramel sauce on top. Place the tart in the freezer to chill for 30 minutes.

12. When ready to serve, remove the tart from the freezer and top with coconut whipped cream and pretzels. (For a pretty presentation, use a combination of whole and crushed pretzels for the garnish.) To remove the tart from the pan, don't top it just yet. To loosen the crust, gently run a butter knife around the edge of the pan. Gently wedge a pie knife under the crust and carefully lift up to remove the tart from the pan. Carefully place the frozen tart on a serving plate and top. Let the tart come to room temperature for 15 to 20 minutes before slicing and serving.

13. Store covered in the refrigerator for up to 5 days.

Note

To make this tart nut-free, use Earth Balance's vegan buttery sticks and follow the nut-free option for the Coconut Caramel Sauce.

Brownie Cheesecake

YIELD: One 8-inch cheesecake   PREP TIME: 15 minutes, plus 2 to 3 hours to soak dates and cashews and 2 hours to chill   COOK TIME: 45 minutes

Jared isn't the biggest fan of cheesecake, but he is a fan of brownies, so this is the only cheesecake he enjoys—so much so that the fact that he's eating cheesecake doesn't even faze him. Whether or not you love cheesecake, if you love brownies, I'm absolutely certain you'll love this cheesecake. Unlike a regular chocolate cheesecake, it has melted chocolate blended into the filling as well, giving it that ultra-rich and fudgy, chocolatey taste and texture that those famous chocolate squares, aka brownies, are known for. I highly recommend serving this cheesecake with a scoop of coconut or cashew milk ice cream if having all the chocolate all at once is too much decadence. This is a rich and decadent treat!

CHOCOLATE OAT CRUST:

2 cups gluten-free rolled oats

1 cup raw cacao powder

1 cup pitted medjool dates, soaked in water for 2 hours and drained

⅓ cup gluten-free oat milk or water

BROWNIE FILLING:

16 ounces raw cashews, soaked in water for 2 to 3 hours and drained

1 cup plain unsweetened dairy-free yogurt

⅓ cup maple syrup

⅓ cup arrowroot powder

5 ounces unsweetened baking chocolate (100% cacao), chopped (about ½ cup)

½ cup raw cacao powder

To make the crust:

1. Line an 8-inch springform pan with parchment paper.

2. In a food processor, pulse the oats and cacao powder to almost a fine powder.

3. Add the soaked dates and oat milk or water and blend until you have a thick and sticky dough, 2 to 3 minutes.

4. Press the dough into the bottom and about three-quarters of the way up the sides of the prepared springform pan. Place the pan in the freezer to chill while you prepare the chocolate brownie filling.

To make the filling:

5. Preheat the oven to 350°F.

6. In a food processor, blend the cashews until smooth, 3 to 4 minutes. Add the yogurt, maple syrup, and arrowroot powder and blend until smooth. There should be no visible pieces of cashew.

7. Melt the chocolate in the microwave or on the stovetop, following the instructions on pages 14 and 15.

8. Pour the melted chocolate and cacao powder into the food processor. Blend until fully incorporated or, for a swirled effect as shown in the photo, pulse 2 or 3 times, just until the chocolate begins to be mixed into the cashew base.

9. Remove the springform pan from the freezer and pour the filling into the pan.

10. Bake for 45 minutes, or until the cheesecake is set around the edges but not at the very center. (The center of the cake will appear slightly glossy, while the edges will be set when the cake is ready to come out of the oven.)

11. Remove the cheesecake from the oven and let it cool on the countertop for 15 minutes, then place it in the freezer to chill for 2 hours.

12. When ready to serve, allow the cheesecake to sit at room temperature for 15 minutes. Remove the sides of the springform pan and carefully place the cake on a plate to serve. Store covered in the refrigerator for up to 5 days or in the freezer for up to a month.

Cake Batter Cookie Pie

YIELD: One 9-inch pie **PREP TIME:** 15 minutes **COOK TIME:** 32 minutes

While this is not really a "pie" per se, it was a common dessert at birthdays we celebrated as kids. In fact, my best friend growing up had a "cookie pie" as her birthday cake each year. I decided to make a cake batter version so that it's like you're having a slice of birthday cake…only in cookie pie form! The texture of this pie is more cookielike than cakelike, but the flavor is nearly identical. It's an easy dessert if making a tiered cake is just not your thing.

1½ cups cassava flour

¾ cup coconut sugar

1 teaspoon baking powder

½ teaspoon baking soda

¾ cup creamy unsalted almond butter

½ cup unsweetened applesauce

2 tablespoons coconut oil, softened

1 tablespoon pure vanilla extract

3 tablespoons vegan sprinkles

Dairy-free vegan ice cream, for serving (optional)

1. Preheat the oven to 350°F. Grease a 9-inch pie pan or cast-iron skillet with cooking spray or coconut oil.

2. In a large bowl, whisk together the flour, sugar, baking powder, and baking soda.

3. In a medium bowl, beat the almond butter, applesauce, coconut oil, and vanilla extract.

4. Fold the wet mixture into the dry until combined, making sure there are no clumps of the dry mixture left.

5. Fold in the sprinkles.

6. Pour the batter into the prepared pan and bake for 30 to 32 minutes, until a toothpick comes out clean when inserted in the middle. The pie will be completely set and bounce back at a light touch.

7. Remove the pie from the oven and let cool in the pan for 15 minutes. If you'd like to remove it from the dish before serving, carefully turn the cookie pie out onto a large plate, then invert it onto a serving plate.

8. Slice and serve with dairy-free vegan ice cream, if desired. Store in an airtight container in the refrigerator for up to 5 days or the freezer for up to a month.

Notes

To make this pie nut-free, use coconut butter or sunflower seed butter in place of the almond butter.

To make it Paleo, use the Paleo baking powder on page 37, but add it to the wet ingredients in Step 3.

Strawberry Pie

YIELD: One 9-inch pie   PREP TIME: 35 minutes   COOK TIME: 50 minutes

One of my favorite fruits is strawberries. A close second to bananas, I might add. Even better if the two are paired together! But for this pie, we'll celebrate strawberries because they definitely deserve the spotlight. This pie tastes like early summer in a bite. With fresh berries and a bit of vanilla, it's refreshing and mouthwatering, and hard to not go back for a second slice! I like to add a scoop of vanilla coconut ice cream or coconut whipped cream to mine. Absolutely heavenly!

FILLING:

3 cups fresh strawberries (about 1 pint), sliced

½ cup coconut sugar

⅓ cup arrowroot powder

¼ cup coconut oil, melted

1 tablespoon pure vanilla extract

Double recipe Paleo Vegan Pie Crust (page 52)

¼ cup maple syrup

2 tablespoons unsweetened dairy-free milk

1. In a large bowl, toss the strawberries with the coconut sugar, arrowroot powder, coconut oil, and vanilla extract until they are completely coated. Set aside.

2. Prepare the pie crust dough according to the directions on page 52, doubling the recipe and, after completing Step 2, dividing the dough into 2 equal portions.

3. Following Step 4 on page 52, roll out one of the dough discs and place it in a 9-inch pie pan, but do not trim any excess dough overhanging the sides of the pan (you'll use that excess dough later to seal the top crust to the bottom crust).

4. Spoon the strawberry filling into the crust, then place the filled crust in the refrigerator.

5. Roll out the second dough disc, again following Step 4 on page 52. Use small cookie cutters to create shapes in the top crust, or simply slit a few air pockets to give the pie ventilation.

6. Remove the pie pan from the refrigerator. Carefully drape the second crust over the strawberry filling, then use your fingers to seal the edges. You can crimp the edges with your fingers or a fork.

7. Preheat the oven to 400°F. Place the pie back in the refrigerator to chill while the oven preheats.

8. Once the oven is preheated, remove the pie from the refrigerator. In a small bowl, whisk together the maple syrup and dairy-free milk. Use a butter brush to lightly brush the top and edges of the pie with the maple glaze.

9. Place the pie on a rimmed baking sheet (in case of drips), then bake for 15 minutes.

10. After 15 minutes, reduce the oven temperature to 375°F and continue baking the pie for 30 to 35 minutes, until the crust is lightly golden. Remove from the oven and let set for 45 minutes before serving. Store covered in the refrigerator for up to 5 days or in the freezer for up to a month.

Note ———————————————————————————————

You can use any dairy-free milk here. If you prefer nut-free, I recommend coconut or oat milk. (If using oat milk and you require it to be gluten-free, be sure to buy a brand labeled as such.) If you prefer Paleo, I recommend coconut, almond, or macadamia nut milk.

Blueberry Crumble Pie

YIELD: One 9-inch pie   **PREP TIME:** 35 minutes   **COOK TIME:** 1 hour

I love my strawberry pie (page 256) and this blueberry pie equally, but if I'm not in the mood for a double crust, this is my go-to recipe. Crumble pies are wonderful because they're so easy; they can be messy and imperfect, and everyone loves them. I mean, who couldn't love warmed berries with a crunchy topping served à la mode?

1 Paleo Vegan Pie Crust (page 52)

FILLING:

3 cups fresh blueberries (about 1 pint)

½ cup coconut sugar

⅓ cup arrowroot powder

¼ cup coconut oil, melted

1 tablespoon pure vanilla extract

CRUMBLE TOPPING:

½ cup coconut oil, softened

1 cup cassava flour

⅓ cup maple syrup

1. Complete the recipe for the pie crust on page 52, using a 9-inch pie pan and following the instructions for blind baking it until par-baked. Set the par-baked crust aside to cool while you make the filling.

2. In a large bowl, toss the blueberries with the coconut sugar, arrowroot powder, coconut oil, and vanilla extract until the blueberries are completely coated. Set aside.

3. Spoon the blueberry filling into the cooled crust, then place the filled crust in the refrigerator while you prepare the crumble topping.

4. In a medium bowl, cut the coconut oil into the cassava flour until the mixture resembles crumbly sand. Add the maple syrup and mix to fully combine. The texture should be clumpy rather than completely crumbly. You should be able to grip the dough and form medium to large clumps.

5. Remove the pie pan from the refrigerator. Sprinkle the crumble topping over the blueberry filling.

6. Preheat the oven to 400°F. Place the pie back in the refrigerator to chill while the oven preheats.

7. Once the oven is preheated, remove the pie from the refrigerator. Place the pie on a rimmed baking sheet (in case of drips) and bake for 15 minutes.

8. After 15 minutes, reduce the oven temperature to 375°F and continue baking the pie for 30 to 35 minutes, until the crust and crumble topping are lightly golden. Remove from the oven and let set for 45 minutes before serving. Store covered in the refrigerator for up to 5 days or in the freezer for up to a month.

Banana Bread Cheesecake

YIELD: One 8-inch cheesecake   **PREP TIME:** 15 minutes, plus 2 to 3 hours to soak dates and cashews and 2 hours to chill   **COOK TIME:** 45 minutes

One of the top recipes on The Banana Diaries *had to be banana bread, so I decided why not make a banana bread cheesecake as an ode to that recipe? This cake tastes like a bite of banana bread that's been topped with a deliciously sweet cashew cream. I personally love my banana bread with chocolate chips, so I've added them to the filling here. You can omit them if you're not a chocolate fan, but if you are, I say go for it!*

CINNAMON OAT CRUST:

3 cups gluten-free rolled oats

1 cup pitted medjool dates, soaked in water for 2 hours and drained

⅓ cup gluten-free oat milk or water

2 teaspoons ground cinnamon

FOR THE TOP:

1 cup sliced bananas

Coconut whipped cream, store-bought or homemade (page 49) (optional)

BANANA BREAD FILLING:

16 ounces raw cashews, soaked in water for 2 to 3 hours and drained

1 cup plain unsweetened dairy-free yogurt

1 cup mashed bananas (about 3 large ripe bananas)

⅓ cup maple syrup (optional)

3 tablespoons arrowroot powder

1 tablespoon pure vanilla extract

2 teaspoons ground cinnamon

⅔ cup vegan dark chocolate chips (55% to 70% cacao)

To make the crust:

1. Line an 8-inch springform pan with parchment paper.

2. In a food processor, pulse the oats to almost a fine powder.

3. Add the soaked dates, oat milk, and cinnamon and blend until you have a thick and sticky dough, 2 to 3 minutes.

4. Press the dough into the bottom and about three-quarters of the way up the sides of the prepared springform pan. Place the pan in the freezer to chill the crust while you prepare the banana bread filling.

To make the filling:

5. Preheat the oven to 350°F.

6. In a food processor, blend the soaked cashews until smooth, 3 to 4 minutes.

7. Add the yogurt, mashed bananas, maple syrup (if using), arrowroot powder, vanilla extract, and cinnamon and blend until smooth. There should be no visible pieces of cashew.

8. Stir in the chocolate chips.

9. Remove the crust from the freezer and pour the filling into the pan.

10. Bake for 45 minutes, or until the cheesecake is set around the edges but not at the very center. (The center of the cake will appear slightly glossy, while the edges will be set when the cake is ready to come out of the oven.)

11. Remove the cheesecake from the oven and let it cool on the countertop for 15 minutes, then place it in the freezer to chill for 2 hours.

12. When ready to serve, allow the cake to sit at room temperature for 15 minutes, then top with the banana slices and coconut whipped cream, if desired. Remove the sides of the springform pan and carefully place the cake on a plate to serve. Store covered in the refrigerator for up to 5 days or in the freezer for up to a month.

Chocolate Hazelnut Tart

YIELD: One 9-inch tart   **PREP TIME:** 15 minutes, plus 2 hours to chill
COOK TIME: 25 minutes

When I studied abroad in Italy, I quickly learned that Italians love the combination of chocolate and hazelnuts just like Americans love chocolate and peanut butter. It is the *combo, and for good reason. Hazelnuts have a unique nutty taste that is downright addicting when paired with chocolate. This tart tastes like eating a spoonful of Nocciolata with a delicious hazelnut cookie crust—a heavenly combo that you'll definitely need to make for parties, celebrations, or whenever the craving hits!*

HAZELNUT CRUST:

10 ounces raw hazelnuts

⅔ cup coconut oil, softened

½ cup cassava flour

¼ cup maple syrup

1 teaspoon baking soda

4 to 6 tablespoons chilled water

CHOCOLATE HAZELNUT FILLING:

1 (13.5-ounce) can unsweetened coconut cream

½ cup raw cacao powder

½ cup vegan dark chocolate chips (55% to 70% cacao)

¼ cup maple syrup

¼ cup creamy unsalted hazelnut butter (see Note)

1 tablespoon pure vanilla extract

¼ cup arrowroot powder

½ cup chopped raw hazelnuts, for garnish

Note

To make your own hazelnut butter for this recipe, preheat the oven to 375°F. Line a rimmed baking sheet with parchment paper. Place 1½ cups whole hazelnuts on the baking sheet and bake for 5 to 7 minutes, until aromatic. Remove from the oven and allow to cool for 5 minutes, then roll the hazelnuts on a clean kitchen towel to remove the skins. Place the nuts in a food processor and process for 2 to 3 minutes, until you have a smooth and creamy butter. Note that this is the minimum quantity of nuts required for the food processor to blend the nuts properly; you will have about ½ cup hazelnut butter left over.

To make the crust:

1. In a food processor, pulse the hazelnuts to almost a fine powder.

2. Add the coconut oil, cassava flour, maple syrup, and baking soda, and blend until the dough becomes thick and sticky, yet still clumpy.

3. Add the chilled water to the dough, starting with 4 tablespoons, and blend again, adding the remaining 2 tablespoons a little bit at a time if the dry ingredients are not fully forming into a consistent dough.

4. Preheat the oven to 375°F and use coconut oil to grease a 9-inch tart pan with a removable bottom.

5. Press the dough into the bottom and up the sides of the prepared tart pan; be sure to press the dough firmly into the fluted shapes around the sides of the pan. Place the crust in the refrigerator to chill for 30 minutes while the oven continues to preheat.

6. Remove the crust from the refrigerator and poke the bottom of the crust 5 or 6 times with a fork. Blind bake the crust for 12 to 15 minutes, until just beginning to turn golden.

7. Remove from the oven and let cool for 15 minutes.

To make the filling:

8. In a large saucepan, bring the coconut cream to a boil.

9. Once boiling, reduce the heat to medium-low and add the cacao powder, chocolate chips, maple syrup, hazelnut butter, and vanilla extract, whisking to combine.

10. Sift in the arrowroot powder, then stir until the arrowroot dissolves. Reduce the heat to a simmer and continue to stir until the coconut cream begins to thicken, about 7 minutes.

11. Once thickened, pour the coconut milk mixture into the prebaked tart crust.

12. Place the tart in the refrigerator to set for at least 2 hours. When ready to serve, remove from the refrigerator. Carefully remove the sides of the tart pan by holding the bottom of the pan and allowing the side to fall over your arm. Carefully place the tart on a plate to serve, then garnish with the chopped hazelnuts. Store leftovers covered in the refrigerator for up to 5 days.

Coconut Cream Pie

OPTION

YIELD: One 9-inch pie   PREP TIME: 15 minutes, plus 2 hours to chill
COOK TIME: 25 minutes

If you're in desperate need of a tropical vacation, this pie is the next best option. I swear, if you take just one bite and close your eyes, it's almost as if you were on a beach in Hawaii (unless you are making this pie while you're in Hawaii, and then you don't even need to imagine it!). I remember the first time I made something with real coconut and had my dad, who is a self-proclaimed connoisseur of coconut confections, try it. He was blown away. That's what real coconut tastes like?! Yep. While most people might be accustomed to artificial coconut flavor, this pie features the real deal, and I know you'll be a fan. This particular pie is my dad's favorite!

1 teaspoon coconut oil, for greasing

1 batch Vegan Oat Crust (page 50)

COCONUT CREAM FILLING:

1 (13.5-ounce) can unsweetened coconut cream

½ cup maple syrup

2 teaspoons pure vanilla extract

½ cup unsweetened shredded coconut, plus extra for garnish if desired

¼ cup arrowroot powder

2 cups coconut whipped cream, store-bought or homemade (page 49), for topping

1. Preheat the oven to 375°F. Grease a 9-inch pie pan with the coconut oil.

2. Press the crust dough into the pie pan, working it up the sides of the pan. Place the crust in the refrigerator to chill for 30 minutes while the oven continues to preheat.

3. Remove the crust from the refrigerator and poke the bottom of the crust 5 or 6 times with a fork. Blind bake the crust for 12 to 15 minutes, until cooked and lightly golden but not browned.

4. Remove from the oven and let cool for 15 minutes. Keep the oven at 375°F.

To make the filling:

5. In a large pot, bring the coconut cream to a boil.

6. Once boiling, reduce the heat to medium-low and add the maple syrup and vanilla extract, whisking to combine.

7. Stir in the shredded coconut.

8. Sift in the arrowroot powder, then stir until the arrowroot dissolves. Reduce the heat to a simmer and continue to stir until the coconut mixture begins to thicken, about 7 minutes.

9. Once thickened, pour the coconut cream mixture into the prebaked pie crust.

10. Place the pie in the refrigerator to set for at least 2 hours before serving. Serve topped with coconut whipped cream and garnished with shredded coconut, if desired.

11. Store covered in the refrigerator for up to 5 days.

Note ───────────

To make this pie Paleo, swap the Paleo Vegan Pie Crust (page 52) for the Vegan Oat Crust. Complete the instructions for a prebaked Paleo crust, using a 9-inch pie pan, then pick up with this recipe at Step 5.

Mini Lemon Tarts

YIELD: 6 mini tarts   **PREP TIME:** 20 minutes   **COOK TIME:** 35 minutes

Who doesn't love mini desserts? These tartlets are the cutest little treats to bring some sunshine to your day! Made with a coconut lemon filling and tinted extra yellow thanks to the turmeric powder, they are the perfect light and refreshing summertime treat.

1 Paleo Vegan Pie Crust (page 52)

1 (13.5-ounce) can unsweetened coconut cream

⅓ cup maple syrup

Juice of 1 lemon

1 teaspoon pure vanilla extract

¼ cup arrowroot powder

2 teaspoons turmeric powder

6 lemon slices, for garnish (optional)

1. Grease six 4-inch tart pans with removable bottoms with coconut oil.

2. Prepare the pie crust: Complete Steps 1 through 3 in the recipe on page 52, then roll out the chilled dough as described in Step 4. Instead of transferring the rolled-out crust to a 9-inch pie/tart pan, use one of the mini tart pans as a guide to create 6 circles, making the dough circle about ½ inch wider all the way around the edge of the tart pan. Use a paring knife to gently cut the dough into 6 circles and carefully drape a dough circle over each tart pan. Press the dough into the bottoms and up the sides of the tart pans; be sure to press the dough firmly into the fluted shapes around the sides of the pans. Place the tart pans on a rimmed baking sheet and set in the refrigerator to chill while the oven preheats.

3. Preheat the oven to 350°F.

4. Remove the crusts from the refrigerator and poke a few holes in the bottom of each crust with a fork. Place the crusts in the oven and blind bake for 10 minutes, until par-baked and just beginning to turn lightly golden.

5. Remove from the oven and let cool for 15 minutes before filling. Reduce the oven temperature to 350°F.

6. In a large bowl, whisk together the coconut cream, maple syrup, lemon juice, vanilla extract, arrowroot powder, and turmeric powder.

7. Divide the filling evenly among the par-baked crusts and place back on the baking sheet. Bake the tarts for 25 minutes, or until the edges of the filling are set and the middle is still slightly wobbly.

8. Remove from the oven and let set for 45 minutes before serving. Carefully remove the sides of the tart pan by holding the bottom of the pan and allowing the side to fall over your hand. Carefully place on a plate to serve. Top with sliced lemon slices, if desired. Store covered in the refrigerator for up to 5 days.

Mini Berry Tarts

YIELD: 6 mini tarts   **PREP TIME:** 20 minutes   **COOK TIME:** 35 minutes

For anyone who's wary of trying a vegan dessert, this is a wonderful introductory recipe. Before I got my younger brother hooked on vegan desserts, he was hesitant to try my creations…until I made these mini berry tarts! Of course, I didn't tell him they were vegan. (I need a fully unbiased opinion!) In fact, I think he thought they were from a bakery. One bite, and then I broke the news to him: these tartlets are indeed vegan, dairy-free, and gluten-free, yet you'd never know from the deliciously oat-y crust and creamy vanilla custard. Don't believe me? Give this recipe a try!

OAT CRUST:

2 cups gluten-free rolled oats

⅓ cup coconut oil, softened, plus extra for greasing

¼ cup maple syrup

4 to 6 tablespoons chilled water

FILLING:

1 (13.5-ounce) can unsweetened coconut cream

⅓ cup maple syrup

¼ cup arrowroot powder

2 teaspoons pure vanilla extract

1 cup fresh berries of choice

To make the crust:

1. Grease six 4-inch tart pans with removable bottoms with coconut oil.

2. Pulse the oats in a food processor until most of the oats have been pulverized into a fine flour but with some larger pieces of oats remaining, about 5 seconds. There should not be any whole pieces of oats remaining.

3. Add the coconut oil, maple syrup, and 4 tablespoons of the chilled water. Pulse again until a thick dough forms. If there is still a lot of dry flour left, add another 2 tablespoons of chilled water and pulse again.

4. Gently press the dough into the bottoms and up the sides of the tart pans; be sure to press the dough firmly into the fluted shapes around the sides of the pans. Using a fork, poke a few holes in the bottom of each crust. Place all 6 crusts in the refrigerator to keep cool while you preheat the oven. Preheat the oven to 375°F.

5. Remove the crusts from the refrigerator. Place the crusts in the oven and blind bake for 10 minutes, until par-baked and just beginning to turn lightly golden.

6. Remove from the oven and let cool for 15 minutes before filling. Reduce the oven temperature to 350°F.

To make the filling:

7. In a large bowl, whisk together the coconut cream, maple syrup, arrowroot powder, and vanilla extract.

8. Divide the filling evenly among the par-baked crusts and place back on the baking sheet. Bake the tarts for 25 minutes, or until the edges of the filling are set and the middle is still slightly wobbly.

9. Remove from the oven and let set for 45 minutes before serving. Carefully remove the sides of the tart pan by holding the bottom of the pan and allowing the side to fall over your hand. Carefully place on a plate to serve. Top with fresh berries. Store covered in the refrigerator for up to 5 days.

Pumpkin Pie

YIELD: One 9-inch pie   PREP TIME: 20 minutes, plus 6 hours to set
COOK TIME: 1 hour 20 minutes

I love all pies, but pumpkin pie holds a special place in my heart. Every Thanksgiving, I guarantee you I'm taking at least two slices of this pie, and yes, that is post–Thanksgiving dinner. This pie is undetectably vegan, Paleo, gluten-free, and nut-free. Do you want to know something even cooler? Every Thanksgiving, someone brings a store-bought pumpkin pie, and every Thanksgiving, only the store-bought pumpkin pie is left. So if you're looking for a holiday dessert that pleases all eaters, this is your pie!

1 Paleo Vegan Pie Crust (page 52)

FILLING:

1½ (15-ounce) cans pumpkin puree
½ cup maple syrup

½ cup canned full-fat coconut milk
1 teaspoon pure vanilla extract
¼ cup arrowroot powder
2 tablespoons pumpkin pie spice

1. Complete the recipe for the pie crust on page 52, using a 9-inch pie pan and following the instructions for blind baking it until par-baked. Save some of the scraps for cutout decorations, if desired. Set the par-baked crust aside to cool while you make the filling. Increase the oven temperature to 400°F.

2. In a large bowl, use a hand mixer to beat the pumpkin puree, maple syrup, coconut milk, vanilla extract, arrowroot powder, and pumpkin pie spice until the filling is smooth and there are no clumps of arrowroot.

3. Pour the filling into the par-baked crust. Cover the edges of the crust with either a pie crust saver or aluminum foil.

4. Place the cutouts on a rimmed baking sheet lined with parchment paper and bake for 7 to 8 minutes, until golden brown, then remove from the oven.

5. Place the pie on a rimmed baking sheet, place the pan in the oven, and bake for 40 minutes. Remove the foil and bake for another 15 to 20 minutes, until the crust is lightly golden on the edges and the filling in the very center is slightly jiggly still but the edges of the filling are set.

6. Let the pie cool, then place in the refrigerator to set overnight or for a minimum of 6 hours before serving. Decorate with the baked cutouts prior to serving. Store covered in the refrigerator for up to 5 days.

Chapter 10

SWEET BREADS & MUFFINS

Cinnamon Raisin Bread

OPTION

YIELD: One 9 by 5-inch loaf (16 slices)   **PREP TIME:** 10 minutes
COOK TIME: 45 minutes

This bread is reminiscent of the yeasted cinnamon raisin bread my mom used to buy us as kids, but a bit chewier. Between the warm raisins and the sweet fragrant cinnamon in every bite, it's an absolute dream. Plus, since it's a quick bread, it's quite simple to put together—no kneading or yeast activation required. I highly recommend toasting up a slice and topping it with a pat of vegan butter, or crumbling it over a bowl of dairy-free yogurt as a morning treat. It's wonderful!

Olive oil or coconut oil, for greasing

3 cups gluten-free rolled oats, ground into a rustic flour (see Notes, page 117)

½ cup cassava flour

¾ cup coconut sugar

1 tablespoon ground cinnamon

1 tablespoon baking powder

2 teaspoons baking soda

1¼ cups Vegan Buttermilk (page 35), room temperature

¾ cup unsweetened applesauce, room temperature

1 teaspoon pure vanilla extract

¾ cup raisins

1. Preheat the oven to 350°F. Grease a 9 by 5-inch loaf pan with olive oil or coconut oil, or line the pan with parchment paper, leaving some paper overhanging the sides for easy removal.

2. In a large bowl, whisk together the flours, sugar, cinnamon, baking powder, and baking soda.

3. Add the vegan buttermilk, applesauce, and vanilla extract to the flour mixture and mix until there are no clumps of dry ingredients remaining and you have a thick batter.

4. Fold in the raisins.

5. Pour the batter into the prepared loaf pan. Bake for 40 to 45 minutes, until a toothpick comes out clean when inserted in the middle.

6. Remove from the oven and let cool for 15 minutes before removing the bread from the pan. Slice and serve. Store the slices in an airtight container at room temperature for up to 3 days or in the refrigerator for up to a week.

Note ———————————————

To make this bread nut-free, follow the nut-free option for the Vegan Buttermilk.

Marbled Pumpkin Bread

OPTION

YIELD: One 9 by 5-inch loaf (16 slices) **PREP TIME:** 12 minutes
COOK TIME: 55 minutes

This bread is one of my favorite recipes in this chapter, although I'm partial to all things pumpkin. I think it's because my love of autumn is even stronger than my love of coffee. (If you know me, you know how hard it would be for me to go a day without coffee!) A classic pumpkin spice batter is swirled into a chocolate-flavored twist on the original, resulting in an incredibly moist and rich bread that is somehow light and easy to eat, too. Creating an elegant marbling effect is actually quite easy, but remember that less is more—just a few swirls will do the trick.

1¾ cups cassava flour

¾ cup coconut sugar

1 tablespoon pumpkin pie spice

1 teaspoon baking soda

1 teaspoon ground cinnamon

1 cup pumpkin puree

½ cup olive oil or melted coconut oil (see Notes)

2 Flaxseed Eggs (page 34)

¼ cup plus 1 tablespoon unsweetened dairy-free milk, room temperature, divided

2 tablespoons maple syrup, room temperature

1 tablespoon Paleo Baking Powder (page 37) (see Notes)

1 teaspoon pure vanilla extract

1 cup vegan dark chocolate chips (55% to 70% cacao), plus more for topping

⅓ cup raw cacao powder

1. Preheat the oven to 350°F. Line a 9 by 5-inch loaf pan with parchment paper, leaving some paper overhanging the sides for easy removal.

2. In a large bowl, whisk together the flour, sugar, pumpkin pie spice, baking soda, and cinnamon.

3. Add the pumpkin puree, olive oil, flaxseed eggs, ¼ cup of the dairy-free milk, maple syrup, baking powder, and vanilla extract and mix until the dry and wet ingredients are completely combined.

4. Fold in the chocolate chips.

5. Scoop half of the batter into a separate bowl. Add the cacao powder and the remaining 1 tablespoon of dairy-free milk to one of the bowls. Mix the batter until the cacao powder is completely incorporated.

6. Pour half of the chocolate batter into the prepared loaf pan, then top the chocolate layer with half of the pure pumpkin batter. Repeat once more to create one more layer of each batter, or four layers total.

7. Run a knife through the top of the loaf pan to marble the bread slightly. Do not overmix, as this will ruin the marble effect. Less is more here. Sprinkle with extra chocolate chips, if desired.

8. Bake for 50 to 55 minutes, until a toothpick comes out clean when inserted in the middle.

9. Remove from the oven and let cool for 15 minutes before removing the bread from the pan. Slice and serve. Store in an airtight container, sliced, at room temperature for up to 3 days or in the refrigerator for up to a week.

Notes ———————————————————————————————————

If you do not need the bread to be 100 percent Paleo, you can swap gluten-free 1-to-1 baking flour for the cassava flour and use any store-bought baking powder in place of the homemade version. Add the baking powder to the dry ingredients in Step 2, along with the baking soda. The bread can be made with all-purpose flour if you tolerate gluten.

You can replace the oil with ½ cup of unsweetened applesauce for an oil-free bread.

You can use any dairy-free milk here. If you prefer nut-free, I recommend coconut or oat milk. (If using oat milk and you require it to be gluten-free, be sure to buy a brand labeled as such.) If you prefer Paleo, I recommend coconut, almond, or macadamia nut milk.

Blueberry Banana Bread

OPTION   OPTION

YIELD: One 9 by 5-inch loaf (16 slices)   **PREP TIME:** 10 minutes
COOK TIME: 45 minutes

My favorite berries to eat and to photograph are blueberries. The wonderful blue and purple hues make everything so much brighter, and of course, I love the fresh berry flavor that elevates an otherwise traditional banana bread. With a purple burst in every bite, this banana bread makes a wonderful morning snack with a cup of freshly brewed coffee.

1¾ cups gluten-free 1-to-1 baking flour or all-purpose flour

½ cup coconut sugar

1 tablespoon baking powder

1 teaspoon baking soda

1 teaspoon ground cinnamon

¼ teaspoon finely ground sea salt

1 cup mashed bananas (about 3 large ripe bananas)

2 Flaxseed Eggs (page 34)

½ cup unsweetened dairy-free milk, room temperature

½ cup unsweetened applesauce, room temperature

1 teaspoon pure vanilla extract

1 cup fresh blueberries, plus more for topping

1. Preheat the oven to 350°F. Line a 9 by 5-inch loaf pan with parchment paper, leaving some paper overhanging the sides for easy removal.

2. In a large bowl, whisk together the flour, coconut sugar, baking powder, baking soda, cinnamon, and salt.

3. In a medium bowl, mix together the mashed bananas, flaxseed eggs, dairy-free milk, applesauce, and vanilla extract.

4. Fold the wet mixture into the dry until combined, making sure there are no clumps of the dry mixture left.

5. Add the blueberries and mix until they're evenly distributed throughout the batter.

6. Pour the batter into the prepared loaf pan and top with additional blueberries, if desired. Bake for 40 to 45 minutes, until a toothpick comes out clean when inserted in the middle.

7. Remove from the oven and allow to cool for 10 minutes before removing the bread from the pan. Allow to fully cool before slicing, about 20 minutes. Store in an airtight container at room temperature for up to 3 days or in the refrigerator for up to 5 days.

Note ———————————————

For a nut-free dairy-free milk, I recommend coconut or oat milk. (If using oat milk and you require it to be gluten-free, be sure to buy a brand labeled as such.)

Double Chocolate Chunk
BANANA BREAD

YIELD: One 9 by 5-inch loaf (16 slices)   **PREP TIME:** 10 minutes
COOK TIME: 50 minutes

If anything has even the slightest leg up on the pure deliciousness of banana bread, it's chocolate chip banana bread. Full of melty chocolate and made with simple ingredients, this bread has a big place in my heart. I recommend warming up a slice and smearing it with nut butter or even coconut butter. The chocolate-banana-coconut combination is absolutely delicious! Given that this bread is both nut-free and gluten-free, it makes it a wonderful and safe snack to take to school or work.

1¾ cups mashed bananas (4 to 5 large ripe bananas)

2 Flaxseed Eggs (page 34)

⅔ cup unsweetened applesauce

½ cup maple syrup

1 teaspoon pure vanilla extract

1½ cups gluten-free rolled oats, ground into a rustic flour (see Notes, page 117)

½ cup cassava flour

½ cup raw cacao powder

2 teaspoons baking powder

1 teaspoon baking soda

¼ teaspoon finely ground sea salt

½ cup vegan dark chocolate chips (55% to 70% cacao)

FOR THE TOP (OPTIONAL):

1 ripe banana, sliced in half lengthwise

½ cup vegan dark chocolate chips (55% to 70% cacao)

1. Preheat the oven to 350°F. Line a 9 by 5-inch loaf pan with parchment paper, leaving some paper overhanging the sides for easy removal.

2. In a large bowl, mix together the mashed bananas with the flaxseed eggs, applesauce, maple syrup, and vanilla extract until well combined.

3. Sift the oat flour, cassava flour, cacao powder, baking powder, baking soda, and salt into a medium bowl. Add any larger bits of oats caught in the sifter to the bowl and whisk to combine.

4. Add the dry ingredients to the wet and mix until there are no clumps of flour.

5. Fold in the chocolate chips.

6. Pour the batter into the prepared loaf pan and top with the sliced banana and ½ cup of chocolate chips, if desired. Bake for 45 to 50 minutes, until a toothpick comes out clean when inserted in the middle.

7. Remove from the oven and allow to cool for 10 minutes before removing the bread from the pan. Slice and serve. Store in an airtight container at room temperature for up to 5 days, in the refrigerator for up to a week, or in the freezer for up to a month.

Lemon Poppy Seed Loaf

OPTION

YIELD: One 9 by 5-inch loaf (16 slices) **PREP TIME:** 10 minutes
COOK TIME: 45 minutes

If you need some cheering up, this lemony quick bread tastes like sunshine in a bite. I truly believe citrus-flavored treats were invented to help us get through the cold winter months. Now, if you prefer not to use poppy seeds, you can swap in chia seeds or omit them altogether. Personally, the poppy seeds remind me of childhood. (So many of my treats do! I think that's where my love of baking comes from. I think it helps me keep a bit of light-heartedness about life!) Whip up the easy sugar glaze to go on top, and you can't help but smile with every bite.

LEMON POPPY SEED LOAF:

3 cups gluten-free rolled oats, ground into a rustic flour (see Notes, page 117)

⅓ cup cassava flour

½ cup coconut sugar

1 tablespoon baking powder

1 teaspoon baking soda

¼ teaspoon finely ground sea salt

3 Flaxseed Eggs (page 34)

1¼ cups unsweetened dairy-free milk, room temperature

⅔ cup unsweetened applesauce, room temperature

2 teaspoons grated lemon zest

6 tablespoons freshly squeezed lemon juice (about 2 lemons)

3 tablespoons coconut oil, melted

1 teaspoon pure vanilla extract

3 tablespoons poppy seeds (see Notes)

GLAZE:

½ cup powdered sugar

1 tablespoon unsweetened dairy-free milk

1 tablespoon poppy seeds, for garnish

To make the loaf:

1. Preheat the oven to 350°F. Line a 9 by 5-inch loaf pan with parchment paper, leaving some paper overhanging the sides for easy removal.

2. In a large bowl, whisk together the flours, sugar, baking powder, baking soda, and salt.

3. In a medium bowl, mix together the flaxseed eggs, dairy-free milk, applesauce, lemon zest, lemon juice, coconut oil, and vanilla extract.

4. Fold the wet mixture into the dry until combined, making sure there are no clumps of the dry mixture left.

5. Add the poppy seeds and mix until they're evenly distributed.

6. Pour the batter into the prepared loaf pan and bake for 40 to 45 minutes, until a toothpick comes out clean when inserted in the middle.

7. Remove from the oven and allow to cool for 10 minutes before removing the loaf from the pan. Allow the loaf to fully cool, about 20 minutes, before making the glaze.

To make the glaze:

8. In a medium bowl, whisk together the powdered sugar and dairy-free milk until there are no more clumps of powdered sugar.

9. When ready to glaze, spread the glaze over the lemon poppy seed loaf, then garnish with the poppy seeds. Slice and serve. Store in an airtight container for up to 5 days at room temperature or for up to a week in the refrigerator. You may also freeze the bread for up to a month.

Notes

For a nut-free dairy-free milk, I recommend coconut or oat milk. (If using oat milk and you require it to be gluten-free, be sure to buy a brand labeled as such.)

For a superfood upgrade, swap chia seeds for the poppy seeds.

Vegan Challah Bread

OPTION

YIELD: 1 loaf (10 slices)   **PREP TIME:** 20 minutes, plus 1 to 1½ hours to rise and proof dough   **COOK TIME:** 45 minutes

My partner, Jared, is a master at making challah French toast. It's one of our favorite breakfasts for birthdays and holiday celebrations. However, when we went plant-based, we not only needed a vegan French toast recipe, but a vegan challah bread to boot. Enter the best homemade vegan challah bread, so good that even Jared's dad (whose favorite bread is challah!) couldn't tell that it was entirely vegan. Making challah is not as complicated as it looks, and it's actually quite fun! I love the braiding part in particular. Use this recipe just to enjoy a slice of challah toast, as a bread for French toast, or even in bread pudding, like the recipe on page 310.

DOUGH:

1 cup warm water (110°F), plus more if needed

6 tablespoons coconut sugar, divided

4 to 4½ cups plus 1 tablespoon all-purpose flour, divided

1 packet active dry yeast

¼ cup coconut oil, melted but not hot

GLAZE:

2 tablespoons maple syrup

1 tablespoon unsweetened dairy-free milk

SPECIAL EQUIPMENT:

Kitchen thermometer

1. Set the oven to the proof setting (or at 80°F) or make sure that you have a warm area (above 79°F) for the dough to rise.

2. To make the dough, whisk together the warm water, 3 tablespoons of the coconut sugar, and 1 tablespoon of the flour in a large bowl.

3. Add the yeast and let activate for 10 minutes. The mixture should start to foam and smell yeastlike. If it does neither, toss it and start again (if the water is too hot, it will kill the yeast).

4. Once the yeast is activated, add the remaining 3 tablespoons of coconut sugar and the melted coconut oil. Whisk until fully combined.

5. Sift in 4 cups of flour in ½-cup increments, stirring after each increment. The dough should be sticky and lumpy. If not, add another ½ cup of flour. If the dough has not absorbed all of the flour, add more warm water in 1-tablespoon increments. Knead the dough until the flour is completely combined.

6. Lightly flour a clean surface and turn the dough onto it. Knead the dough until it is smooth and springy, about 5 minutes. Once the dough is kneaded, lightly grease a clean bowl and place the dough inside. Cover the bowl with a clean kitchen towel and place in the oven or in a warm spot away from drafts. You can also place it in a safe spot outside if it's hot enough.

7. Let the dough rise until doubled in size, 30 minutes to 1 hour. Once it's doubled, punch it down and lightly flour a clean surface.

8. Knead the dough again for 2 to 5 minutes, then use a bench scraper or knife to slice the dough into 3 equal pieces. Roll each into a long strand (12 to 16 inches).

9. Take the strands and press them together at one end. Wrap one strand over the other to create a braid shape, then press the other ends of the strands together. You can leave it as a long loaf or wrap the loaf into a "C" shape to create a circle, as shown in the photo.

10. Place the loaf on a baking sheet and cover with a clean kitchen towel. Place the covered baking sheet by the oven, away from drafts, to proof for 30 minutes. Preheat the oven to 350°F.

11. When the loaf has proofed and the oven is preheated, bake the loaf for 20 to 25 minutes, until lightly golden. Remove from the oven and set aside while you make the glaze.

12. Mix the glaze ingredients together in a small bowl. Lightly brush the top of the loaf with the glaze mixture.

13. Let cool on the pan for 10 minutes before slicing and serving. Store in an airtight container at room temperature for up to 3 days or in the refrigerator for up to a week.

Chocolate Pistachio Muffins

YIELD: 12 muffins   PREP TIME: 10 minutes   COOK TIME: 35 minutes

I discovered my love of chocolate paired with pistachios when I was making homemade pistachio butter a few years ago. I accidentally burned the pistachios, and after I ground them up in the food processor, I ended up with a nut butter that was more brown than green. I decided to add some cacao powder to cover up the slightly burnt taste, and I was instantly hooked. Ever since, I have added chocolate to almost all of my pistachio creations. These muffins have the perfect ratio of chocolate to pistachio and are incredibly easy to make. Warm one up in the morning to go with a bowl of coconut or cashew milk yogurt, or pack one for a mid-afternoon snack. It's a perfect portion of decadence!

2½ cups gluten-free rolled oats, ground into a rustic flour (see Notes, page 117)

½ cup raw cacao powder

½ cup coconut sugar

1 tablespoon baking powder

2 teaspoons baking soda

3 Flaxseed Eggs (page 34)

1 cup Vegan Buttermilk (page 35), room temperature

½ cup unsweetened applesauce

1 teaspoon pure vanilla extract

¾ cup coarsely chopped raw pistachios, plus whole shelled pistachios for garnish if desired

1. Preheat the oven to 350°F. Place 12 cupcake liners in a standard-size muffin tin.

2. In a large bowl, whisk together the oat flour, cacao powder, sugar, baking powder, and baking soda.

3. In a medium bowl, mix together the flaxseed eggs, vegan buttermilk, applesauce, and vanilla extract.

4. Fold the wet mixture into the dry until combined, making sure there are no clumps of the dry mixture left.

5. Fold in the pistachios until the nuts are distributed evenly throughout the batter.

6. Using a ⅓-cup measuring scoop or a 3-tablespoon cookie scoop, fill each cupcake liner three-quarters of the way full. If desired, sprinkle each muffin with a few pistachios. Bake for 30 to 35 minutes, until a toothpick comes out clean when inserted in the middle.

7. Remove from the oven and allow to cool for 10 minutes before flipping the muffins onto a cooling rack. Turn them right side up and let cool completely. Store in an airtight container at room temperature for up to 5 days, in the refrigerator for up to a week, or in the freezer for up to a month.

Banana Nut Muffins

OPTION

YIELD: 12 muffins   **PREP TIME:** 10 minutes   **COOK TIME:** 35 minutes

This recipe makes it onto my meal-prep list every week. And it's not just because it is one of the easiest recipes in this book or because the muffins themselves make for an "indulgent"-tasting breakfast or snack, but because it satisfies many allergy needs: dairy-free, egg-free, gluten-free, grain-free, soy-free, and even an option for nut-free! I recommend including the walnuts if you're not doing nut-free, but if you are, you can substitute pumpkin or sunflower seeds. Even chia seeds would be fun for a banana faux–poppy seed muffin. Make these for the week ahead as an easy breakfast or snack that you and your family can enjoy!

1¾ cups mashed bananas (4 to 5 large ripe bananas)

½ cup creamy unsalted almond or sunflower seed butter

3 Flaxseed Eggs (page 34)

2 teaspoons Paleo Baking Powder (page 37) (see Notes)

2 teaspoons pure vanilla extract

¾ cup coconut flour

1 tablespoon ground cinnamon

½ teaspoon baking soda

¼ teaspoon finely ground sea salt

1 cup raw walnut pieces and/or halves

1. Preheat the oven to 350°F. Place 12 cupcake liners in a standard-size muffin tin. (To make your own parchment paper liners, as pictured, see the note, opposite.)

2. In a large bowl, stir the mashed bananas, almond butter, flaxseed eggs, baking powder, and vanilla extract until combined.

3. Sift in the coconut flour, cinnamon, baking soda, and salt and stir to combine. Mix the batter until it is thick and no dry clumps remain.

4. Fold in the walnut pieces.

5. Using a ⅓-cup measuring scoop or a 3-tablespoon cookie scoop, fill each cupcake liner three-quarters of the way full. Bake for 30 to 35 minutes, until a toothpick comes out clean when inserted in the middle.

6. Remove from the oven and let cool for 15 minutes before removing the muffins. Serve warm or cold (but they are best enjoyed when warm!). Store in an airtight container at room temperature for up to 3 days, in the refrigerator for up to a week, or in the freezer for up to a month.

Notes

If you do not need the muffins to be 100 percent Paleo, you can use any store-bought baking powder in place of the homemade version. Add it when you add the other dry ingredients in Step 3, along with the baking soda.

For nut-free muffins, use sunflower seed butter and swap your favorite seeds for the walnuts.

To make your own parchment paper cups, as pictured, cut twelve 3-inch squares of
parchment paper. Gently press the middle of each square down into the muffin cavities,
continuing to press and smooth out the paper into a circular shape in the bottom of each
cavity. Crease the natural folds around the sides of the cupcake cavities and spoon the batter
into the parchment paper liners.

Blueberry Oat Muffins

OPTION

YIELD: 12 muffins   **PREP TIME:** 10 minutes   **COOK TIME:** 35 minutes

If you're a little bored with oats, these blueberry oatmeal muffins will definitely respark your joy. Like an elevated bowl of oatmeal with blueberries, these muffins are topped with a deliciously crunchy cinnamon streusel that truthfully could be eaten and enjoyed on its own! When blueberry season hits, this is always the first recipe I make.

1¾ cups gluten-free rolled oats, ground into a rustic flour (see Notes, page 117)

⅔ cup coconut sugar

1 tablespoon baking powder

2 teaspoons baking soda

½ cup Vegan Buttermilk (page 35), room temperature

⅓ cup vegan butter or coconut oil, melted

2 Flaxseed Eggs (page 34)

1 teaspoon pure vanilla extract

1 cup fresh blueberries

OAT CRUMBLE:

½ cup gluten-free rolled oats, ground into a rustic flour

3 tablespoons maple syrup

2 tablespoons coconut oil, melted

1. Preheat the oven to 350°F. Place 12 cupcake liners in a standard-size muffin tin.

2. In a large bowl, whisk together the oat flour, coconut sugar, baking powder, and baking soda.

3. Add the vegan buttermilk, melted vegan butter, flaxseed eggs, and vanilla extract and mix until well combined.

4. Fold in the blueberries.

5. Using a ⅓-cup measuring scoop or a 3-tablespoon cookie scoop, fill each cupcake liner three-quarters of the way full.

6. Prepare the oat crumble by mixing together the oat flour, maple syrup, and melted coconut oil until well combined. Sprinkle the mixture over each muffin, about 2 teaspoons per muffin.

7. Bake for 30 to 35 minutes, until a toothpick comes out clean when inserted in the middle of a muffin.

8. Remove from the oven and let cool for 15 minutes before removing the muffins. Serve warm or cold (but they are best enjoyed when warm!). Store in an airtight container at room temperature for up to 3 days, in the refrigerator for up to a week, or in the freezer for up to a month.

Note _____

To make these muffins nut-free, follow the nut-free option for the Vegan Buttermilk and use Earth Balance's vegan buttery sticks or coconut oil.

Chocolate Chip Raspberry Muffins

OPTION OPTION

YIELD: 12 muffins   **PREP TIME:** 10 minutes   **COOK TIME:** 35 minutes

I know everyone loves strawberry and chocolate, but to me, raspberries and chocolate are the real dynamic duo. The raspberries offer not only sweetness, but just enough tartness to make these muffins satisfying rather than feeling like you just consumed a ton of sugar to start your day. I love eating one fresh out of the oven or reheated and split open to smear with a pat of vegan butter. They make a wonderful breakfast, snack, or treat when berries are in season!

1¾ cups gluten-free 1-to-1 baking flour or all-purpose flour

⅔ cup coconut sugar

1 tablespoon baking powder

2 teaspoons baking soda

½ cup Vegan Buttermilk (page 35), room temperature

⅓ cup vegan butter or coconut oil, melted

2 Flaxseed Eggs (page 34)

1 teaspoon pure vanilla extract

1 cup fresh raspberries

½ cup vegan dark chocolate chips (55% to 70% cacao)

1. Preheat the oven to 350°F. Place 12 cupcake liners in a standard-size muffin tin.

2. In a large bowl, whisk together the flour, coconut sugar, baking powder, and baking soda.

3. Add the vegan buttermilk, melted vegan butter, flaxseed eggs, and vanilla extract and mix until well combined.

4. Fold in the raspberries and chocolate chips.

5. Using a ⅓-cup measuring scoop or a 3-tablespoon cookie scoop, fill each cupcake liner three-quarters of the way full. Bake for 30 to 35 minutes, until a toothpick comes out clean when inserted in the middle of a muffin.

6. Remove from the oven and let cool for 15 minutes before removing the muffins. Serve warm or cold (but they are best enjoyed warm!). Store in an airtight container at room temperature for up to 3 days, in the refrigerator for up to a week, or in the freezer for up to a month.

Note

To make these muffins nut-free, follow the nut-free option for the Vegan Buttermilk, and use Earth Balance's vegan buttery sticks or coconut oil.

Chocolate Cinnamon Rolls

OPTION

YIELD: 10 to 12 rolls   PREP TIME: 30 minutes, plus 90 minutes to rise and proof dough   COOK TIME: 35 minutes

If anything can beat out a homemade cinnamon roll on a Saturday morning, it's a homemade chocolate cinnamon roll! By now, I'm pretty sure you can tell the love I have for chocolate. These yeasted rolls are filled with a deliciously rich chocolate center and smeared with chocolate glaze (as if having chocolate only once in the roll counts as a chocolate cinnamon roll!). I have even included instructions for prepping these rolls ahead of time (because let's be honest, we don't always have the time or patience for a two-and-a-half-hour cinnamon roll making session). That way, when you wake up, all you need to do is bake and eat!

DOUGH:

1¼ cups unsweetened coconut milk

¼ cup melted vegan butter or coconut oil

¼ cup coconut sugar

4¼ cups all-purpose flour, divided, plus more for the work surface

1 packet active dry yeast

⅓ cup unsweetened applesauce, room temperature

1 teaspoon pure vanilla extract

FILLING AND GLAZE:

5 ounces vegan dark chocolate chips (55% to 70% cacao), divided

¼ cup melted vegan butter

3 tablespoons ground cinnamon

1 tablespoon coconut oil, melted

SPECIAL EQUIPMENT:

Kitchen thermometer

1. Grease a medium bowl with olive oil or coconut oil; set aside.

2. In a microwave-safe bowl, heat the coconut milk and melted vegan butter until the mixture reaches 110°F; use a thermometer to measure the temperature.

3. Pour the heated mixture into a large bowl and add the coconut sugar and 1 tablespoon of the flour. Whisk together, then add the yeast, mix lightly, cover, and let activate for 10 minutes in a warm area. You should see the yeast begin to foam, and it will smell yeastlike. If this does not happen, the yeast was not activated and you must scrap the mixture and start again.

4. When activated, add the remaining flour, applesauce, and vanilla extract and knead the dough lightly for 2 to 4 minutes. Place the dough in the greased bowl, cover with a clean cloth or plastic wrap, and place in the oven or in a warm area to rise until doubled in size, about 1 hour.

5. After an hour, lightly punch down the dough. Lightly flour a clean surface and place the dough in the middle. Sprinkle a little flour on top of the dough and flour a rolling pin. Roll out the dough into a rectangle measuring 8 by 12 inches. Grease an 8-inch or larger round or square baking pan with olive oil or coconut oil.

6. Melt 2.5 ounces of the chocolate following the instructions on pages 14 and 15. Lightly brush the dough with melted vegan butter, then brush with melted

chocolate, leaving a ½-inch border around the edges of the dough. Sprinkle the cinnamon evenly over the chocolate.

7. Tightly roll the dough lengthwise, moving away from you. Slice into 10 to 12 cinnamon rolls and place in the greased baking pan.

8. Cover again with a clean towel or wrap in plastic and place in a warm spot away from drafts. Let the rolls proof for 30 minutes. Preheat the oven to 350°F.

9. Bake the rolls for 25 to 30 minutes, until golden.

10. Remove from the oven and let cool in the pan for 5 to 10 minutes while you prepare the glaze.

11. To make the chocolate glaze, melt the remaining 2.5 ounces of chocolate following the instructions on pages 14 and 15. Stir in the melted coconut oil and use a brush to spread the glaze over the rolls.

12. Store in an airtight container in the refrigerator for up to 4 days. To reheat, place a roll on a baking sheet lined with parchment paper and warm in a preheated 350°F oven for 5 to 7 minutes.

Notes

To make these rolls nut-free, use Earth Balance's vegan buttery sticks or coconut oil.

If making a day ahead of time, complete Step 8 through the second rise, then cover the rolls and place them in the refrigerator overnight. When ready to bake, allow the rolls to sit in the oven (turned off) with the light on for 20 to 25 minutes. Then remove the rolls from the oven and allow them to rest over or by the oven as it preheats.

Paleo Cinnamon Rolls

OPTION

YIELD: 10 to 12 rolls   **PREP TIME:** 30 minutes   **COOK TIME:** 35 minutes

These cinnamon rolls are for my grain-free and Paleo folks. Or if you're just looking for a new and different cinnamon roll recipe, these rolls are also for you! Entirely nut-free and grain-free, this recipe is a great option for those with any of the top eight allergens. What's even better? Unlike regular cinnamon rolls, this Paleo version is entirely yeast-free, meaning there's no "knead" for rising time (baking pun, but there is a bit of kneading still—ha!). These quick cinnamon rolls make a speedy yet delicious weekend brunch or holiday breakfast option for all eaters.

DOUGH:

2½ cups cassava flour, plus more for the work surface

½ cup coconut flour

2 tablespoons coconut sugar

2 Flaxseed Eggs (page 34)

½ cup Vegan Buttermilk (page 35), room temperature

½ cup unsweetened applesauce, room temperature

2 tablespoons Paleo baking powder (page 37)

1 teaspoon pure vanilla extract

½ cup coconut oil, softened

FILLING:

¼ cup coconut oil, melted

⅓ cup coconut sugar

¼ cup ground cinnamon

GLAZE:

½ cup coconut butter, melted

1. Preheat the oven to 375°F. Line an 8-inch square baking pan with parchment paper.

2. In a large bowl, whisk together the cassava flour, coconut flour, and coconut sugar.

3. Add the flaxseed eggs, vegan buttermilk, applesauce, Paleo baking powder, and vanilla extract and mix until well combined.

4. Add the softened coconut oil and knead it into the dough.

5. Use cassava flour to lightly flour a piece of parchment paper and a rolling pin. Place the dough on the floured parchment and roll it out into a rectangle measuring 8 by 12 inches.

6. Brush the dough with the melted coconut oil, then sprinkle the coconut sugar and cinnamon on top, leaving a ½-inch border around the edges of the dough.

7. Use the parchment paper to gently but tightly roll the dough lengthwise, moving away from you. Slice into 10 to 12 cinnamon rolls and place in the prepared baking pan.

8. Bake for 30 minutes, or until lightly golden.

9. Spoon the melted coconut butter over the rolls for the glaze. Serve warm.

10. Store in an airtight container in the refrigerator for up to 5 days or in the freezer for up to a month. To reheat, place a roll on a baking sheet lined with aluminum foil and warm in a preheated 350°F oven for 5 minutes.

Note ——————————————————————————————

To make these rolls nut-free, follow the nut-free option for the Vegan Buttermilk.

Chocolate Babka

OPTION

YIELD: Two 9 by 5-inch loaves (16 slices each)   PREP TIME: 20 minutes, plus 65 minutes to rise and proof dough   COOK TIME: 45 minutes

I first tried babka a few years ago, when Jared's family brought it to a family celebration. I knew about babka, of course, but I didn't realize it was so good. I simply had to re-create it! However, I'm not one for long processes of breadmaking; my patience dwindles after a while. So I decided to make a babka that doesn't require refrigeration or oodles of proofing time. This version is surprisingly straightforward, and I've outlined the directions so that it will be seamless for you to replicate. A warning before you begin: this bread is highly addicting. One bite and you won't be able to stop!

DOUGH:

¾ cup unsweetened dairy-free milk

3 cups plus 1 tablespoon all-purpose flour, divided

⅓ cup plus 1 tablespoon coconut sugar, divided

2¼ teaspoons RapidRise instant yeast (see Notes)

¼ cup unsweetened applesauce

¼ cup vegan butter or coconut oil, melted

1 teaspoon pure vanilla extract

2 teaspoons olive oil, divided, for greasing

CHOCOLATE FILLING:

½ cup chopped vegan dark chocolate (80% cacao) (about 5 ounces)

½ cup unsweetened coconut cream (see Notes)

¼ cup coconut sugar

1 tablespoon coconut oil, melted

SPECIAL EQUIPMENT:

Kitchen thermometer

Notes

Though instant yeast technically doesn't require rehydration, I rehydrate it for extra insurance. Instant yeast can act differently from brand to brand, so I suggest you use the brand I used when testing this recipe: Fleishmann's RapidRise. However, if you have only dry active yeast on hand, you can use that. Just be sure to add 10 to 15 minutes to the initial rise time.

To get ½ cup of coconut cream, place a 13.5-ounce can of coconut cream in the refrigerator for 1 hour. Once chilled, remove the can from the refrigerator and scoop out the fat until it measures ½ cup, making sure to leave any water behind. From my experience, even cans of coconut cream contain some coconut water. Using this technique with cans of coconut cream ensures that you'll have the thickest, richest cream possible and that you'll end up with the right amount for the recipe. You can do the same with a can of full-fat coconut milk, but you may need more than one can.

To make this bread nut-free, use Earth Balance's vegan buttery sticks or coconut oil. For a nut-free dairy-free milk, I recommend coconut or oat milk.

1. Set the oven to the proof setting (or at 80°F) or make sure that you have a warm area (above 79°F) to place the dough to rise.

2. To make the dough: Heat the dairy-free milk to 110°F and pour it into a large bowl.

3. Add 1 tablespoon of the flour and 1 tablespoon of the coconut sugar to the milk and whisk to dissolve. Then add the yeast and mix it into the milk mixture; set aside to activate for 5 to 7 minutes. You should see the yeast begin to foam, and it will smell yeastlike. If this does not happen, the yeast was not activated and you must scrap the mixture and start again.

4. Once the yeast is activated, add the remaining ⅓ cup of sugar, the applesauce, melted vegan butter, and vanilla extract. Mix to combine.

5. Gradually sift the remaining 3 cups of flour into the wet mixture in 1-cup increments, mixing the dough with a spoon to combine the flour with the wet mixture. Once the flour is fully incorporated, gently knead the dough in the bowl to make sure everything is combined. Shape the dough into a ball.

6. Grease a clean bowl with 1 teaspoon of the olive oil, then place the dough in the bowl and cover it with a clean kitchen towel or cloth. Place the bowl in the oven or in a warm area to rise until doubled in size, about 45 minutes.

7. While the dough is rising, prepare the chocolate filling: Begin by melting the chocolate in the microwave or on the stovetop, following the instructions on pages 14 and 15. Pour the melted chocolate into a medium bowl and add the coconut cream, coconut sugar, and coconut oil and whisk until combined. Set aside in a warm area.

8. Preheat the oven to 350°F. Grease two 9 by 5-inch loaf pans with the remaining 1 teaspoon of olive oil.

9. When the dough has doubled in size, remove it from the oven. Lightly flour a clean work surface and rolling pin and place the dough on the floured surface.

10. Roll the dough into a large rectangle measuring 9 by 17 inches, with one of the long sides toward you. Using a butter brush or spoon, spread the chocolate filling onto the dough, making sure it reaches the edges.

11. Begin to roll the far side of the dough toward you, as if you were making cinnamon rolls. Continue rolling until you have a 17-inch-long cylinder.

12. Using a sharp knife, cut the cylinder in half lengthwise. Cross one strand over the other in the middle. Gently twist the strands together to form a spiral. Cut the spiral in half crosswise and place in the prepared loaf pans, then cover with a clean kitchen towel or cloth.

13. Place the covered loaf pans by the oven, away from drafts, to proof for 20 minutes.

14. Once proofed, bake the loaves for 45 minutes, or until browned and puffy. The babka should be slightly firm to the touch and sound hollow when tapped.

15. Remove from the oven and let the bread cool for 10 minutes before removing from the pans. Slice and serve.

16. Store in an airtight container at room temperature for up to 3 days or in the refrigerator for up to a week.

Double Chocolate Chip Scones

OPTION

YIELD: 8 scones   PREP TIME: 10 minutes   COOK TIME: 25 minutes

I absolutely love a scone with a cup of freshly brewed coffee. During the week, I try to stay on the healthier side—you know, oatmeal, toast, fruit, that sort of thing. But come the weekend, I'm ready for a bit more sweetness in the morning! These scones are a real treat, yet they're made with simple ingredients, like oat flour, coconut oil, and coconut sugar. Plus, they're easy to make on a weekend morning. I like to drizzle mine with a bit of melted chocolate, but that's totally optional!

2½ cups gluten-free rolled oats, ground into a rustic flour (see Notes, page 117)

¾ cup raw cacao powder

½ cup coconut sugar

1 tablespoon baking powder

2 teaspoons baking soda

½ cup coconut oil, chilled

1 cup Vegan Buttermilk (page 35)

3 Flaxseed Eggs (page 34)

½ cup vegan dark chocolate chips (55% to 70% cacao)

1. Preheat the oven to 350°F. Line a baking sheet with parchment paper.

2. Set aside 2 tablespoons of the rustic oat flour. Put the rest of the oat flour, the cacao powder, sugar, baking powder, and baking soda in a large bowl and whisk to combine.

3. Cut the chilled coconut oil into the flour mixture using a fork or pastry cutter.

4. Add the vegan buttermilk and flaxseed eggs and use a spoon to mix the wet and dry ingredients together until you have thick and sticky dough.

5. Fold in the chocolate chips.

6. Lightly flour a clean work surface with the reserved oat flour. Scoop the dough out of the bowl onto the floured surface and shape it into a circle about 8 inches in diameter. Use a frosting scraper or sharp knife to divide the dough into quarters and then eighths.

7. Using a spatula, gently place the scones on the prepared baking sheet. Bake for 20 to 25 minutes, until a toothpick comes out clean when inserted in the middle of a scone.

8. Remove from the oven and let the scones cool for 10 minutes before removing from the pan. You can let them continue cooling on a cooling rack or serve them while still warm.

9. Store in an airtight container at room temperature for up to 3 days or in the refrigerator for up to a week. To reheat, place on a baking sheet lined with aluminum foil and warm in a preheated 325°F oven for 5 to 7 minutes.

Note

To make these scones nut-free, follow the nut-free option for the Vegan Buttermilk.

Chocolate Chip Oatmeal Cups

OPTION

YIELD: 10 oatmeal cups   **PREP TIME:** 10 minutes, plus 2 hours to soak dates
COOK TIME: 22 minutes

While you may not have the time to prepare a recipe like Double Chocolate Chip Scones (page 304) on a weekday morning, you can definitely enjoy these date-sweetened oatmeal cups throughout the week. This is the ultimate meal-prep breakfast when you want something easy, portable, and delicious. Make it on a Sunday afternoon, and you'll have breakfast all week long. I suggest serving these oatmeal cups with a bit of dairy-free yogurt or dairy-free milk and some fresh fruit (or extra chocolate chips!).

1 cup pitted medjool dates, soaked in water for 2 hours and drained

2 cups gluten-free rolled oats

2 teaspoons baking powder

1 teaspoon baking soda

½ teaspoon ground cinnamon

1 cup unsweetened dairy-free milk

2 Flaxseed Eggs (page 34)

½ cup vegan dark chocolate chips (55% to 70% cacao)

1. Preheat the oven to 350°F. Place 10 cupcake liners in a standard-size muffin tin.

2. In a large food processor, pulse the dates until they're a smooth and sticky paste.

3. In a large bowl, whisk together the oats, baking powder, baking soda, and cinnamon.

4. Add the date paste, dairy-free milk, and flaxseed eggs to the dry ingredients and stir until combined into a thick batter.

5. Fold in the chocolate chips.

6. Using a ⅓-cup measuring scoop or a 3-tablespoon cookie scoop, fill each cupcake liner three-quarters of the way full. Bake for 20 to 22 minutes, until lightly golden.

7. Remove from the oven and let the oatmeal cups cool for 10 minutes before removing from the tin. You can let them continue cooling on a cooling rack or serve them while still warm.

8. Store in an airtight container at room temperature for up to 3 days or in the refrigerator for up to a week.

Note

For a nut-free dairy-free milk, I recommend coconut or oat milk. (If using oat milk and you require it to be gluten-free, be sure to buy a brand labeled as such.)

Baked Strawberry Donuts

OPTION OPTION

YIELD: 10 donuts   **PREP TIME:** 10 minutes   **COOK TIME:** 24 minutes

You might think donuts would be a whole long process, but they are actually quite simple to make, even gluten-free! Yes, you could fry them, but I prefer them baked with a dash of nutmeg to give them that bakery flavor. (That secret is between you and me!) I discovered after much testing that since strawberries are moist, the batter has a hard time cooking. However, if the strawberries are coated in a bit of flour before being added to the batter, the donuts bake through wonderfully.

½ cup sliced strawberries

1 cup plus 1 tablespoon all-purpose flour or gluten-free 1-to-1 baking flour, divided

½ cup coconut sugar

2 teaspoons baking powder

1 teaspoon baking soda

¼ teaspoon ground nutmeg

¼ cup unsweetened applesauce

¼ cup vegan butter or coconut oil, melted

¼ cup Vegan Buttermilk (page 35)

2 teaspoons pure vanilla extract

SPECIAL EQUIPMENT:

One 12-cavity or two 6-cavity metal or silicone donut pan(s)

1. Preheat the oven to 350°F. Grease 10 cavities of one 12-cavity or two 6-cavity donut pan(s). If you have only one 6-cavity pan, you will need to bake the donuts in 2 batches.

2. In a small bowl, toss the strawberries with 1 tablespoon of the flour until they're evenly coated.

3. In a medium bowl, whisk together the remaining 1 cup of flour, the sugar, baking powder, baking soda, and nutmeg.

4. Add the applesauce, vegan butter, vegan buttermilk, and vanilla extract to the dry ingredients and mix until well combined. You will have a thick batter. Fold in the coated strawberries.

5. Either pipe or spoon the batter into the prepared pan(s), filling each cavity about three-quarters of the way full. Bake for 20 to 24 minutes, until the donuts are puffy and golden.

6. Remove from the oven and let the donuts cool for 10 minutes before removing from the pan(s). Allow to cool completely on a cooling rack before serving.

7. Store in an airtight container at room temperature for up to 3 days or in the refrigerator for up to a week.

Note

To make these donuts nut-free, use Earth Balance's vegan buttery sticks or coconut oil and follow the nut-free option for the Vegan Buttermilk.

Bread Pudding

OPTION

YIELD: 7 servings   PREP TIME: 10 minutes   COOK TIME: 35 minutes

This recipe is a bit of an outlier since we're not making any bread here. Instead, we're using bread as the basis for a dessert! If you find yourself with bread staling quicker than you like, you can use it to make this recipe. This is what bread pudding was invented for—to make use of day-old (or week-old) bread. My grandma often used old bread to make bread pudding for my grandpa. It was one of his favorite dishes. When I was eight, I decided to surprise him with bread pudding for his birthday. Being the confident little baker that I was, I declined my grandma's help and insisted I could do it myself (though she kept an eye on me so I was safe!). Well, I confused flour with sugar and didn't realize it until our first bite of the pudding. Needless to say, I was pretty disappointed and embarrassed, but my grandpa just laughed, and we got ice cream instead. Rest assured, I will not let you mix up flour and sugar here! This vegan bread pudding is incredibly easy and straightforward. It's wonderful for a sweet brunch or dessert, especially when sprinkled with a little powdered sugar and/or topped with fresh berries and coconut cream.

1 teaspoon coconut oil, for greasing

2 cups unsweetened dairy-free milk

2 Flaxseed Eggs (page 34)

⅓ cup coconut sugar

1 tablespoon pure vanilla extract

1 tablespoon arrowroot powder

4 cups cubed gluten-free bread (see Notes)

1. Preheat the oven to 350°F. Grease a 9 by 6-inch baking dish with the coconut oil.

2. In a medium bowl, whisk together the dairy-free milk, flaxseed eggs, sugar, vanilla extract, and arrowroot powder. Set aside.

3. Place the cubed bread in the prepared baking dish. Pour the milk mixture over the bread and toss to fully cover the cubes of bread in the milk mixture.

4. Bake for 30 to 35 minutes, until the bread has absorbed the liquid.

5. Remove from the oven and let cool for 10 minutes before serving. This bread pudding is best served warm.

6. Store in an airtight container in the refrigerator for up to 5 days. To reheat, place the desired amount in a baking dish and warm in a preheated 350°F oven for 5 to 8 minutes.

Notes

For a nut-free dairy-free milk, I recommend coconut or oat milk. (If using oat milk and you require it to be gluten-free, be sure to buy a brand labeled as such.)

If you don't have arrowroot powder, you can substitute cornstarch.

For the gluten-free bread, any vegan store-bought brand will do. Vegan Challah Bread (page 286) works wonderfully here and is not difficult to make.

Acknowledgments

To the *Banana Diaries* community, I am so profoundly grateful for each and every one of you. I still pinch myself because it all feels like a dream! Thank you for taking that first chance on my recipes, for trusting me to deliver you some vegan (and Paleo at times!) goodness, for the sweet messages daily through email and DM, and for helping me create one of the most positive and loving communities I've had the privilege of being a part of. I could not be living this dream without you. I know I will never be able to thank you enough, but I hope this book is a start. Thank you, from the bottom of my heart.

Jared, you are such a light in the dark. Not only are you the biggest inspiration for *The Banana Diaries*, but you also just inspire me in everyday life. Thank you for supporting my dreams even when it felt impossible to reach, for trying each and every one of my recipes (they weren't all winners at first—ha!), for making last-minute grocery trips as I'm in mid-chocolate pour, for making sure I ate more than just sweets in the making of this book, and for constantly showing me love and compassion through not only the process of *Baked with Love*, but for the daily routine of my job and career. You're my best friend, my partner, and my rock.

Mom and Dad, you both mean to me more than I can express in words. The things I'm most proud of in myself are the things you've taught me. Thank you for always supporting me through it all. You taught me from a young age that when you work hard and put your all into it, you're rewarded, and that could not be more true. Thank you for showing me such unconditional love and for showing me that you can absolutely make your dreams a reality.

Brooke and Erik, I'm laughing as I write this because I can't take myself seriously at all when I'm with you two. I'm so beyond grateful I have you two as siblings. Through thick and thin, you both have managed to make me crack up with laughter when I'm down, stressed, or struggling, and I'm forever grateful for that. I love you both so much, and am so incredibly grateful for how you both support me. Even through the fights, I know we can all rely on each other, and I'm so thankful for that.

Gie, I am beyond grateful for you. Thank you so much for being the coolest grandma on Earth. I mean, what nearly 80-year-old Italian who's never tried a Paleo vegan dessert in her life would be so willing to take a bite of my creations?! I feel so incredibly lucky. Not only that, but you've inspired some of my best recipes on the blog (and in this book!), and I'm forever grateful for that.

Alex, you are such an incredible human. Thank you so much for literally keeping me sane throughout this entire process (and helping me grow, both in my business and as a human!!). You did more than just keep me on (and even ahead!) of schedule with this book; you showed me what's possible when I have the systems in place, been such a wonderful mentor in helping me to achieve goals I had never dared to approach before, and been there for me even on the weekends (when we both should have been resting!). I am so lucky to be able to work with you.

Lauren and Caroline, you guys have seen it all. Thank you so much for being my friends through high school and beyond (and for loving me enough to try my gluten-free vegan creations, even when I was first starting out!).

Tori and Adri, I love you both so much! Thank you for seeing me through my darkest moments and my best. I'm so lucky to have such an incredible support system. Your friendship means the world to me. P.S. Thanks for being SO EXCITED about *The Banana Diaries* when I first told you I was starting a blog—to have your support from day one has meant more than you'll know. Love you both!!

Emilie, Sarah, and Sky, *le mie amiche, vi adoro!* You guys are the best. So beyond grateful for all of the crazy adventures, laughs, cries, and hugs we've had. I cannot wait for what's to come for us.

Shuangy of *Shuangy's Kitchen Sink*, thank you for being my best friend, not only in blogging but in life. Your friendship means the world to me. You somehow manage to deliver the truth in the most loving way, and that is a skill not many have! I love so much how our relationship is about supporting each other's dreams. I cannot imagine doing this thing without you. You're truly the best.

Natalie of *Feasting on Fruit*, thank you for being such an incredible friend and e-coworker. Our FaceTime dates are truly some of my favorite and keep me so grounded in this wild online world. I'm beyond grateful for your support and love always.

Rachel of *Bakerita*, you are truly such a gem of a human. I still vividly remember our first call when I said I wanted to start a blog and the support you gave me was just mind-blowing. You inspire me every single day with your work ethic, passion, creativity, artistic skill, recipes, and most of all, your heart. Thank you.

Holly, my editor at Victory Belt, thank you so much for helping me put all of these words together! You are truly a miracle worker; thank you for fielding my slew of emails and really going through these pages with a fine-tooth comb. Your attention to detail is truly remarkable, and I'm so grateful for it because it's made the best possible cookbook for *Baked with Love*. You are Superwoman, I'm convinced!

Lance, Susan, and the entire Victory Belt team, you are all incredible. I'm so beyond grateful I've had the opportunity to work with you all. Your positivity, help, professionalism, and dedication to putting this book together truly has just blown me away. I feel so lucky to have been able to work alongside you. This is the dream team!

Recipe Index

BASICS

Flaxseed Egg

Vegan Buttermilk

Paleo Powdered Sugar

Paleo Baking Powder

Vegan Buttercream Frosting

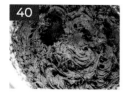
Paleo Vegan Chocolate Buttercream Frosting

Vegan Cream Cheese Frosting

Chocolate Hazelnut Spread

Coconut Caramel Sauce

Berry Jam

Coconut Whipped Cream

Vegan Oat Crust

Paleo Vegan Pie Crust

BROWNIES & BARS

56
Peanut Butter Swirl Brownies

58
Caramel-Filled Brownies

60
Birthday Cake Bars

62
Oatmeal Chocolate Chunk Bars

64
Kitchen Sink Blondies

66
S'mores Brownies

68
Red Velvet Brownies

70
Almond Butter Blondies

72
Chocolate Cheesecake Bars

74
Pecan Pie Bars

76
Cookie Dough Fudge Bites

78
Chocolate Granola Bars

80
Chocolate Peppermint Bars

82
Lemon Bars

84
Flourless Chickpea Brownies

86
Vegan Shortbread Millionaire Bars

88
Candy Bar Blondies

90
Snickerdoodle Blondies

COOKIES

94

Chai-Spiced
Snickerdoodles

96

Macadamia Nut
Cookies

98

Peanut Butter
Cup Cookies

100

Brownie
Chocolate Chip
Cookies

102

Oatmeal Raisin
Cookies

104

Peanut Butter–
Filled Chocolate
Cookies

106

Everything but
the Kitchen Sink
Cookies

108

Chocolate Chip
Biscotti

110

Double
Chocolate Chip
Cookies

112

Frosted Soft
Sugar Cookies

114

Chocolate
Peppermint
Cookies

116

Monster Cookies

118

Chocolate-
Topped
Shortbread
Cookies

120

Chocolate Chip
Cookie Cups

122

Peanut Butter
Raspberry
Thumbprint
Cookies

124

Chocolate &
Vanilla Linzer
Cookies

126

Mini Teddy Bear
Cookies

128

Sugar Cookie
Cutouts

130

Ginger Molasses
Cookies

132

Flourless Peanut
Butter Chocolate
Chip Cookies

CUPCAKES

136

Caramel-Filled Cupcakes

138

Chocolate Chip Banana Cupcakes

140

Carrot Cake Cupcakes

142

Boston Cream Pie Cupcakes

144

Funfetti Cupcakes

146

Hot Chocolate Cupcakes

150

Vanilla & Chocolate Marbled Cupcakes

152

Ice Cream Sundae Cupcakes

154

Zesty Lemon Cupcakes

156

Raspberry Coconut Cupcakes

158

Peanut Butter–Filled Cupcakes

160

Pecan Cupcakes

162

Red Velvet Cupcakes

164

Mocha Cupcakes

166

Strawberry Vanilla Cupcakes

168

Cookies 'n' Cream Cupcakes

170

Pumpkin Cupcakes

CAKES

174
Chocolate Hazelnut Cake

178
Lemon Blueberry Cake

182
Chocolate Mousse Cake

186
Molten Lava Cakes

188
Peanut Butter Banana Cake

190
Chai Pumpkin Cake

192
Coconut Lemon Cake

196
Paleo Chocolate Cake

198
Chocolate Peanut Butter Fudge Cake

202
Flourless Chocolate Cake

204
Birthday Cake

206
Eton Mess

208
Cookie Dough Cake

212
Chocolate Chip Banana Bundt Cake

214
Sweet Potato Cake with Maple Cream Cheese Frosting

218
Blueberry Coffee Cake

222
German Chocolate Cake

226
Strawberry Shortcake Cake

228
Mini Blueberry Mug Cake

PIES, TARTS & CHEESECAKES

232
Chocolate Peanut Butter Cheesecake

234
Banoffee Tart

236
Salted Caramel Pear Tart

238
Cookies 'n' Cream Cheesecake

242
Cannoli Tart

246
Neapolitan Cheesecake

248
Raspberry Tart

250
Chocolate Caramel Pretzel Tart

252
Brownie Cheesecake

254
Cake Batter Cookie Pie

256
Strawberry Pie

258
Blueberry Crumble Pie

260
Banana Bread Cheesecake

262
Chocolate Hazelnut Tart

266
Coconut Cream Pie

268
Mini Lemon Tarts

270
Mini Berry Tarts

272
Pumpkin Pie

SWEET BREADS & MUFFINS

276

Cinnamon Raisin
Bread

278

Marbled
Pumpkin Bread

280

Blueberry
Banana Bread

282

Double
Chocolate Chunk
Banana Bread

284

Lemon Poppy
Seed Loaf

286

Vegan Challah
Bread

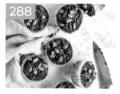
288

Chocolate
Pistachio Muffins

290

Banana Nut
Muffins

292

Blueberry Oat
Muffins

294

Chocolate Chip
Raspberry
Muffins

296

Chocolate
Cinnamon Rolls

298

Paleo Cinnamon
Rolls

300

Chocolate Babka

304

Double
Chocolate Chip
Scones

306

Chocolate Chip
Oatmeal Cups

308

Baked
Strawberry
Donuts

310

Bread Pudding

Allergen Index

 Gluten-free   Nut-free   O = Option

 Paleo   Peanut-free

Recipe	Page	Gluten-free	Nut-free	Paleo	Peanut-free
Flaxseed Egg	34	✓	✓	✓	✓
Vegan Buttermilk	35	✓	O	O	✓
Paleo Powdered Sugar	36	✓	✓	✓	✓
Paleo Baking Powder	37	✓	✓	✓	✓
Vegan Buttercream Frosting	38	✓	O	O	✓
Paleo Vegan Chocolate Buttercream Frosting	40	✓	O	✓	✓
Vegan Cream Cheese Frosting	42	✓	O	O	✓
Chocolate Hazelnut Spread	44	✓		✓	✓
Coconut Caramel Sauce	46	✓	O	O	✓
Berry Jam	48	✓	✓	✓	✓
Coconut Whipped Cream	49	✓	✓	✓	✓
Vegan Oat Crust	50	✓	✓		✓
Paleo Vegan Pie Crust	52	✓	✓	✓	✓
Peanut Butter Swirl Brownies	56	✓		O	O
Caramel-Filled Brownies	58	✓	O	✓	✓
Birthday Cake Bars	60	✓	O	✓	✓
Oatmeal Chocolate Chunk Bars	62	✓	O		✓
Kitchen Sink Blondies	64	O	O		✓
S'mores Brownies	66	✓	✓		✓
Red Velvet Brownies	68	O	✓		✓
Almond Butter Blondies	70	✓	O	✓	✓
Chocolate Cheesecake Bars	72	✓			✓
Pecan Pie Bars	74	✓		✓	✓
Cookie Dough Fudge Bites	76	✓	O	✓	✓
Chocolate Granola Bars	78	✓	O		✓
Chocolate Peppermint Bars	80	✓	✓		✓
Lemon Bars	82	✓	✓	O	✓
Flourless Chickpea Brownies	84	✓	✓		✓
Vegan Shortbread Millionaire Bars	86	✓	O	✓	✓
Candy Bar Blondies	88	O	O		O
Snickerdoodle Blondies	90	✓	O		✓
Chai-Spiced Snickerdoodles	94	O	O		✓
Macadamia Nut Cookies	96	O			✓
Peanut Butter Cup Cookies	98	O	O		O
Brownie Chocolate Chip Cookies	100	O	✓		✓
Oatmeal Raisin Cookies	102	✓	O		✓

Recipe	Page	🌾	🥜	🔪	🥜
Peanut Butter–Filled Chocolate Cookies	104	O	O		O
Everything but the Kitchen Sink Cookies	106	O	O		✓
Chocolate Chip Biscotti	108	O			✓
Double Chocolate Chip Cookies	110	O	O		✓
Frosted Soft Sugar Cookies	112	✓	O		✓
Chocolate Peppermint Cookies	114	✓	O		✓
Monster Cookies	116	O	O		O
Chocolate-Topped Shortbread Cookies	118	✓		O	✓
Chocolate Chip Cookie Cups	120	O	O		✓
Peanut Butter Raspberry Thumbprint Cookies	122	O	O		O
Chocolate & Vanilla Linzer Cookies	124	✓	O	O	✓
Mini Teddy Bear Cookies	126	✓	O	O	✓
Sugar Cookie Cutouts	128	✓	O	O	✓
Ginger Molasses Cookies	130	✓	O	O	✓
Flourless Peanut Butter Chocolate Chip Cookies	132	✓	✓	O	O
Caramel-Filled Cupcakes	136	O	O		✓
Chocolate Chip Banana Cupcakes	138	O	O		✓
Carrot Cake Cupcakes	140	✓	O		✓
Boston Cream Pie Cupcakes	142	O	O		✓
Funfetti Cupcakes	144	O	O		✓
Hot Chocolate Cupcakes	146	✓	O		✓
Vanilla & Chocolate Marbled Cupcakes	150	O	O		✓
Ice Cream Sundae Cupcakes	152	O	O		✓
Zesty Lemon Cupcakes	154	O	O		✓
Raspberry Coconut Cupcakes	156	O	O		✓
Peanut Butter–Filled Cupcakes	158	✓	O	O	O
Pecan Cupcakes	160	O			✓
Red Velvet Cupcakes	162	O	O		✓
Mocha Cupcakes	164	O	O		✓
Strawberry Vanilla Cupcakes	166	O	O		✓
Cookies 'n' Cream Cupcakes	168	O	O		✓
Pumpkin Cupcakes	170	O	O		✓
Chocolate Hazelnut Cake	174	✓		✓	✓
Lemon Blueberry Cake	178	O	O		✓
Chocolate Mousse Cake	182	✓	O		✓
Molten Lava Cakes	186	✓	O	O	✓
Peanut Butter Banana Cake	188	O	O		O
Chai Pumpkin Cake	190	O	O		✓
Coconut Lemon Cake	192	O	O		✓
Paleo Chocolate Cake	196	✓	✓	✓	✓
Chocolate Peanut Butter Fudge Cake	198	✓	O		O
Flourless Chocolate Cake	202	✓	✓	✓	✓
Birthday Cake	204	O	O		✓

Recipe	Page	🌾	🥜	🧁	🌽
Eton Mess	206	✓	✓		✓
Cookie Dough Cake	208	O	O		✓
Chocolate Chip Banana Bundt Cake	212	✓	O		✓
Sweet Potato Cake with Maple Cream Cheese Frosting	214	✓	O	✓	✓
Blueberry Coffee Cake	218	✓	O		✓
German Chocolate Cake	222	✓		✓	✓
Strawberry Shortcake Cake	226	✓	✓	✓	✓
Mini Blueberry Mug Cake	228	O	O		✓
Chocolate Peanut Butter Cheesecake	232	✓			O
Banoffee Tart	234	✓	O	O	✓
Salted Caramel Pear Tart	236	✓		O	✓
Cookies 'n' Cream Cheesecake	238	✓			✓
Cannoli Tart	242	✓		O	✓
Neapolitan Cheesecake	246	✓			✓
Raspberry Tart	248	✓	✓	O	✓
Chocolate Caramel Pretzel Tart	250	✓	O		✓
Brownie Cheesecake	252	✓			✓
Cake Batter Cookie Pie	254	O	O	O	✓
Strawberry Pie	256	✓	O	O	✓
Blueberry Crumble Pie	258	✓	✓	✓	✓
Banana Bread Cheesecake	260	✓			✓
Chocolate Hazelnut Tart	262	✓		✓	✓
Coconut Cream Pie	266	✓		O	✓
Mini Lemon Tarts	268	✓	✓	✓	✓
Mini Berry Tarts	270	✓	✓		✓
Pumpkin Pie	272	✓	✓	✓	✓
Cinnamon Raisin Bread	276	✓	O		✓
Marbled Pumpkin Bread	278	✓	O	✓	✓
Blueberry Banana Bread	280	O	O		✓
Double Chocolate Chunk Banana Bread	282	✓	✓		✓
Lemon Poppy Seed Loaf	284	✓	O		✓
Vegan Challah Bread	286		O		✓
Chocolate Pistachio Muffins	288	✓			✓
Banana Nut Muffins	290	✓	O	✓	✓
Blueberry Oat Muffins	292	✓	O		✓
Chocolate Chip Raspberry Muffins	294	O	O		✓
Chocolate Cinnamon Rolls	296		O		✓
Paleo Cinnamon Rolls	298	✓	O	✓	✓
Chocolate Babka	300		O		✓
Double Chocolate Chip Scones	304	✓	O		✓
Chocolate Chip Oatmeal Cups	306	✓	O		✓
Baked Strawberry Donuts	308	O	O		✓
Bread Pudding	310	✓	O		✓

General Index

butter (*continued*)

Vegan Buttercream Frosting, 38–39

Vegan Cream Cheese Frosting, 42–43

C

cacao powder

about, 13

Brownie Cheesecake, 252–253

Brownie Chocolate Chip Cookies, 100–101

Caramel-Filled Brownies, 58–59

Chocolate Cheesecake Bars, 72–73

Chocolate Granola Bars, 78–79

Chocolate Hazelnut Cake, 174–177

Chocolate Hazelnut Spread, 44–45

Chocolate Hazelnut Tart, 262–265

Chocolate Mousse Cake, 182–185

Chocolate Peanut Butter Cheesecake, 232–233

Chocolate Peanut Butter Fudge Cake, 198–201

Chocolate Peppermint Bars, 80–81

Chocolate Peppermint Cookies, 114–115

Chocolate Pistachio Muffins, 288–289

Chocolate & Vanilla Linzer Cookies, 124–125

Double Chocolate Chip Cookies, 110–111

Double Chocolate Chip Scones, 304–305

Double Chocolate Chunk Banana Bread, 282–283

Flourless Chickpea Brownies, 84–85

Flourless Chocolate Cake, 202–203

German Chocolate Cake, 222–225

Hot Chocolate Cupcakes, 146–149

Ice Cream Sundae Cupcakes, 152–153

Marbled Pumpkin Bread, 278–279

Mini Teddy Bear Cookies, 126–127

Mocha Cupcakes, 164–165

Neapolitan Cheesecake, 246–247

Paleo Chocolate Cake, 196–197

Paleo Vegan Chocolate, 40–41

Peanut Butter Swirl Brownies, 56–57

Peanut Butter–Filled Chocolate Cookies, 104–105

Peanut Butter–Filled Cupcakes, 158–159

Red Velvet Brownies, 68–69

Red Velvet Cupcakes, 162–163

S'mores Brownies, 66–67

Vanilla & Chocolate Marbled Cupcakes, 150–151

Cake Batter Cookie Pie recipe, 254–255

cake flour

about, 10

Birthday Cake, 204–205

Boston Cream Pie Cupcakes, 142–143

Caramel-Filled Cupcakes, 136–137

Chai Pumpkin Cake, 190–191

Chocolate Chip Banana Cupcakes, 138–139

Coconut Lemon Cake, 192–195

compared with all-purpose flour, 28

Cookie Dough Cake, 208–211

Cookies 'n' Cream Cupcakes, 168–169

Funfetti Cupcakes, 144–145

Ice Cream Sundae Cupcakes, 152–153

Lemon Blueberry Cake, 178–181

Mini Blueberry Mug Cake, 228–229

Mocha Cupcakes, 164–165

Peanut Butter Banana Cake, 188–189

Pecan Cupcakes, 160–161

Pumpkin Cupcakes, 170–171

Raspberry Coconut Cupcakes, 156–157

Red Velvet Cupcakes, 162–163

Strawberry Vanilla Cupcakes, 166–167

Vanilla & Chocolate Marbled Cupcakes, 150–151

Zesty Lemon Cupcakes, 154–155

cakes

baking pans/tins for, 22

Birthday Cake, 204–205

Blueberry Coffee Cake, 218–221

Chai Pumpkin Cake, 190–191

Chocolate Chip Banana Bundt Cake, 212–213

Chocolate Hazelnut Cake, 174–177

Chocolate Mousse Cake, 182–185

Chocolate Peanut Butter Fudge Cake, 198–201

Coconut Lemon Cake, 192–195

Cookie Dough Cake, 208–211

Eton Mess, 206–207

Flourless Chocolate Cake, 202–203

German Chocolate Cake, 222–225

Lemon Blueberry Cake, 178–181

Mini Blueberry Mug Cake, 228–229

Molten Lava Cakes, 186–187

Paleo Chocolate Cake, 196–197

Peanut Butter Banana Cake, 188–189

Strawberry Shortcake Cake, 226–227

Sweet Potato Cake with Maple Cream Cheese Frosting, 214–217

Candy Bar Blondies recipe, 88–89

Cannoli Tart recipe, 242–245

Caramel-Filled Brownies recipe, 58–59

Caramel-Filled Cupcakes recipe, 136–137

Carrot Cake Cupcakes recipe, 140–141

carrots

Carrot Cake Cupcakes, 140–141